Conquistador

By Griff Hosker

Published by Sword Books Ltd 2021

SWORD
BOOKS

Copyright ©Griff Hosker First Edition 2021

Contents

Prologue

The Year of Our Lord 1511, Devon

I am Thomas Penkridge, and my story begins when my father, John the Falconet, so named because he was a gunner and fired a falconet gun, took me to sea. I had lived with my grandmother and grandfather until the sweating sickness took them. We had lived in a small house with just enough land to give us milk and enough food to get by. The meat we ate was made up largely of rabbits I trapped and hunted. I had a good eye! When I was left alone a neighbour gave me a roof over my head until my father returned from the sea. My father had been a gunner for old King Henry, but he had fallen out with one of the King's captains and came back to the home of his parents and, I think, also for me. He told me that Captain Edward Edmundson was a bad captain and used men badly. My father had stood up for a man who was mistakenly punished and had been whipped for it. He was not a man to forgive easily. My father was a proud man and having fallen out he would not serve again with the captain of the king's ship. Being a highly skilled man he had made enough money serving King Henry, the first of the Tudors, to enable him to pay a blacksmith to make him a falconet. He helped to keep the price down by having the two of us act as the smith's assistants. I learned then about guns. I knew what it took to make one and how easy it was to destroy one! It took time, for my father knew that the gun would make us more money than it cost us to make and he wanted it to be perfect. Few ships had guns and my father was clever. He knew that captains would flock to hire him and his artillery piece. He trained me to be one of his gunners and, in later life, that proved to be a life saver, quite literally. However, I get ahead of myself.

We did not need to take the falconet with us when we sought work. In Devon, where we lived, my father was famous, some might say infamous. As well as being a gunner he was also something of a brawler and had been brought up before the magistrates more than once. Thanks to his service to King Henry he did not have to endure gaol, but he was punished and was often ordered to walk twenty miles to the cathedral to atone for his sins. Some men said it was because my mother died giving birth to a stillborn sister and her death made him the way he was. I do not know. My father was the way my father was when I knew him. I never saw the brawler but I did see a man with a wicked sense of humour who was reputed to be the finest gunner in the King's navy. Now we had a new king, the eighth King Henry, and many of my father's friends thought he ought to seek a position on a ship. He had friends for although he brawled, he was as loyal a man as ever walked the roads of Devon.

One night, when he had enjoyed cider and ale, a fearful combination, he confided in me his reason for not serving in the navy again, "Tom, I have served the king and been rewarded but if I was to serve a merchant then I might have a share of the profits. One day I would have my own ship. We will look for a suitable sea captain. I want one whose dreams and ambition match mine!"

I had seen but thirteen or fourteen summers then, I was not sure, and all I cared about was that I had adventure. I did not relish being a farmer and I knew that, as a gunner, I would have an easier life than that of a sailor. I would only be needed when we fought and with my father firing the falconet, we would always be victorious. I could see no flaw in the plan. Having my father home was all that I cared about.

As soon as we met Captain One-Eyed Peter, I knew he would be the man my father would follow. We had heard that there were merchant ships in Falmouth harbour and went down to speak with them. There had been a wild storm to the south of us and many battered ships had found their way into Falmouth harbour. As was usual when that happened then, inevitably, men deserted their ships. For some, it was because their purses were full and for others because they had suffered enough at the hands of a precocious and unforgiving sea. The captains were hiring and as usual, it was the Infanta Inn that they used. It was the largest in Falmouth and had rooms for the richer captains.

As we trudged down the road to Falmouth my father explained, "Some captains are very successful, Tom. They choose the right cargoes and manage to evade the pirates to bring them to port just when the prices are at their highest. Others choose the wrong cargo and return to find that they are so low in value that for many of the goods they have brought, they get virtually nothing for them. The better cargoes come from exotic places which are further away. Africa and the Indies are the best, but Africa is plagued with Barbary pirates and Spain protects the Indies. I want a rich captain. He need not dress well but he will have a good sword and he will like fine food and drink. When at sea sailors eat and drink poorly so that when they return those who are rich enjoy themselves. You keep quiet in the inn and watch. Your lessons in becoming a good gunner begin this day"

That day I saw a performance by my father. We had both dressed in our best. We wore good hose and my father's doublet was well made. He also had the best of boots and we both had fine hats upon our heads. We had little money left now that we had paid for the falconet, but we were dressed well, and we ate the best of food. My father used the money, to his mind, wisely and he was convinced that we would soon be hired.

Due to the presence of so many ships the town was full. William Wootton, the landlord of the Infanta Inn, had hired a couple of men to guard the door and keep out those whose purses were not full enough. Both local men, they knew my father and nodded, "Morning, John, it is like a cockfight in there!"

My father laughed, he was used to such events, but he was a large man, as big as the two men who were there to keep us out. "I will get their attention."

We pushed our way through the noisy gathering. It was like a hanging day. Instead of heading to where they sold the drinks my father pushed his way to the centre of the room and, putting his hands on his hips, used the voice which I came to realise could be heard above a howling gale in a wild sea. "Gentlemen, your attention!" To emphasise his words, he stamped hard on the wooden floor with his sea boots and the crack was like thunder. The whole, enormous room went silent. He smiled as he spoke, "I am John the Falconet and I served in Henry Tudor's navy until I fell foul of a man not fit to be a gong scourer or leech collector!" They were the worst two jobs that anyone could have and showed the contempt my father had for the captain. "I now have my own falconet and as I am the finest of gunners then any captain who hires me is buying the best. I will entertain offers from any captain who wishes to hire me, my falconet and my son! I shall be at the table by the window!" The fact that there were two men seated there did not worry my father, as he strode towards the table both of them nodded and then vacated the table rather than risking a confrontation with this most famous of brawlers.

He sat and waited. The noise soon rose to its previous level. We did not have long to wait, and a thin-faced captain came over with a jug of ale and a beaker for my father. He poured the ale and said, "I am Captain

William Coverdale and I have a fine vessel, a carrack, *'The Maid of Wight'*. I would like to hire you and I will pay you well."

My father looked at the man's sword which even I could see was cheap and his badly made boots and, after drinking half of the ale, said, "No, for you are a cheap man. Your sword and the fact that you do not offer my son an ale show that. Begone!"

The man flushed and as those on the nearby tables had heard, fled to the sound of laughter. My father dismissed another three with equal alacrity. All were for differing reasons and none as rude as the one afforded to Captain Coverdale. I wondered if we would ever find one which was suitable. I was enjoying the day for I had enjoyed three small ales as well as a dish of fried limpets brought as an inducement by one captain.

I had noticed One-Eyed Peter for he wore no patch over his damaged orb and the scarred evidence of some nautical battle drew my attention. I was young and such things fascinated me. The maimed men who begged in the streets always made me look at them. One-Eyed Peter had a good sword with a magnificent basket hilt, and he had a fine scabbard too. He wore sea boots which were skilfully made. When he came over after the fourth sea captain was sent away, I saw that he had no jug of ale in his hand but a bottle of brandy and a platter of bread.

"My name, John the Falconet, is One-Eyed Peter of Kent. I do not bring ale for your son but as he has enjoyed three beakers already and has not only a rosy glow but a distant look in his eye, I bring some bread for him to soak up the drink and for you some Spanish brandy."

My father was particularly fond of brandy and he emptied his ale and held out his beaker, "The Captain is right, Tom, now eat bread so that we may talk."

The captain poured them both a healthy measure. Brandy was not cheap and showed that the captain was successful. "I have heard of you, John. You were not boasting. I hate men who do so but equally, I do not trust unduly modest men. I am the most successful captain on the south coast. I bring in the richest cargoes and I came here today to hire a gunner. I will be honest, I found none, and I was about to leave when you entered. I wanted to judge you before I spoke, and I admired the way you dismissed those others. Had you taken a berth with any of them then I would not have even entertained making you an offer."

"And are you making me an offer?"

He poured more brandy and nodded to me and the bread, I ate! "Perhaps but I need to know how you stand on the matter of taking from others."

My father frowned, "Stealing? Piracy?"

"Those are harsh terms, John the Falconet. Let us say we find some foreign ship, not English mind, one which was poorly captained and sailed. What if their lords and masters forbade trade with England? Would it not be our Christian duty to relieve them of their cargo and take it back to England?" He paused to see my father's reaction. "I do not speak of neighbours of England, but the Indies and Africa have many men of dubious character. What if we were to visit these new worlds and bring back cargoes which would make the lives of those who live in King Henry's realm better?"

My father had spoken to me of the restrictive practice of Spain and the Barbary Coast. English ships were banned from trade so that spices and the new produce of these worlds was very expensive. One-Eyed Peter must have heard that for I knew it would appeal to my father and when he nodded, it was confirmed.

"As you say, it is not only our Christian duty but our patriotic duty to make the lives of those who live in England better. Of course, you would need my falconet, *Mary*, for I have seen some of these Spanish carracks, they now call them galleons. What would be our pay?"

"A hundredth of the profits."

My father held out his beaker and it was refilled, "A twentieth!"

"A tenth and you provide the shot and powder. That is my last offer. I need you but not to put me in the alms-house!"

My father put out a huge paw and grinning, shook the hand of One-Eyed Peter. It took a week for us to sell our furniture and house. We used the money to buy the powder and have the cast iron balls made by the blacksmith who, once again, gave us a lower price by using our labour. I had almost doubled in size since my father had returned and much of that was due to the work in the smithy. By the time we reached Falmouth again, the *'Falcon'* was ready for sea and I left Devon for what might be the last time aboard the English carrack. There was something special about sailing aboard a ship that had almost the same name as our gun! Who knew what the future held? At least I was with my father and I had a family; that was all that mattered. I looked at England and thought of the family I once had. They were dead now and lay in English cemeteries. Perhaps one day, when I had made my fortune, I would return to visit their graves and erect better gravestones for I was determined to make something of myself.

Pirate

Chapter 1

I had seen ships before when I had been taken to watch my father leave for the sea but this time, I had a personal interest in them for one would be my home for the foreseeable future. I recognised the vessel from my father's description and the bird at the bowsprit. It looked to be tiny and I wondered how the men I saw swarming over her as she prepared for sea could possibly fit within! The ship was named before my father and his gun were hired but sailors are superstitious, and it was considered lucky that he sailed on the *'Falcon'* and that his gun was called a falconet. My father had named the gun, **Mary**, in honour of my mother. The first voyage we undertook was a legal one, or that was what I thought. It had taken some time to become used to the cramped conditions on the carrack. I did not know, at first, how lucky we were. My father and I had a cabin in the bow castle. It was just large enough for our two hammocks and neither of us could stand inside but it was dry, and we were protected from the worst of the elements. We were next to the store for the cannonballs and above the powder store. My father was unhappy with the position of the powder. It was not fear of explosion for, as he told me if it exploded prematurely then the whole ship would be destroyed. It was more practical than that. He did not wish it to become damp. The reason for our cabin was the falconet which was tied by ropes to cleats. The carpenter made a carriage for us and wheels. My father had the gun fitted with wheels so that we could position it anywhere on the ship but the two gun holes we would use most often were close to the bows. It was there we placed the metal rings with which we secured the gun to the gunwale. My father told me that the recoil would send the gun back across the deck and we would have to haul it into position. I realised that we would need a crew to work the gun. The two of us could not manage it alone.

For the first five days at sea I was learning how to sail and by that, I mean not to vomit. My father spent every moment he could teaching me how to be a gunner. It was not easy as the stink from the gunpowder made me retch until I grew used to the smell. He showed me, without actually using powder and ball, how to load the gun and showed me where he would touch the linstock. He even showed me the wedges he would use to raise and lower the barrel so that he could hit that at which he fired.

"As soon as the captain gives us men to help us work the gun we shall test fire it. Until then you must learn to find your way around the ship. You have entered a different world with names and words which are unfamiliar to you. Come, I will start your lesson."

He led me around the carrack which now appeared bigger than I had first thought when I had seen her tied to the land. The bow castle and stern castle were the places the officers and skilled men such as the carpenter, master, sailmaker and the like, slept. The crew slept either on deck or, if we had no cargo, below deck. I learned my way around the ship and the terminology of sailing. There were sheets and cleats, cross trees, main masts, bowsprits, stern castle, bow castle and a thousand others as foreign to me as Greek. I learned them when I was not learning to move the gun around the ship. Six days in, the captain provided my father with the start of a crew. To that end, two ship's boys were assigned to help us. Ned and Hob were younger than I and their fathers were members of the crew. They, along with my father, helped me to learn the nautical terms and I was able to help them understand my father's strange language.

They would be the ones sent to fetch and carry the ball and powder from the store. On the first calm day we enjoyed we fired the gun for the first time. We did not waste our valuable cannonballs when we practised but smaller smooth rocks were brought aboard for the purpose. When they were used there were other stones kept in the hold as ballast and I was grateful that Ned and Hob were the two who had to fetch them for I hated descending into the Stygian bowels of the ship. One thing I noticed was the large crew who lived aboard. For such a small ship the twenty sailors seemed excessive. Most ships our size had a crew of half or less. It meant more profits for the captain. Our captain was rich and yet he employed more men. I wondered at that for the men would be crowded in their quarters in the sterncastle.

The storm which had brought the ships to port had also left wreckage in the sea and we had targets aplenty as we practised. My father showed his skill as he sent the round stones to within a few feet of the wreckage and, when the stone he used was round enough and smooth enough, he was able to hit the target which always brought a cheer from the crew. The captain seemed satisfied and after four days we stopped wasting powder. My father had paid for it and until we had a profit from our work, we would only use it in anger. I learned that while the gun could send a ball more than a mile, the odds of hitting anything more than five hundred paces away was slim. My father spoke as he worked us and he sounded more like a schoolmaster then than a gunner.

"There are tricks you can do, Tom. You can drop a ball down onto a ship and such a ball, if it is inaccurate might tear a hole in a sail or snap a rope. With luck, you can nick and weaken a mast. There is also the technique of bouncing the stone along the water, as you boys did when you skimmed stones across the village pond. Those lessons will have to wait until we use the gun in anger. You are all three learning and that is good. I will pass on as much knowledge as I can so that you, Tom, will become a better gunner than I." I did not believe that possible and I was in awe of my father.

The other lesson I had was in food and the eating of it. The fresh food had all gone by day four and from then on, we ate cold rations of beer, stale bread, called biscuits, salted pork and, as it was late summer, apples from the barrel. The sailors and ship's boys ran lines astern baited with some of the maggots they found in the apples, the bread or the meat and they caught fish. I had yet to be hungry enough to eat the fish raw as they did but I did not doubt that one day I would succumb. Until then I improvised, and I learned to soak the bread in the beer to make it palatable and to eat an apple at the same time. The other learning experience was emptying my bowels and making water. The latter was easy once you mastered the art of standing on the gunwale, holding on to the foresheet and ensuring that the wind was behind. If any pee landed on the deck then Jacob, the First Mate, would inflict a savage punishment of a stroke with the knotted rope he carried. I never had to suffer that for it was Hob who transgressed. The emptying of the bowels was harder for after lowering your breeks you had to hold on to a handy rope or cleat and try to match the movements of the ship with your rear end hanging over the sea. That this was not an easy task was manifested by the stains which, until we had a storm, marked the side of the ship. Luckily, my new diet meant I did not have to endure the torture often.

The sea, to me, seemed vast and empty. We rarely saw another sail let alone a ship. My father took the time to explain that to me. "Most ships hug the coast and there you will find many ships. We are taking the shorter route and using the wind. We use the open waters and can save up to seven days, but the deeper seas are perilous." He turned and faced aft, I was becoming familiar with such terms now, "After this voyage,

10

Captain Peter has a mind to sail west to the Indies and there we shall have to endure deeper and lonelier seas where we might not see another vessel for three weeks. Regard this as a taste of what is to come."

When we did see a ship, we were close to the estuary which led to Bordeaux. The Captain was obviously seeking wine. Although Gascony had been taken over by France less than sixty years earlier there were still close relations with England and English ships could still trade with Bordeaux. I wondered about this for the First Mate, Jacob, told me that King Henry had allied with the enemies of France and we were at war. No one, least of all the captain seemed concerned but I was apprehensive.

The estuary was very wide, and we had a relatively safe passage up the river. As we were against the current, we would be travelling slower than when we returned. I was just looking forward to hot food and so I was eager to visit my first foreign land. As we sailed up the river it smelled and looked completely different to the Devon I knew. The birds which flew above us had some similarities to ours, but they were different. The ships were also of a different type. Whilst the hulls were largely similar the rigging was different. My father told me that they were lateen sailed and had a flatter bottom for they were not intended for deep-sea work. They travelled the coast and into the sea known as the Mediterranean. It was all an adventure to me, and I loved my new life. The port of Bordeaux made Falmouth look like a fishing village. There were huge warehouses and houses which seemed to rise like cliffs and some towered over our masts. My father and I had no task save to prepare to go ashore and it was others who secured the ship to the quay.

Our clothes marked us as sailors and English ones at that but, as I said, even relations with France were strained here in Gascony we were treated well. Everything was new to me and while the rest of the crew prepared the hold for the cargo the captain went ashore to buy the wine we would take back with us. My father took me around the city for my education. There had been no school in the village and, indeed, my father could neither read nor write and yet he felt he had an education. As he said it was an education in the world and he taught me to use my eyes and ears to learn. "Listen more than you speak and do not judge until you are certain that they will be good judgements."

"When will that be?"

He laughed and ruffled my hair, "That is the trick, my son, to know the moment! Until you know then do not judge at all."

We did not have many coins and so we looked and did not spend much. One thing we did buy was a large earthen pot. I was told that we would use this from now on when we made water. "Sea water corrodes the cannon and fresh water is too valuable to waste on the gun. We swab out the barrel with pee." Every moment spent in my father's company was a preparation for life and I loved it.

My father had invested in the pot because he was certain that our profits from this voyage would enable us to build up our fortune. We did stop in a tavern where my father bought some wine. He watered mine. He also ordered the local bread and ham. Fresh bread was something we would have to forego for months at a time and my father said that French bread was particularly good. As we drank and ate he spoke to me, "Tom, I am unhappy that I have left the service of the king. We are both English and never forget that but there are too many captains like Edmundson, and I had to leave. I know that I neglected you when I went to sea but I felt I had to serve my country. Perhaps God made me leave the service of the king so that I could look after you. When I learned that my parents had died, I was mortified that you were alone. It resolved me to looking after my own interests and yours. My aim is to make us rich men. I hope that you pick up the skills as a gunner for a man needs a trade. We watch out for each other no matter what happens!"

I nodded, "Aye, father, and I am glad that you came back for me. I was not lonely, and Nan and Grandfather loved me and cared for me each and every day. I knew that I was loved but I am happy that we are together." That small meal bonded us together.

We returned to the ship having bought some essentials as well as a good knife for me. We were close enough to Spain for such items to be cheaper than in England. I had a small eating knife, but the one I bought was a working knife and, if needs be, a killing knife for the world in which I now lived was a dangerous one. With double edges and a long blade it would sit in the sheath I bought on my belt and be a constant companion.

The cargo arrived a couple of days later and I was surprised that it did not fill the hold. My father shrugged, "The captain knows his business and there may be other ports he might visit." He did not look me in the eye when he spoke but down at the deck! I was not convinced especially as we sat in the port, where we had to pay mooring fees for another couple of days. We saw other English ships leave and I wondered at that. If they were the first into a home port, then they would get a better price than us. We left on the same tide as a far French ship that was heading for Dieppe. *'Roi Francis'* was bigger than us and far fatter. I thought that our captain was a fool for although the river was wide the Frenchman sailed so that we could not overtake him, and we had to wait until the sea to do so. We should have left earlier and we would have saved time.

Once out to sea we used every inch of canvas and with a hold just a quarter full, we flew. It was when the crew removed the figurehead that I began to wonder about the captain. He hoisted a flag with the cross of Genoa upon it. When we had sailed into the harbour, we had flown the red saltire, the flag of Gascony. I thought it was a courtesy but now I wondered. When my father had me fetch Ned and Hob and we prepared *Mary* to be fired then my suspicions were confirmed. The captain intended piracy. My father must have known but it may have been that as France had taken over lands that were traditionally English, he felt justified. It was when I began to grow up and lose some of my naïvety.

The crew armed themselves and I saw three harquebuses taken out and fitted on their stands on the starboard side. The harquebus was a gunpowder weapon and had a long narrow barrel that fired a lead ball or a stone. They were a close-range weapon and took as long to reload as our falconet. My father said that they were useful only in their unpredictability. The three weapons would send balls into the enemy and they could go anywhere. The men also wore helmets. They were the types known as morions and had no visor. The captain had a cabacet helmet which was a more expensive version and offered protection to the ears. We were going to war. My father had us attach the ropes holding the falconet to the deck and to the aperture on the starboard side also. The captain had planned this and confirmed that he must have told my father what he intended. My father did not seem put out by this act of piracy. We began a turn and with a fast wind astern we headed north and west. I spied, on the horizon, a ship which wallowed a little. As we drew closer, I saw that it was the Frenchman we had seen in Bordeaux.

My father's voice was no longer that of a schoolmaster but one of command, "Now pay attention, all three of you. We fire this gun today in anger. Watch everything that I do, Tom, for one day you shall be a gunner too." He picked up a one-pound ball and rolled it in his hands, "Always choose your best ball for the first shot. When the barrel becomes choked with soot then it does not fly as true. Today, we intend to make this Frenchman stop." He smiled, "The French are at war with us and this is our patriotic duty!" We watched him load the gun and ram it home. We would have to do this eventually. He had lit his linstock as soon as we had seen the Frenchman and now it was glowing red. I held it for him, well away from the powder as he finished his preparations. I held the swab which had been soaked in the urine from the pot. It stank but not as much as the gunpowder.

I did not mind what we were doing for I was young, but I knew that the captain was hiding behind a flag. The French ships began to become suspicious of our sudden approach from seaward. They must have known us from the port and yet we had not only changed our flag we had come from an unexpected quarter. She did not have sea room and there was little that she could do except, perhaps, run for La Rochelle but that was too far away, and she waddled like a milk cow as every inch of sail was put upon her.

I heard as we closed to within ten lengths of her, the Captain's voice, "Show us your skill master gunner. I would have her hit but not harmed."

I saw that the Frenchman had no gun ports and that was why the ship had been selected; she was unarmed. It meant my father could discharge his weapon with impunity.

"Run her out, boys." The falconet was a light gun and although the three of us could easily haul her towards the open port, a couple of sailors came to help us this first time. I think they were excited to see her in action. My father looked down the barrel and using the wedges adjusted the aim. The use of the correct wedges was critical in the aiming of the cannons. I stood ready with the linstock. My father had explained to me the mechanics of the gun. He wanted to impress the captain and so he waited until we were a thousand feet from the Frenchman and when he was satisfied, he took the linstock from me and applied it to the hole. We knew what to expect but the cloud of smoke which followed the tongue of flame still made us jump. My ears hurt and I determined to tie something around them the next time we fired. The ball went into the side of the Frenchman but appeared to do little harm. We knew what we had to do, I took the swab and applied it. I rammed it in the barrel to stop any sparks remaining. Steam hissed. I gave the swab to Hob as my father handed me the linstock and he chose a second ball. Ned picked up one of the half-pound bags of black powder. I was able to watch the flight of the second ball as it spun towards the ship for I had my hands over my ears. With the Frenchman under full sail, it was obvious that the ball would hit but my father would not be happy with a hole in a sail. He had aimed at the mainmast knowing that a misdirected flight would enable it to hit the foremast or lateen. God and the wind were with us and I saw it crack into the mainmast. Of course, it would not destroy the ship but the splinters which flew from the mast showered those nearby and even at just less than a thousand feet I heard the cries.

"Well done, John!" The Captain put the rudder over and aimed for the stern of the ship. He held a speaking trumpet to his mouth and shouted something in French. I guessed it was an order for the Frenchman to hove to and lower the flag.

"Run her out again boys!" As soon as *Mary's* black snout emerged the Frenchman reefed his sails and lowered his flag. The threat was enough. He could not know that we had just loaded a ball. We could have filled the barrel with the small shot used by the harquebus. At close range, my father had told me, they could clear the deck of an enemy ship and the Frenchman would fear the ammunition called grapeshot.

It was only when we came next to her that I saw the disparity of size. She rode lower in the water because her hull was full, and we rode higher for we had few barrels and yet she still towered over us. Two of the crew scrambled up the side to secure us tightly to her and then the captain and ten of his men followed. The large crew was now explained.

I was not privy to the conversation, but my father told me what would be happening. The French crew would be rounded up and the two men with the harquebuses who had boarded with the other crew would be aiming their weapons at them. The ship would be searched for treasure while some of the French crew would be ordered to bring up barrels from below their decks. Our hold was already open and the crew were ready to receive the barrels. One-Eyed Peter was clever. The wind was pushing the two ships towards the French coast and the teeth like rocks which awaited us. The French would hurry to obey the orders of One-Eyed Peter for they would know that our smaller ship could not possibly take all the barrels.

My father shook his head as we waited, "We will have to take out the ball and the powder when we are in port. I don't like leaving a loaded weapon on deck but that was a good ball I used." My father was a craftsman. He knew his trade and that day saw the start of an education which, in many ways, saved my life.

When the hold was full and we were much lower in the water, the captain and his boarders returned. I saw the French line the sides and shake their fists at us. I could not understand their curses, but I knew that they swore. I discovered why as we began to pull away and head back to England. I saw, aboard the Frenchman, sheets and ropes flapping in the wind. Our crew had cut them. They would delay the Frenchman. We did not want to be pursued by French ships from La Rochelle. With the standard of Genoa lowered and the falcon figurehead replaced we became the peaceful merchant ship once more. The Captain was so pleased he sent a bottle of brandy he had taken from the Frenchman to us and with half a beaker inside me, I slept well.

We did not land at Falmouth but Dover instead. There was a method in the Captain's planning. King Henry had troops fighting in Calais, and Dover, protected by its mighty castle, was a safe anchorage. There, we would escape close scrutiny and we would get a good price for our wine for London was the best market. I asked my father why we did not sail up the Thames to make even more profit. He told me that the journey up the congested and twisting river was not worth it. We would make enough. We had paid for just one-tenth of the cargo we sold. It was assumed we had acquired it all legally. We all shared in the plunder from the ship. As with all the profits, One-Eyed Peter took half, my father, our share and the men shared the rest. They were happy. Four of the crew deserted as soon as they had been paid but the captain did not seem dismayed. As my father said, many sailors wished to serve a successful captain and we would find four more easily.

When the coins came in my father and I both became rich. We had not been poor before but now the coins we were paid gave us money to put into a small chest and to fill our purses. We went into Dover town and bought ourselves better clothes, boots, and weapons. I bought a sword. It was shorter than the one used by my father, but now I saw the necessity for it. We were pirates and one day I would need to fight! Most of the money, however, we stored in chests. Our cabin was our home and our castle. There was an unwritten law that no matter what we did to others we never stole from a crewmate. Jacob was the First Mate on the ship and he told me that the punishment was to be thrown overboard. None had ever stolen.

As we had a smaller crew once we had refitted the ship we sailed south to Oporto. With a smaller crew, I was not sure if we would be able to be pirates. As it turned out this was a legal voyage. The captain wanted some Portuguese wine and Portugal was an ally. He would not be robbing a Portuguese ship. However, what we did do was spend some time in port in case a French ship arrived when we might repeat our earlier attack. We spent a fortnight at anchor. The wine would not go off and it gave the Captain the opportunity to find four crewmen and to find other places for us to raid.

We found two men who had fallen out with their captain. One-Eyed Peter established that they were not averse to piracy and Jack and Edgar joined us. The captain, along with Jacob, came to the bow to speak with my father. They were all of an age and seemed to get on. Often, whilst at sea, my father would stand with them at the stern and talk.

"John, there are opportunities it seems to the east, and India. The spice trade is lucrative. We could make money!"

My father nodded, "I have not sailed that far. Have you?"

Both men shook their heads but the captain seemed keen, "Although the Portuguese and the Spanish have forts there now and twixt here beyond those dangers is the land of Africa and it has many treasures for us."

Jacob shook his head, "The southern seas, I have heard, are dangerous and there are huge sea monsters and fish as large as ships there. It would take us many months to sail there and then return."

My father nodded, "That makes sense to me. We will be home in ten days or so when we leave here. We can make twelve voyages a year where, from what you say, we might only manage one going east."

Jacob agreed, "Aye, Captain, this is no galleon, and our hold is not large enough to make the risk worth it."

The captain was sensible enough to take heed of the advice offered. I think he knew the wisdom of it. "Then we head west. The Spanish have found lands there. They thought they had found a short journey to the Indies, but they have not. We can reach their islands in three weeks. The waters may not be known to us but as we are not at war with Spain we can trade or take."

Jacob stroked his grey flecked beard, "Take what, Captain? They do not have wine, do they?"

The captain grinned, "The rumour is that the people there, the ordinary ones, wear gold as though it was not precious, and they have exotic spices and foods too although I know not what they are."

My father was a thoughtful man, and he was the cleverest man I knew. He nodded towards some of the larger ships in the harbour, "Until we do know what there is for us to take would it not be wiser to continue to do as we are? While England is at war with France, we can take from them and each time we dock we can find out more about these new lands to the west of us. Do you not need charts?"

Jacob was the one who advised on maps and he nodded his head in agreement, "John is right, Captain. We cannot buy them for they are preciously guarded. We would have to take them. The last Frenchman we took had good maps of this coast which we added to ours but once we sail beyond Ireland then we would be sailing blind."

"Then we seek charts. From now on we sail further to the west when we return home in case we can find a vessel which has such maps."

That struck me as an unlikely plan. When we had sailed the longer crossing, we had seen nothing except for dolphins and fish! However, it was a plan.

We made two more peaceful voyages and whilst they brought us some profit, we had not yet earned enough for my father to have a second falconet made. That was the plan of both him and the captain. One-Eyed Peter had seen the benefit of the gun in that single action. As Jacob told us before the gun the *'Falcon'* had been forced to use her harquebuses to subdue ships and they had been resisted. Men had been lost. Eventually, other ships would mount guns but, for the moment, we were rare. We also took on four more men and when we did so then I knew that we intended piracy once more.

We sailed to Lisbon this time. Our voyage south on the empty seas showed us nothing but an empty sea. I had thought Bordeaux and Oporto were large and busy, but Lisbon dwarfed the two of them. We seemed like a fishing coble amongst the huge galleons and galleys which filled the harbour. The harbour was alike a small sea it was so vast. My father had seen the port before and he pointed at the largest ships, "They have come from the Indies. They might have sailed for a month or more without sighting the shore. They will have sailed around the southern tip of Africa. be able to sail there is beyond me."

It was not just the ships that were exotic. We had seen Moors in Oporto but here there were all hues and shades of men from olive-skinned through to ebony black and even yellow-hued with eyes which appeared narrow. The world was, indeed, wider than I could have imagined.

Once again, the captain was scouting rather than buying. We had brought some Nottingham Lace to sell and some Kentish hops. He was a good merchant for he knew what was valuable elsewhere in the world.

The hops made for good beer and the lace was light and Iberian ladies craved its delicacy. It made an excuse for our presence.

One of the crew, Rob, also known as Robin Top Man, was small and incredibly strong. He had earned his name by climbing to the top of the mainmast and working there. It was a skilled job. I discovered, in Lisbon, that he had another skill. He was a burglar and was adept at breaking into houses and buildings not to mention ships. There was a Spanish ship in port. She was a galleon, but she had been damaged in a storm far out to sea. She had come from Isla Juana which had been discovered by Columbus some twenty years earlier. Now the man who disembarked from the ship, Diego Velázquez de Cuéllar, had established a settlement. We did not see him or the treasures he had brought back but other captains marvelled at them and their tales seemed as fantastical as the stories of sea monsters. One-Eyed Peter sent Rob to sneak aboard and find any charts. He returned with the charts and I managed to sneak a peek at them when they were shown to my father. To me they were disappointing. They were incomplete and I wondered how they would be of use.

My father explained, "They are a starting point. When we sail to the west, we will add details to them and, perhaps, steal some more. The captain has been speaking with the sailors who returned from this new land and while their masters might be close-mouthed the sailors, for the price of a jug of wine, are less guarded. We know that the voyage will take three weeks out and less than that to return for the winds, generally, come from the west."

"We will sail there then?"

He nodded, "Not until the summer. We might sail close to these coasts in winter and autumn but not an unknown sea which causes so much damage to ships which are like floating towns!"

When we left it was because the Captain had identified another target which docked not far from us. The *'Orleans'* had returned from the Indies. She was a cross between a galleon and a carrack and dwarfed our vessel, but not only did she have no guns but half of her crew had also been lost at sea. Attacked by Arab pirates already, she had spent a week making running repairs to her sails and hull. After speaking with the survivors we learned that she was heading for the Loire and so all that we had to do was to wait off the coast. Under crewed, she would be slower than we were. It would be like a nippy terrier attacking a cow. Although bigger than our carrack we were more agile and could dance around her.

This time my father might have to fire several balls. Over the last weeks we had been making bags of shot to use in case we were attacked and, as a last resort, we could use them to clear the enemy decks. Hob and Ned had collected river stones when we had docked. They were free ammunition and would be just as effective as specially made lead balls. My father had worked out how to use the roll of a ship to lob such missiles into a ship. The ropes, sheets and sails were all vulnerable as well as men working the rigging. It was the day before the Frenchman was due to depart that we headed out towards the sea.

We waited for the ship just a mile offshore. The falcon had gone and, once more we bore the cross of Genoa. Hob and Ned spent most of their lives doing every menial task which could be found, especially by their fathers, so that when they were asked to tend the gun with two of the new men, they were delighted. I think both saw themselves, like me, as an assistant gunner. I suspect there might come a time when my father and I would have to perform more seamanlike duties but for now, we were in such demand that we had a leisurely life.

Rob was the lookout, and it was he who shouted, "Sail, ho!" which alerted us to the Frenchman. He knew the ship we sought and as soon as he gave the call then the sails were allowed to billow, and we began to load the gun. We had learned from the first engagement and it took less time for us to ready the gun at the gun hole. Ned was tasked with raising it. The captain hoped that it would come as a shock when the hole was opened, and the black gun emerged. My father patted *Mary's* barrel almost affectionately, "Fire true, my sweet."

Being at the bow we could see all the movements of the Frenchman and it was clear that he suspected nothing. I think that the angle and the wind meant he could not see our flag. We inexorably drew closer to him and when it was obvious that we were on a converging course he put on more sail. It made no difference for we had the weather gauge, and we were both lighter and faster, not to mention more manoeuvrable. This time it was the Frenchman who opened fire. He, too, had harquebus but whoever fired the two of them had panicked for even *Mary* was not yet in range of the small weapons but they were within point-blank range of our falconet.

The Captain shouted, "Ready when you are, Master Gunner!"

My father raised his hand in acknowledgement and then said, "Run her out!"

We hauled and the polished black barrel peered out of the gun hole. That was the moment when we announced our intentions. Until then we were just an ordinary pirate ship who would try to board and engage in hand-to-hand fighting. Even with many of her crew lost already, the galleon still had more men than we did. That was about to change.

My father chose his moment well and the ball cracked into the mainmast. This time it was a little lower than before. We saw men take cover.

"Reload!"

We had practised these actions so many times that none of us had to think about it. With cloths tied about our ears, we looked like gunners. My father had drilled us every day so that we were perfect. He fired again but this time he aimed at the gunwale. It was like skimming stones on the sea. The ball struck the top of the wood and showered those nearby with deadly splinters. It then ricocheted into the foremast, gouging a chunk out of it before hitting the bow castle where I could see four men with crossbows.

The captain put us close enough so that he could use his speaking trumpet and yet we were beyond the range of the crossbows and harquebus.

I gathered the meaning of the words but this time the French captain suddenly put his rudder over to try to crush us. One-Eyed Peter was too quick for him and *'Falcon'* too lively. We danced out of the way and he shouted, "They need a couple more balls, Master Gunner!"

"Reload!"

This time he chose one of the bags of balls instead of a cannonball. I saw that we were going to cut across the galleon's bows and that would take us within forty feet of the massive vessel. For the falconet that meant we would not miss and cause a great deal of damage. As the bowsprit loomed above us, he held his hand out for the linstock. We were helped by the fact that as we turned our ship heeled over sharply and he fired *Mary* directly up at the crossbows and harquebus aimed at us from the huge bow castle. I had never seen the effect of this bag of balls before for we had yet to fire it. The balls ripped the gunwale and bow castle apart and tore into the ten men who were gathered there with weapons at the ready. Their screams and the blood which arched above them told me the effect.

Suddenly, the ship's flag came down and the captain ordered the sails to be reefed. They were surrendering and my father was saved from having to load the gun again. Hob still washed out the barrel. My job would be, when the gun cooled down sufficiently, to clean away all the powder which had gathered. We did not use seawater for the salt would weaken the barrel. Instead, we used the urine and I used that to clean out the hole and the barrel. It was pungent although necessary work. Already I had become accustomed to the stink of the gunpowder,

All the time we were securing the gun and closing the gun hole the rest of the crew were ensuring that we were well tied to the ship. Jacob had told me that in times past the crew of the captured ship could expect a watery grave for no prisoners were taken. One-Eyed Peter was a practical man, he did not want ships to fight to the death because they feared being captured. Of course, he knew that he had a limited time to make his money for captains would spread the word about the carrack with the falconet and that, I think, was why he planned on the newly established Spanish colonies to be his next target. It took longer to unload the cargo this time for One-Eyed Peter had to be selective in what we took. He picked the most easily transported items and those which would bring the greatest profit. It was almost dark as we sailed away. Once more the ship would take some time to be able to continue for, apart from the injuries and deaths they had suffered, our men had also damaged their rigging. They would have more repairs to effect. We took the harquebuses and undamaged crossbows. They would be useful.

Rob came to see us as we headed north and west. He strode over to *Mary* and patted her, "Master Gunner, I would not like to be on the wrong end of this. The men you hit before they surrendered," he shook his head, "four were dead and without faces while the others will all be crippled. Even those who were struck by splinters will be scarred for life."

My father nodded and, taking a cloth, wiped the place Rib had touched, "We should make the most of it for when other ships learn how to use these at sea then we will have bloody battles!"

I had not thought of that. I just saw the easy victories and the riches that would come our way.

Chapter 2

We made even more profit from this voyage and when I saw the gold and helped to count it out, I asked, "Do we leave the sea now, father? We are rich enough to buy a farm or a large house."

He laughed, "I am no farmer and what would I do in a large house? I would spend all my time in the alehouse and become John the Brawler once more. After I left the navy and took on your upbringing, I put the brawling behind me and, besides, do you not wish to see this new land in the west? When we were in Lisbon, I heard the Spanish sailors speak of a place called El Dorado, a city of gold to the west. It is said that the roads are paved with precious metal and all wear rubies and pearls about their necks. They have fetched back great quantities of gold and silver, but they say it is a drop in the ocean. It is the poorer tribes they have encountered, and they seek a land further west. I should like to visit it."

The other crewmen had heard the same and this time there were no desertions for they all wished to go to the Indies. The word spread and other sailors tried to sign on. One-Eyed Peter was no fool and he did not take any on for he would have to keep them over the winter. Instead, we headed for Devon and Cornwall once more. The captain was a Cornishman, and he knew of a deserted cove where we could beach *'Falcon'* and clean the weed and barnacles from her hull. We could apply a poisonous coating that would slow down the deadly worms which might threaten her. The ship would have to be in perfect condition to face the Atlantic Ocean. Ropes, crosstrees, and masts would be replaced. Spares would be bought for when next we went to sea; we would be crossing the great ocean and we had to be able to repair our ship. My father and I returned to the blacksmith who had made **Mary** for he would have another made. The cost would be borne by the captain and my father jointly. I had improved so much that he made me his assistant. He would still direct me when we used the guns, but it would be me who used the linstock on the second gun. I felt I had taken the first step to becoming a man.

The village looked suddenly much smaller when we returned. Until I had left, the only big place I knew was Totnes. We had walked from Totnes in order to pay for the falconet. The first one had taken most of his savings; this one took so little that we barely noticed. That was the difference between the money saved while a gunner on a King's ship and a pirate.

The blacksmith, Egbert, noticed a difference in me immediately, "The sea air has done him a power of good John. He will soon be the size of you!"

My father beamed with pride, "Aye, and he will be a gunner too,"

The smith nodded, "Then this gun will be for him?"

My father nodded, cautiously, "Perhaps!"

"In which case, I shall work a design in the barrel for him. Perhaps his grandmother's name? She was very fond of him."

My father smiled, "Aye, Betty, I like that. She could not abide Elizabeth, could she, but Betty, now there is a name for a gun?"

We left the village and walked back to Totnes where we would stay the night before returning to the ship. The smith had said that the work would take him a month which was not excessive for what he needed to do. My father and I would build the trunions and the wooden frame for the gun while the ship was being cleaned. The landlord of the inn, Alf, was wary of my father for his brawling past. He still drank heavily but this was a different John the Falconer and halfway through the evening Alf came over with a couple of drinks.

"These are from me, John! Have you found religion for you are not the same man who came here a couple of years since and almost destroyed my inn?"

He put his arm around me, "No, I found my son. I don't know why I fought so much. Now I am more at peace with myself."

The next day as we walked to the beach and joined the rest of the crew I said, "You know, father, I think you brawled so much because of mother and her death. That is what Grandmother thought and she was wise."

"Aye, perhaps you are right. They say a man may have many women, but he only has one love of his life and that was your mother. You remind me of her. We have a new start, my son, and when we go to the new world it will be as though someone has wiped our slate clean and we can begin again fresh. There is nothing left for us in England. I am still English, but I want new horizons and a future for both of us."

By the time we reached the ship, I was desperate to board her and leave England, but we had a winter of work ahead of us and I knuckled down with the rest. The cove we found must have been some sort of port in ancient times for there were the remnants of old stone dwellings close to the beach. With the addition of branches and pieces of old damaged sail, we made ourselves homes which, whilst not comfortable, would keep us dry and away from the worst of the autumn and winter storms which, inevitably, came from the west.

My father and I, with One-Eyed Peter's permission, painted an eye on each of the gun holes at the bows. It looked effective and managed to make the holes for the guns disappear. That was when my father and I joined the rest of the crew cleaning the hull. With the carrack canted on her side, we scraped away the stinking weed and crustaceans which clung to her hull. Jacob checked for worms and any dubious sections were removed and we replaced them with fresh wood. When we had completed that then the progress on the rest of the hull slowed. When we had completed one side then Jacob brewed up a foul-smelling concoction which we painted on the hull. We then had to wait for it to dry before we could refloat her and then bare the other side.

I said all the crew but that was not true. One-Eyed Peter took Hob with him and they left us. He did not tell us where he was going for he was the captain and did not need to tell us. My father and Jacob, when we ate our evening meal, speculated that he was finding out more about the seas to the west. If we did not have maps and charts, then he would seek men who had sailed west and mine their conversations for nuggets of gold.

It was while scraping the hull that I got to know the crew. They varied in age and background. Some had been married men, but they had left home. Two because they had married a scold. Others had left the home because they did not like to work for another. Most were young men like me. They wanted adventure and, despite the risks, they wanted the opportunity to become rich. Life in England could be perilously short. The sweating sickness had been around for a few years and whilst not as dangerous as the plagues which regularly visited the land, the illness took apparently healthy men. The sea for all its dangers seemed free of such pestilence.

We celebrated Christmas in our huts. The hull was clean and our task after the twelfth night was to begin to paint the upper part of the ship with the protective concoction and renew the ropes and sheets. One-Eyed Peter and Hob returned a week before Christmas with a cart, another sailor, drink, and food including half a dozen noisy, caged, geese. We built a pen for the geese which we would fatten up and, as we had some sacks of flour, built a brick oven which would save a long walk to the nearest town to buy bread twice a week. I was sick of fish and shellfish. The occasional bunny we had trapped had been a highlight. The geese would feed us for the whole of the Christmas celebrations.

However, all our attention was on the swarthy and ancient sailor who had come with the captain. He had a wooden leg and that fascinated me as I had never seen one. He looked older than any of the rest of the crew and that included old Jacob. He was thin and emaciated. Captain One-Eyed Peter himself made the old man comfortable in the best of the huts, the one reserved for him and so we were denied the chance to question him.

Hob, of course, was under no such restriction and as he and Ned were my friends, while we collected the inevitable shellfish from the beach, he told us of his adventures with the captain.

"We went to London! The Captain hired a horse and a pony, and we stayed in inns all the way to London. I did not mind sleeping on the floor nor fetching and carrying for the captain for we ate well, and it was not just small beer I was given!"

Ned shook his head, "I wish that it had been me who was selected!"

Hob and Ned were good friends and, in many respects still children, "He picked the cleverest! We visited the sea captains and the inns they frequented. There were many and we gathered information. The captain wrote and I kept the papers safe and then when we were at Tilbury, we heard of this man we brought, Juan de Burgos. One of the captains said that he was a Spaniard who had sailed with Columbus. We heard that he was begging in Shoreditch and we sought him out. That was but eight days since. As soon as we found him the captain quickly clothed and fed him. We rode the horses to Portsmouth where we took a ship to Falmouth. It was there we bought the geese and the other supplies."

I was eager to know about the Spaniard, "And the Spaniard, what did you learn of him?"

"His English is not good, but he seems like a nice man. He has lost most of his teeth and when he smiles it is like looking into an old graveyard. He looks thin now but when we discovered him, he was a walking corpse. One-Eyed Peter has filled him with food, and he was even given a bed!"

"Then he must be important."

Hob nodded as he scooped up a crab to drop it into the bucket we were using to collect the shellfish, "He sailed with Columbus and was with three other expeditions, the last one just two years since. He has been beyond the islands which they first discovered to the land which lies to the south and west. It was there he lost his leg. He was foraging in the jungle there when a cat, twice the size of a man attacked him. It took his leg before his comrades could come to his rescue. The captain of his expedition took off the rest of the leg below the knee and they sealed it with fire. The wood of his leg comes from that land and it is marvellously hard. When he returned, he was paid off."

"Then how did he end up in London?"

Hob tapped his nose, "The same reason the captain sought him. Another Englishman found him in Cadiz and sought his knowledge. He brought him back to England, but the captain had the sweating sickness and died a day after they arrived. The Spaniard's English was poor then and he could not tell his story. The only work he could find was as a gong scourer and even that did not last long. By the time his English was good enough for him to tell his tale all that it brought him was the coppers he earned from telling his story which is how we found him. Men thought it a fantasy."

"And he would go back with us, even though it cost him dear?"

"Aye, Tom, for he said that the rivers ran with gold and he would go back to become a rich man."

I did not believe that the rivers ran with gold but if he was willing to go back so readily then there must be something in his story. We did not get to speak to him for One-Eyed Peter and Jacob were closely closeted with him. The papers and charts were amended and improved. My father thought it boded well for our expedition. The man would know where their ships sailed, and it was their ships we would take. With two falconets we would be more powerful than any ship they had in that part of the world. We had established that much from speaking with Juan. I liked the old man for despite the loss of his leg he was always cheerful and hopeful of a golden future. One-Eyed Peter saw in him an investment and he had us all working hard to keep the old man happy whilst improving the ship. The cart proved useful for my father and I were able to use it to fetch the falconet, my new gun, *Betty*. My father had made the trunions and they were already aboard the now refloated, *'Falcon'*.

Alf had done a good job. He had etched the name *Betty* in the bronze, using a copper and iron mix to do so. It looked effective and my father was more than happy to pay the price. My father and Alf had grown up together and were still friends. I had also known the smith all my life.

27

My father and I knew that we would not see him again for a long time, if ever. Alf understood, all too well, that we were sailors, and the seas were perilous. It was a poignant parting but there were no tears, just firm arm clasps and meaningful looks. With the cast iron balls he had made for us we left with a wagon and horse we had hired.

"What about powder, father? Will we be able to procure it in the west?"

He shook his head, "I doubt it and if we do then it will be more valuable than gold. I would suggest to the captain that we fill the hold with it but that would just make us a floating bomb!" He chuckled at his own black humour. "We can make our own for that is the best way. Sulphur and charcoal can be obtained anywhere but the saltpetre is more difficult. It can be found but you have to know where to look, or you could manufacture it. We could always make our own, but it takes ten months to do so. We might be better off taking saltpetre. I will speak with One-Eyed Peter. I do not mind paying for it as we are well rewarded."

"And when we are as rich as King Henry, father, what then?"

He smiled, "Speaking to Juan I know that the people of the west are primitive but hard working. Perhaps I will become king of the new land." He smiled, "That is for the future. Let us take it one step or should that be one voyage at a time. You are enjoying life are you not?"

"Of course, life is an adventure."

"Then let us live it!"

The captain was happy for us to take saltpetre with us as we would not need huge quantities and when my father and I had fitted **Betty** he and Jacob went to Falmouth to arrange for the supplies and the saltpetre we would need to be ready and waiting for us when we sailed there to take on our supplies. We were almost ready to sail.

When Juan was not sitting with the captain he liked to sit with Hob, Ned, and me at the bows. There were two reasons I think: firstly, he was an old man and had no children. Ned and Hob were like the children and grandchildren he never had and secondly, he was interested in the falconet. He knew of the harquebus and told us how simply firing it terrified the natives into submission. When he saw the cannonball we used he was impressed. We used the time to learn the others' language. His English improved and we learned Spanish. It was not idle chatter for he told us of the jungles, natives, and creatures we would meet. The cat which had savaged him was just one of many. He said it was the size of a lion. Then there were crocodile-like creatures. I had seen a stuffed crocodile once and I thought they were terrifying. He spoke of snakes as long as a ship and insects whose bites could kill. He told us of the heat and the humidity which slowly suck the life out of a healthy man. It seemed to me that there were more reasons not to sail than to risk all.

He shook his head, "Tomas," when he said my name it always sounded formal and grand, the O sound seemed to go on forever and the S at the end was sibilant, "there are treasures there such as you cannot imagine. We have yet to begin to find them. Further west are cities made of gold and silver. On our expedition, we took prisoners with golden coins in their ears and noses yet they have neither iron nor copper. Their weapons are bone, stone, or wood. Why a single knight could often capture a whole village for their weapons could not even begin to dent his mail and they are terrified of horses, even a small one for they know not what they are and the men who lead the expeditions are like knights of old. We call them Conquistadors, conquerors for that is what they do, they conquer and take. They are unbeatable."

His words set me thinking. Perhaps we needed armour and mail. We could take horses and then I sank back to earth. We were not going to conquer a land like the Spaniards. We were going to rob them and return east. My father's dream of becoming a king had seduced me. We were pirates; nothing more and nothing less!

It was April by the time we were ready to sail. We would not need the whole hold for our supplies and some of the crew would be able to sleep where we would normally carry our cargo. They tried it out on the voyage to Falmouth and seemed quite happy to be almost entombed in the dark. I would not have relished that for our little cabin was dark enough, but they seemed quite relieved to have the warmth and dryness it afforded. We headed for Falmouth where, after we had loaded the supplies, the captain allowed the crew ashore, over two nights, to enjoy their last hot meal for some time. We had barrels of ale on board as well as water and salted meat not to mention dried beans. Our hold did not carry cargo, just supplies. One-Eyed Peter had also spoken with Juan and he had extra weapons and helmets bought for us. My father and I sat together in the inn. We were both reflective for this might be our last night in England for months or even years. Our goodbye to Alf seemed to presage what would be a goodbye to England. One-Eyed Peter was philosophical and thought that we would easily be able to return, sell what we had and then sail west for more profits. Speaking with Juan had made me realise that even if that did happen, we would be away for a year, perhaps two. The ale tasted sweeter knowing that the next ale we drank might be old, stale and almost sour. The hot food tasted like ambrosia as we knew there would be none until we reached the other side of the world. Even the people we saw made us homesick before we had even left. The girls who served the drinks would be the last white women we would see until we returned. We really were going to a new world.

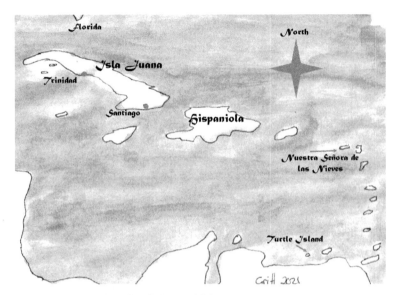

The Caribbean 1515

Chapter 3

The weather was not propitious when we left. It was not a gale, but the sea was lively with steep waves and deep troughs, and we secured our precious falconets with double restraints and canvas. We had not yet had the time or the place to test fire *Betty* and I was eager to do so. That would have to wait until the seas had abated and we could see the full effect. Juan had told us that often a ship would be becalmed, and my father saw that as the best opportunity to see how good *Betty* was. Until we sailed much further west Juan was not needed by the Captain and so he sat with us at the bow. We had made canvas covers to keep the seawater from the metal, but we still polished them dry each day and while we did my Spanish improved as did Juan's English. Hob and Ned were quite envious for they were kept busy sailing the ship. Only my father, Juan, and I had the luxury of idleness. After two weeks of such sailing and enduring all that the ocean had to throw at us, we suddenly found ourselves becalmed and I was delighted. It was a cloudless sky, and my father used some wreckage we had discovered in the sea just four days into our passage. Hob and Ned used the small boat to row eight hundred feet from us and spread the wreckage out to give us multiple targets. We spread sand around the gun and, of course, we were barefoot to have a better grip. My father warned me to watch my feet for if the wheels of *Betty* hit them then I would be crippled for life!

The crew, shirtless, lined the larboard side as we prepared *Betty* for her first firing. I was not yet a real gunner, and we all knew that but I was well able to load and aim a gun albeit roughly. My father, when Hob and Ned returned, allowed me to aim at one of the targets. We loaded with round cobbles slightly smaller than our iron balls. They were the bounty from the beach. We did not wish to damage the gun and I knew that the cobbles would be much more inaccurate than the round iron balls. This would just give us a rough idea of what the gun could do and would allow me to practise. Every gun was unique and having been made by hand would all handle differently. Normally the tasks of loading and firing were done by the team, but my father let me do them all. We were going nowhere and, as Juan had told us, this calm could last for days. I had watched my father do all that I did but I did not know why. This would be my chance to learn and, from the corner of my eye, I saw him watching me carefully.

I had learned to tie a cloth around my ears and as I fastened it the sounds were muffled and, in many ways, that helped for it concentrated the rest of my senses on the cannon and the target. I applied the linstock. There was the normal delay and then the flame belched forth like a roaring dragon and I watched the arc of the ball as it soared and fell. It landed a good fifty feet beyond the wooden target. I was disappointed. I saw my father speaking to me and I took off the cloth.

"Alf has made **Betty** more accurate than **Mary**. That is good to know. Next time adjust your aim a little."

I almost hit the target with the second shot, but I was still more than ten feet from it. It took four shots for me to hit wood and by that time my father deemed we had used enough of our powder, but I could tell that he was happy. I spent the rest of the day cleaning out the gun so that by the time I had finished she was like new. I was a satisfied gunner.

That was the last day that Juan was able to spend with us for Juan had said that the calm seas were just a week or so from the first of the ring of islands we sought. Their position gave them their name, the Leeward Islands. We had a map, of sorts. Thanks to Juan some of the gaps had been filled in already. We knew we had to sail through a couple of rings of islands. Isla Juana lay to the north close to Hispaniola and, as we were headed for what we hoped would be the middle, we could add to our knowledge. Everyone on the ship was desperate for a landfall. The water was long past stale, and the ale was merely vinegar. I had overcome my revulsion and eaten raw fish just to alleviate the monotony of the ship's biscuits and salted ham. The salted ham almost mocked us for it increased the thirst we felt and all we could use to refresh it was stale water or vinegary ale.

We caught sight, briefly, of a sail to the west of us. Ned was atop the mast and it was he who spied it. The winds were gentle and from the south-west but despite all the canvas we could manage the sails disappeared, but it was a hopeful sign. Ned thought that the ship was heading north. Juan, One-Eyed Peter, and Jacob scrutinised the map carefully for a clue of our position. Navigation, without fixed points of land, was not a precise science. We sailed under reefed sails for we might find an island, Juan said there were many, or we might find a ship. Either was desirable. It was the former we found. It was a tiny rock in the blue sea with a few trees growing out of lush undergrowth, but it was land, and we could anchor and step ashore.

Juan had warned us that the natives whilst easily cowed were sneaky and treacherous. The island looked uninhabited, but it would not do to take that for granted. The boat which was sent ashore had armed men in it and we watched offshore from just a hundred paces, as they dragged the boat onto the sand and drew their weapons. While one watched the boat the other three disappeared into the greenery. They were not away long, and they waved to show that it was safe. We had just one boat and we had to wait for it to return.

I was desperate to get ashore, but my father shook his head. "There is little point. We seek to top up the water barrels and cook a hot meal. The captain wishes to examine the ship for damage and then we will sail. We are still unsure of our position. Be patient. It is good just to see something which is not the sea."

The captain was of the same mind. The water which they managed to find was rainwater trapped in rock pools. It freshened our barrels of water and that was all. The men sent ashore managed to hunt some birds and a shellfish and bird stew was concocted. Juan did not go ashore and so the men were told not to add any greens as they could be poisonous. We needed a larger island where we could all go ashore, and Juan would identify what was edible and what was not. The two-day stay at the island, however, was a relief. We bobbed at anchor and we had hot food. We had slightly fresher water and we could see land. After the vast ocean across which we had travelled that was reassuring.

When we sailed, we still headed due west. Juan was confident that by doing so we would cross the path of a ship sailing from what he called the mainland, north to Isla Juana. That was the largest Spanish settlement and acted as a revictualling centre as well as a gathering point for ships heading back to Spain. They would travel in convoys for mutual safety and protection. We were in the Spanish sea and they felt safe. We would not risk a convoy but if we could find a single ship then we would pounce.

We spied the caravel just before noon the next day. She was heading, as Juan had predicted, north and that gave us a good indication of our position. We flew no flag and I do not think that the ship was in any way suspicious of us. As we drew closer and they saw the larger crew then they became wary and, using all their sails they tried to outrun us. The clean hull and the care we had lavished upon *'Falcon'* paid off and we soon overhauled them. It was Juan who commanded them to stop but the answer and the crack from the harquebus was a clear answer.

"Master gunner, load and run out one of your guns, if you please."

My father nodded and said, "I do not think that we shall have to fire today, we shall let them see **Betty**."

I hoped he was wrong for I wished to fire my gun in anger. I chose the best ball and did it all as carefully as though I was going to fire. Ned opened the gun hole and we pulled **Betty's** black snout to menace the caravel. We were less than ten lengths from them and gaining when they saw the gun and they took in their sails, defeated. We tied up next to her. She was heavily laden, and our deck rose above her. As the hold was opened my father said, "I do not think that she would be able to sail across the sea for she is smaller than we are, and I think she has been built over here. Our captain may have chanced upon a perfect plan. If we can collect enough treasure from these smaller ships, then we can do so without suffering injuries and sail home rich men."

We took their food and water first followed by wine and ale. Then the chests were fetched up. The ship had come from the south and there was treasure on the small ship. As it turned out it was not a fortune but enough to put us in profit already. There were many pearls as well as some gold and silver. There were sacks of food which none of us recognised but Juan did and he said we could either eat them or, if we sailed back soon, sell them. We barely filled a quarter of our hold which confirmed that it was unlikely that the caravel would sail all the way to Spain. With the ropes on the Spaniard slashed to give us time to escape we headed west until the caravel disappeared from view and then we headed south and west. Rob the top man came forrard to make water.

"What is the captain's plan, Rob?"

As he pulled up his breeks and turned, he said, "He is a clever one and no mistake! He wanted the Spaniard to think we headed west but Juan Peg Leg advised him that there were islands he knew of to the south. When we took the stores from the caravel, we also took their charts and their captain had obligingly marked their course. Juan knows where we are. He is taking us to a placed called La Tortuga!"

"The turtle," I said. Juan's lessons had paid off.

Rob looked at me in surprise, "Aye, he said it was an uninhabited island with water and it looks like a turtle. He says we can anchor there and use it as a base. It is far from prying Spanish eyes and he is sure that they have not colonised it and it is just marked as an island with water on their maps."

Juan was right but it was not the best of places. We found it after a two-day search; the map we had was not as accurate as we might have liked but there was a good anchorage and with the sails furled, we would be hidden from all but the closest scrutiny. There was a supply of water on the island, but it was a small one. The captain set to building a blockhouse from the timber we found. It was a place to store some of our supplies. We had taken salted meat from the Spaniard. It was not ham but it tasted good and it freed up space in our hold. The chests we had taken were inventoried and they were left in the crude blockhouse. For the three days it took to build we slept and ate ashore. It was a luxury and then we headed north towards Hispaniola for that was where the gold was.

It took almost a week to reach the huge island and we saw few ships in that time. We were to the east of the main route used by the Spanish ships but the one we had taken already had shown One-Eyed Peter that there was little gold to be had there. Hispaniola was the largest Spanish island and there we would find ships sailing back to Spain laden with treasure. Heading north we travelled for many days and nights. We approached the harbour of Santo Domingo at night and saw that it was filled with ships. There were too many for us to take and Juan said that there were guns protecting the anchorage. We headed for the channel between Hispaniola and the island of San Juan Bautista. The smaller island had no gold and, therefore, few defences.

As dawn broke, we loaded both guns as well as the smaller firearms and the crossbows we had taken from the Spanish ship. Our sails were furled for we could loose them quickly. Whichever ship we tried to take would be both bigger and slower than we. We could catch them. It was not long before noon when the sun baked the whitening deck of our carrack and ensured that any bared feet upon it were burned, that we saw the galleon as it headed north and west. It was on our larboard side and Hob spotted the sails on the horizon. It crossed our course. Juan had told us that the ships used that particular course as it afforded the fastest crossing.

The captain shouted, "Right boys, this is a big one and may have guns. Today our Master Gunner will show his skill and we shall be like a terrier taking on a bear. We will dance around and nibble pieces from her until she surrenders. John the Falconet, we are in your hands! Let fly the mainsail!"

We had not just Ned and Hob with us, the Captain had given us four of the crew. All were new men, and they were strong. Their job would be to haul the falconets into position. My father and I, helped by the two boys, would be responsible for the firing. We each had a linstock and I blew on it to make it glow. The gun holes with their painted eyes were still closed as we stalked the unsuspecting galleon. We were coming from their starboard quarter and they would assume that we were Spanish despite the lack of flag.

The lookout was Rob whose legs were wrapped around the crosstree. He shouted, "I see gun holes, Captain!"

That was disturbing, "How many?"

"There look to be two on the starboard side."

I looked at my father who said, "They will be falcons or, perhaps a saker." He shrugged, "They fire a ball which can be between two and four pounds."

"Should we not stand off then? We are outgunned." I did not want my first action to end in failure.

"Where there is risk there is also reward and I am a Master Gunner. Do not worry, Tom, I do not fear this Spaniard."

As we closed with the laden ship the Spanish captain became suspicious and I saw the black snouts of the guns as they were run out. We had the wind gauge and One-Eyed Peter seemed unconcerned. We stalked our prey, and I knew there would be no invitation to surrender. We would worry them to death. Now that we were closer, I saw that whilst she was larger, she was also lower in the water. Her guns would be able to rake us and if they had two on the starboard side then there would be two on the larboard. In a duel, we would lose.

My father shouted, "Captain, take us towards their stern!"

"Aye, John!"

I saw him aim, the range was long, more than six hundred paces but the stern was the largest target. The harquebus on the galleon popped ineffectually at us as my father fired. The one-pound ball struck the stern but did little damage. He began to reload and said, "I am trying to disable her. A ship with no rudder cannot manoeuvre."

The range had closed, and his second shot was more accurate. He struck just above the rudder. The Spanish captain now saw what we were attempting, and crossbow bolts flew at us. If they struck any flesh, then it would be down to pure luck. I clutched the cross at my neck. We were less than three hundred feet from her stern when the third ball smashed into the rudder. The effect was astounding. The Spanish now had just the wind and the sails to steer the ship. That would take the crew all their time and they would not be able to use crossbows. Even as we passed the stern, I saw men using ropes to clamber down and begin to repair the damage. Had my father had grapeshot ready we could have hurt them, but our harquebuses and crossbows felled one sailor and drove the rest back aboard.

"Captain, bring us around again!"

The Captain waved and we turned across the wind which closed us. "Tom, now it is Betty's turn. Aim for the rudder. At the moment it can be repaired. Can you fire three balls?"

"Aye, father, that we can, eh boys?" I was a youth and yet the two men on the gun and Ned yelled and cheered as though I was a veteran.

It took time for us to turn and I had a good sight of the target which wallowed as the Spanish tried to evade us. Men lined the sides of the ship and I saw that they were all armed. Like my father's first shot my initial attempt hit high but had the effect of splintering the gunwale and clearing it of men, who took shelter.

"You need to use the roll of our ship Tom!"

I nodded as the next ball was loaded. The range was shortening, and my second ball hit the rudder full-on destroying it. They would not be able to repair it. My third one was almost point-blank, and I struck the stern below the waterline.

"Well done, my son! That will put the fear of God into them. Captain, once more and we will see if they wish to surrender."

One-Eyed Peter waved his hand in acknowledgement and he put the *'Falcon'* about to allow my father to have another shot. This time he had grapeshot ready as well as the ball. His first shot was with a cannonball and he fired on the up roll so that the ball smashed into the ornate balustrade which ran around the sterncastle. Splinters both large and small smashed through the ornate sterncastle. He waited for his second shot until we were within a hundred feet and he put both ball and grapeshot in the barrel. Once again, he waited for the carrack to roll and when he had an angle on the gun he fired. Double shotting the gun meant we did not have as much power, but the effect was devastating. We were square on to his stern and the smaller balls added to the one-pound cannonball we used cleared the quarter deck. The flag was hauled down and the sails were reefed.

"Prepare to board. While we are aboard, Master Gunner, I will have Jacob stand off and you can ensure that the Spaniard tries no tricks!"

"Aye, Captain!" He turned to me and said, "There will be no tricks for we have killed the officers. The crew will happily comply, but I worry that we are close enough to Hispaniola for the gunfire to have been heard. If they send ships for us, we may find ourselves trapped. You had better reload **Betty**."

We had just finished reloading the guns when One-Eyed Peter cupped his hands and shouted for Jacob to close with the Spanish ship. We had just two men and two boys left to work the sails and it took us longer than my father liked. The delay, however, allowed our boarders to gather the treasure at the tumblehome. The hold was opened, and we lowered in barrels and chests. We later discovered that our captain had been judicious. He took the treasure that was gold and silver, not to mention spices as well as food supplies and gunpowder. The other items which, while they would fetch a high price in England, he left aboard because they were too bulky. We might be thieves, but we were choosy ones. It was late afternoon by the time we were loaded and that proved costly. My father's prediction was accurate, ships appeared on the horizon from the west. The gunfire had been heard and there was a response. We cast off. There had been no need to damage the ship further for she was shipping water and her rudder would have to be replaced.

As soon as he was aboard the captain had the hold secured and then shouted, "Make all sail and head east!"

My father grinned, "Clever. They will know we are English from our words and when we head east, they will think that we are heading home. As the east will be darker sooner than the west we can disappear, and we can head back to Isla la Tortuga."

Rob was the lookout and he shouted down that the Spanish ships had stopped to aid the damaged galleon. We turned south and headed for home, our new lair. The next day the captain came to see both my father and me. He was delighted with the success we had enjoyed, "Can you repeat that next time we attack?"

My father shrugged, "So long as they have no guns facing us then aye. Our falconets are an irritant. If the Spaniard had turned and used his own guns, then he could have blown us out of the water. We need falcons and a much bigger crew if we are to take on galleons!"

"Then we will only attack ships without guns."

"Do you not intend to return to England, Captain?"

He grinned and with his one eye it always gave him a lopsided look, "We have not even filled a quarter of our hold. When we are full then we sail home, and I shall buy a bigger ship!"

It showed his ambition, but ambition can overreach itself!

Chapter 4

We evaded any pursuit and four days later reached our island; it was so small that I could see why it had been overlooked. We saw no evidence that anyone else had landed there and nothing appeared to have been touched. It took a whole day to unload and when that was done, we had to build ourselves a second blockhouse for the supplies we had taken. The treasure was a different matter. We divided it up in the usual way. One-Eyed Peter suggested that what we did not wish to carry with us we should bury and hide. After much debate, which went on longer because we now had drink and that made some men more argumentative, we agreed to bury most of the treasure. Some men chose to keep their treasure with them, but the majority helped to dig the hole and line it with wood before putting a lid upon it and covering it with earth.

Altogether we spent three days on the turtle. We ate hot food and devoured all the perishable food we had taken from the Spanish ships. It was good that we had Juan with us, for the food was new and we could not discriminate between the leaves that were used to roll together and light, and gnarled and nobbled roots we could peel and boil. Some of the tastes were quite pleasant, like the soft red fruits filled with tiny seeds but the small red pods which looked similar were anything but pleasant. Despite Juan's warnings that they were hot, we all tasted them. I was lucky, I just nibbled the end, but Hob took a large bite and discovered that even ale would not take the taste away. Even the touch of them burned and I wondered why any would take what was clearly a poison. After that we took Juan's advice and if he said something was sweet then we ate it. Gradually we would become used to the new tastes for we could not find the food we were used to!

One-Eyed Peter then decided our next raid. We would head south to where Juan said was the mainland and head to the nearby Isla Margarita which was the main Spanish base in the area. Firstly, it would be a shorter voyage and secondly, there was more likelihood of finding gold or silver there. As my father pointed out they might not have got around to mounting guns there to defend against us. We had a sound reason for risking the Spanish base. The island and the mainland, according to Juan, were renowned for pearls. They were a highly transportable commodity.

We headed south and had a much shorter voyage to reach the mainland. The land we saw was made up of lush jungle and then rising highlands which grew to mountains. We saw fishing boats as we headed for the fishing village of Puerto La Cruz. Juan had it marked on the map and it was the closest settlement to our own island. It took a day to reach it and we anchored at night, hidden by the dark but able to identify the village by the fires and the smell of woodsmoke. One-Eyed Peter came up with a clever plan. He sent four men ashore and two others brought back our boat. The Captain and another three men joined the first four so that we had ten men ashore. Jacob was left in command of the ship and our job was to sail close to the shore and threaten the village with our falconet and harquebuses. We hoped that they would have pearls but, if not, then they would have food and animals. Both were acceptable to us. I thought we could have sailed home anyway. We had more treasure already than we had dreamed. We were being greedy.

As we waited in the dark, I listened to my father, Juan and Jacob talking. I realised that although we were breaking a commandment and stealing, not to mention killing, I was happy with my new trade as a gunner. I liked my life, and the theft did not seem so terrible when I realised that the Spanish had already stolen it from the Indians! Juan had told me some of the atrocities which the Spaniards had committed and our little piece of piracy did not seem so bad. The way I saw it even if we had to spend six months or so living close to danger and taking Spanish ships we would have more than enough treasure to take home and become rich men. Then my father and I could leave the sea. I did not see myself as a pirate for the rest of my life; this was just something I had to do to better myself. One-Eyed Peter wished to buy a bigger ship so that he could rob on a larger scale, but my father and I were getting adventure from our systems and becoming richer in the process. The piracy did not sit well with a king's man who had fought and hunted pirates in the past.

The crew who remained on board did not sleep. We had enjoyed two leisurely days and we were all too excited. Some were gambling while others were carving pieces of bone. We had taken salted carcasses and the bones, once cooked could be carved. Some made fishhooks whilst others chose to fashion brooches and pins. Few sailors were idle. As for me? I polished *Betty*.

The sun came up and, as the villagers emerged, our ship was bathed in sunlight and we were seen. The Indians ran to get their weapons and, from both sides of the forest came One-Eyed Peter and our men! We had the cannons loaded but there was no need for the sight of ten men with swords was enough for them to drop to their knees. If the Indians could speak Spanish it was rudimentary and bearing in mind what we had been told of the Spanish and their treatment of the tribes, our men just ransacked the village. They found food and, from the way One-Eyed Peter waved the bag in the air, he had found pearls too. With our own boat and a commandeered fishing boat, they sailed back to *'Falcon'* and we loaded the food. It was enough for a week and the pearls were a welcome surprise. We set sail and headed north and east. Isla Margarita would be a different prospect!

We reached the island in the midmorning. It became clear that it was not one huge island, but two larger ones separated by a patch of water big enough for a small caravel to pass through. Other islands lay between the two main islands and the mainland. We passed a couple of small settlements on the smaller of the islands. This time there were Spanish settlers as well as Indians. As we neared the main settlement on the larger island, we saw a stockade and a Spanish flag that fluttered above it. In the harbour were a handful of ships, mainly carracks which the Spanish called carabela and one caravel. None were as large as *'Falcon'* but the two falcons which guarded the anchorage precluded an attempt to take the ships. We continued along the island and then headed north and then west to circumnavigate it.

My father left me to speak to Jacob and the captain. What struck me about the island we passed was that it looked prosperous. Small boats and their crews were harvesting pearls and, I suspect, seafood. The island had patches of cultivation. We had seen none on the mainland. Hispaniola and San Juan Bautista had also been prosperous-looking places. If the other islands they had taken were as rich then this would be a good place to raid. I began to envisage us leading a fleet of ships such as ours with, perhaps, six guns on each vessel. We could rule the seas.

When my father came back, he said, "I do not think we will need our guns today. One-Eyed Peter intends to land, tonight, at one of those settlements we saw on the south side of the island. He will leave just Jacob, the boys and us aboard. Now that we have the fishing boat, we can land our men quicker. He will raid them and be back aboard before dawn. We will then head back to our island."

I nodded for it seemed to me to be a good plan. "And we can repeat this."

He smiled, "You have a good mind, Tom. Aye, we can spend a few days back on the turtle and then return here. After that, the captain wishes to sail north again for bigger prizes. We have already taken more than he dreamed but he sees the chance to increase our bounty."

The raid yielded not only pearls, bags of them, but also animals, a pair of goats and some fowl. We lost not a man for although the Spanish had crude weapons they were outnumbered and did not put up a struggle. As Juan told us, they had felt safe and secure. The danger to the Spanish came from the Indians and they had been cowed ten years earlier. Diseases brought from Spain as well as the superior weapons had decimated them and until they had modern weapons would not be a threat.

Back on our island home, we made pens for the fowl. Some of them were similar to the ones we had back in England but others were covered in bright and garish feathers. We learned that the taste was the same. We would have fresh eggs and the goat gave us milk. The insects they ate were totally different to anything we had in England and I was glad we had fowl for they ate many of the biting and crawling insects. The one creature I hated was the land crab. I am not sure it was a crab for it did not walk sideways but it had pincers and a bite could incapacitate a limb for days. I learned to stamp on any I saw and, at night, I ensured that my bed was clear of both snakes and land crabs. I took to sleeping under a blanket. It was hot but it kept the biting insects from me. It was better at sea for they did not sail! We had sacks of food we had taken, and it was Juan who told us what they were and how to cook them. I did not care. It was hot food and anything that was not raw fish or salted ham was welcome. We spent a week back on our island. The goats were allowed to wander freely, and the fowl seemed happy to roost by the blockhouses. There was shade for them and a proliferation of insects. I wondered if we should not build permanent homes for even after we sailed back to England, we could always use this as our island home here in the New World.

Now that we knew the waters a little better Captain Peter was able to save time and over the next week, we repeated our raids on other parts of Isla Margarita and the mainland. We suffered our first wounds and injuries when we did so and it was a warning. The Spanish began to fight back and defend themselves. Jack and Edward, two of the sailors, suffered nasty cuts in the fights. As we headed back to our home, I knew that we would not be able to repeat our raids for the people to the south of us would now be wary.

The two men were tended to and One-Eyed Peter held a council of war. "We have two choices, we either return to England with what we have, or we sail north and try to take another of their galleons. John the Falconet and young Tom have shown that they have the skill with the falconets, and our ship can dance around our foes. What say you?"

My father and I said nothing. We had been flattered and if we suggested sailing back to England then it would seem that we doubted our own ability, but we were both ready to return home. We had our treasure, and this seemed just a little greedy to us.

When we declined to answer then the captain began to give his reasons for his choice to stay for one more raid. One-Eyed Peter was persuasive, and all the crew agreed. This time we would not leave the island without protection. Edward and Jack were still recovering from their wounds, indeed, Jack's leg showed little sign of recovery and the Captain promised to try to find some medicine. The rest of us were well rested and, leaving the fishing boat we had captured for the two wounded men, we set off in good heart.

The islands which the Spanish had settled were in a half-moon to the east and so instead of sailing across the empty ocean, we sailed close to the islands in the hope of picking up a ship. Hob, Ned, and Rob were all good lookouts and it fell to Rob to spy the sail on the eastern horizon. We loosed all the sails and used the wind to try to close with her but she must have been swifter than we and she disappeared. We resumed our course north and, the next morning as the sun came up, we were still alone on the sea. Then Ned spotted a sail. This time, when we loosed the sails we sped so swiftly across the sea that by the time we were sighted by the Spanish caravel, it was unable to evade us.

We had learned our lesson and we neither opened fire nor revealed our guns. We sailed as close as we could to them, knowing that they had no guns, and we had a larger crew. One-Eyed Peter's lessons with Juan had paid off and he was able to converse with the Spanish captain well. We secured ourselves next to her and with our hold open took her cargo of sugar. Although it filled almost half of the hold it would fetch a high price in England. Indeed, I wondered if the captain would simply sail back to the turtle, collect our men and treasure and sail back to England for we had that which we had sought, a valuable cargo! Once more her sheets and ropes were cut and, as we had not fired our guns, Captain Peter was confident that we would be undiscovered for a little while longer.

It was noon when we spied our next sail, and this ship, a large galleon from the look of her, was lumbering north towards Hispaniola. The winds were from the east and so the captain took us east so that we could have the weather gauge. That suited me for it meant it would be my gun, *Betty* which fired. We were like a fisherman hauling in a large and juicy fish. No matter what the Spaniard did we were still overhauling the vessel.

"Master gunner, let the Spaniard know our intentions. Fire one at her stern as soon as you are able."

"Aye, Captain!"

My father turned to me, "Wait until we are a thousand feet from her, Tom. It matters not where you hit. I think she will surrender soon enough. I fear that our ship has become known." We had ceased flying false flags and removing the falcon figurehead since we had crossed the great sea.

"Aye!" I adjusted the barrel and waited with the linstock at the ready. I had watched my father and knew that a gunner could fire his gun at the top of the roll to make it arc down or on its way up to shatter the top of the stern. I intended to hit square in the middle. That would be where the captain's cabin lay and my ball might career through the galleon causing untold damage.

I had just applied the linstock when I heard Rob shout, "Sail to the east! No, make that three sails!"

The smoke from *Betty* obscured the ship briefly and when it had cleared, I saw that the galleon, rather than continuing to flee had turned to allow her starboard side to swing around. My ball hit the stern, but it did not do that which I wished. It merely went from starboard to larboard and even worse I saw that this galleon was armed and there were three black muzzles each of which belched at us. My father fired his gun, and I began to reload mine. Only one of the Spanish balls hit us but it must have been a four-pound ball for it hit the gunwale and splintered it before ricocheting into the mizzen mast. One of the chunks from that gun speared Juan who was next to One-Eyed Peter. *Betty* was ready before *Mary* and I applied the linstock. Our smaller guns could fire faster than the heavier falcons on the galleon. My ball hit just forrard of the sterncastle and was close to one of the three falcons. It must have had an effect for only two guns fired in response, but the gun crews had their eye in and at a range shorter than six hundred feet inflicted damage. One hit the mainmast. I heard a cry as Rob plummeted to his death. My father's gun fired, and he managed to hit close to one of the other guns.

I began to hope we might win this battle when, from the stern, I heard the captain shout, "It is a trap! Those three ships behind have guns. They mean to take us. We will fly for La Tortuga!"

The ship heeled as we turned. The galleon was now less than three hundred feet from us, and our own guns would not bear. The two falcons must have been loaded with a special kind of shot for the crash when they hit was louder than any gun I had heard before. *Mary* was hit and one of the balls smashed through poor Ned's head. It missed me by a couple of feet before slicing into the foremast, which, with a creak and a groan, began to fall. *Mary* did for my father. The barrel hit his chest and he fell to the deck. Before I could even get to him the cross tree from the foremast hit him. His skull was caved in and King Henry's gunner died silently. The second ball had finished off the work of the earlier one and the mainmast tumbled down to crash down the length of the carrack. It brought down the mizzen mast and I heard cries as men died. Then the three ships which had ambushed us fired. The wind had already begun to turn us and I held the linstock ready. Only Hob and I were still alive at the bows and I knew not how many others had survived. That we would be taken was clear, but I determined to avenge my father. I had not even said goodbye to him. He lay crushed, his hand resting in death on *Mary's* barrel.

As we turned, for the mizzen mast acted as a giant rudder, I saw one of the three caravels come into view. I fired and then saw that each of the caravels had emulated us and mounted a pair of guns at the bows of each of the caravels. They were small guns, even smaller than the falconet but the range was so close that they could not miss. Even as my ball destroyed the bowsprit of one of them the six guns fired a ragged volley. They were less than a hundred feet from us and when they hit the side they tore through the already damaged timbers. One must have struck the powder which was stored as far away from the falconets as possible. I was about to order Hob to abandon ship when the stern of the ship exploded. It seemed to rise up from beneath my feet and flames singed my sea boots. Wood and pieces of metal scythed through the air and I felt myself tumbling through the air as *'Falcon'* died. I was completely deafened by the explosion and all appeared silent. As I flew through the air, I saw the sea beneath me and then I descended.

My grandfather had ensured that I could swim, and I said a silent prayer of thanks when I hit the water and began to sink. I unfastened my belt, and my sword and dagger sank to the bottom of the sea. With that weight gone I kicked hard and, as I kicked off my water-filled boots, began to rise. As my head broke the surface, I saw the remains of *'Falcon'* slipping beneath the waves. The wreckage was all around me and I grabbed hold of a piece of the foremast. As I did, I saw Hob bob up from the depths. I was delighted that I was not alone and as I reached out to grab his arm I said, "Hob, we must swim away. If we can get back to the …" I said no more for as I pulled, I realised Hob was a corpse. His body had been cut in two and it was just his torso I held. I let go of his hand and his dead face fell forward.

I turned away from the sinking ship and, holding the wood before me, began to kick. My father had spoken of sailors who had survived for days after being in a sea battle and that was in the cold waters around England. The waters here were warm and I knew that there were many islands. If I swam east, then I would find one. I know not how long I swam but when a Spanish voice shouted at me, I almost swallowed the ocean. I lost my grip on the wood and sank a little. I swallowed water and when I rose, I found myself gaffed like a fish and I was hauled aboard the caravel I had damaged.

I was under no illusions. I would be executed but I determined to give them no satisfaction. I would not beg for my life. I was English and these were Spanish dogs. I was unceremoniously hauled to my feet and dragged before the Spanish Captain who wore a breastplate and had a sword hanging from an ornately decorated belt. He had his hands on his hips and he had a cruel smile on his face.

When he spoke it was in Spanish which, thanks to Juan, I understood, "So you are the only survivor. That is a pity. I hoped to hang you all as pirates!" He walked over to me and turned my hands over. They were black, despite my dunking, for gunpowder stained. "You fed the guns?"

I shook my head and said, as defiantly as I could manage, "No, I am the gunner who did that!" I pointed to the bowsprit.

"Impossible, you are a youth!" One of his own gunners, he also had the blackened fingers, spoke although I did not catch all his words for my ears were still not working properly. His face when he turned had a little more respect upon it, "Enrico here says it is true for he saw you with the linstock in your hand." Juan had taught me well and I found I could understand almost all the words the Spaniard used although I had to work out linstock. "How is it that a callow youth such as you were able to damage my ship?"

"My father was a master gunner and he taught me well."

I expected death. I could see a rope coiled in a seaman's hands and I was prepared to die. I did not want to and I knew that with the sins I had committed and without confession, I would not go to heaven but life held nothing for me anyway. I stood straighter.

The Captain said, "Bind him and secure him below decks. I would speak with him further when we reach port."

I was dragged off. I had a reprieve but what fate awaited me? All chance of returning to England with a fortune was gone and it seemed that my future was bleak. I would either be hanged as a pirate or sent as a slave to row in a galley. Neither prospect appealed to me.

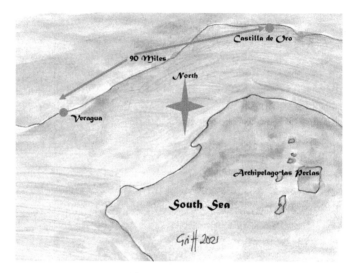

Panama 1519

Slave

Chapter 5

I was locked in the chart room. I thought to cause mischief and destroy the maps and charts, but something prevented me and that, I believe, saved my life. If I had done then their short fuse might have made them execute me out of hand. I had no idea how long I was there for I was brought neither food nor water. It was dark when the door finally opened, and I was dragged out of my cell. I knew that we had been still for some time and that meant we were no longer at sea. I saw that we were in port. I was taken up on deck and metal shackles were fitted to my hands and feet. Some of the crew spat at me while they were fitted. The captain who had ordered me bound was not there and I wondered if I was bound for the slave markets. Two soldiers came aboard, and they hauled me down the gangplank. I was still barefoot although my clothes had dried. I was taken through a new town. It had stone as well as wooden buildings. I knew not which island we were on nor which city it was.

I attempted to speak to the Spanish soldiers, "Where are we?" I know not if it was my accent or just the fact that I had dared to speak but not only did neither reply the one on my left backhanded me with his right hand. My ears rang and I decided that silence was the best policy.

The building they dragged me to was an official one for there were two armed guards outside and the flag of Spain flew from the top. The two soldiers did not come with me but handed me over to the sentries at the door.

"Here is the pirate his excellency wished to see."

"Leave him with us."

The older officer who took me appeared a little more curious than the other two. As he led me into the building he said, almost to himself, "Now why did Don Martín decide that you should not be hanged? What is it about you that saved your life? Perhaps you are a gift for his uncle."

"A gift?"

He laughed, "So you do speak our language. Aye, the captain who took you is the nephew of Don Martín Fernández de Enciso. He is Alcalde Mayor here in Santo Domingo."

At least I now knew where I was. This soldier was a little gentler than the other two. We reached a small chamber next to two huge doors.

He sat me on a seat at a table and said, "Wait here. Do not try to run for it will not go well for you."

He disappeared and I looked around for any kind of food or drink. There was none. The officer came back a short time later and I said, "I have not had anything to drink for a whole day, perhaps longer. I am not sure what day it is."

He nodded and disappeared. He returned with a wineskin and a beaker. He poured some wine into it. "I would not drink the water here, not unless it was boiled first. Drink this. I do not think that you are marked for death but who knows?"

Eventually, the doors opened, and my guard smiled and said, as he pushed me towards it, "Trust to God and speak the truth for that is the best way."

Inside there were just two men. I learned later that one was the Alcalde Mayor, Don Martín Fernández de Enciso, who had recently returned from Spain and that the other was a man who had stowed away on his ship, Vasco Núñez de Balboa. I learned all of this from my guards later on. The latter was a younger man and I got to know him quite well.

It was the Alcalde Mayor who spoke, "Are there any more of you English pirates left?"

Despite the Spanish soldier's advice, I could not betray Jack and Edward. When we did not return to the island, they would be able to dig up the treasure and sail… I know not where but I would not be the cause of their capture. "There was only one ship, Excellency."

He grunted, "At least you have manners!" He poured himself a large glass of wine. He looked to me to be a very serious man while the other, de Balboa, looked to have a look of mischief in his eyes. The Alcalde Mayor went on, "My nephew asserts that despite your youth you are a gunner. Such men, or even youths, are rare."

I nodded and risked speaking, "My father trained me and I fired *Betty* for six months or more."

The Alcalde Mayor frowned and tried to get his tongue around the strange word, "*Betty*?"

"My gun!

De Balboa laughed, "Then he really is a gunner! They all address their weapons as though they are women."

"Hmm. You know that the penalty for piracy is death?"

I nodded, "I know."

"If I were to spare your life what then?"

I frowned for I was confused, "Why, I would be grateful, of course!"

"Would you fire guns for the captain here?"

I looked at de Balboa who was studying my face, "I am English, and I would never fire a cannon at my countrymen."

De Balboa nodded, "No, it would be here, and it would only be Indians and natives who would be your target."

I was taken aback, "Me, become a conquistador?"

The Alcalde Mayor frowned at the impertinence while de Balboa laughed, "Do not get ideas above your station, Englishman! You will never be a conquistador, but I could use you. You have not answered the question."

"The answer is yes for I wish to live, and I like being a gunner, besides I have seen the treasures of this land and I would like some for myself."

The Alcalde Mayor smacked his hand on the table, "The treasure belongs to the King of Spain! You will be a dog on a very short leash." He turned to de Balboa, "Is that clear?"

"Of course."

"Then you may have him, now take him from my presence. He stinks!"

De Balboa stood, "Come, my pungent friend, let us remove your shackles, give you a bath and dress you in decent clothes!"

I came to know Captain Vasco Núñez de Balboa quite well. He was the real pirate and One-Eyed Peter had been a poor imitation! He was a very clever man with a wicked sense of humour which I discovered when I was taken to the room I would share with the rest of his expedition. I rarely got my real name, Tom or even English, which some of the Spanish like to use, instead, de Balboa introduced me as Conquistador and the mockery of a name stuck. I was, in reality, little more than a slave. I was the lowest of the low and had I not had a skill with guns then I would have been executed. I knew that my father's lessons had saved my life and I thanked him in my head. I learned to live with the shame of slavery and vowed, to myself, that one day I would free myself and sail back to England. It kept me going.

The members of the proposed expedition all lived in a wooden building close to the port. I guessed that it was a warehouse of some description. The captain did not take me there directly. After my shackles and fetters were removed, I was taken to the stables and, when I had taken off my clothes, I was dunked in the horse trough. A rough piece of soap was provided and I vigorously washed myself in the horse water. There were fresh clothes provided for me; they were Spanish and not made of the best material but they were serviceable and I was alive! The last vestige of my English past was burned on the fire. The clothes were clean and that was all that mattered. I was given, not boots but sandals. Finally, I was fed. I confess that I did not taste any of the food for I was starving and I just gobbled it down. The ale was swallowed almost in two gulps and, as I ate, I saw the amusement on the face of de Balboa.

"You know, English, I know your hunger. When I stowed away on the Alcalde Mayor's ship, I even contemplated eating the ship's rats. You will do well on my expedition. You know what it is to go hungry and yet you did not give up. That bodes well for we shall have a hard time where we are going."

I thought my Spanish had been good, but Captain de Balboa soon destroyed that illusion. Each time I mispronounced a word or used the wrong one he corrected me and made me say it properly. By the time we reached our destination, I was perfect.

"Captain, where is our destination and why do you need me?" It took three goes to get the word destination pronounced satisfactorily.

"We sail to pick up the men left by the Captain Alonso de Ojeda, at Nueva Andalucía on the Gulf of Urabá. There are men left there and the Alcalde Mayor wishes me to find a better site for the settlement. You ask why we need you? We have guns but what we lack are gunners. This land devours men and we need a fresh supply. There are those who can haul and serve the guns but, from what I have been told, you have skill. Do you?"

I knew that this was no time to be modest. "I hit that which I choose."

"Your father was a good gunner. I hear he destroyed the rudder of the **'San Nicholas'**."

I guessed that was one of the first ships we had taken, and I shook my head, "My father's gun hit the stern but I was closer when it was my turn to fire and I hit the rudder."

I pronounced rudder incorrectly and was given another lesson. "So you are definitely the one for the job. There will be little opportunity for you to practise before we leave for the guns are stored, in pieces, aboard my ship. Now that you have eaten, I will take you to meet the other men

I will be taking." He smiled and his smile seemed to me to be like that of the wolf just before it devours you. "As with you, I have been given little choice in the men I take. Most of them are the sweepings of Santo Domingo, but I will mould them to my will."

The captain was right and the men with whom I sailed were the roughest bunch of men I had ever encountered. I realised then how lucky I had been to serve on *'Falcon'* where everyone was friendly. The twenty odd men in the room all stared at me when I entered and when Captain de Balboa introduced me their stares changed to unashamed laughter. Even as I felt myself colouring, I reminded myself that my father, Hob, Ned, all my former shipmates would happily swap their positions with me for they were dead. I had been given an old cloak which doubled as a blanket and I found a straw bed as far from the others as possible. I would try to be invisible.

I recognised one face. It was the gunner from the ship which had taken me aboard and he came over. I had not looked at him closely before but now I saw that he was an older man, older than my father and Jacob had been. He smiled, "So, my commendation worked, and you were saved." He held out a hand, "I am Enrico, and I was the one who saw you fire the falconet. A little gun but you fired it well. It took me ten years to become as skilled and yet you are just a youth. You must have some natural talent."

I did not understand all his words, but I gathered his meaning. "Thank you, Enrico. Tell me, how did you and your fleet manage to trap us?"

"After your first raids, ships searched for you. A carrack with a bird figurehead is unusual. We thought you had sailed back to England and then a caravel spotted a strange sail and Don Martín, the nephew of the Alcalde, devised the plan. He used the galleon, *'Santa Maria'* to lure you. Your captain was clever and your father skilled, but we knew that your guns, whilst accurate, would not be able to sink the galleon and her task was to be the bait. Your captain liked to attack from windward and that was where we waited. As soon as we heard the guns then the caravels tightened the noose. You were doomed as soon as you attacked. Don Martín hoped to capture you and hang the whole crew for it was his uncle's ships you took."

If we had sailed with the sugar back to our island, then we might have evaded the trap. Fate had intervened and my old life was over. I had to adapt and make the best of my new life.

"Are we the only gunners?"

"We are. Captain Pizarro had two gunners with him but who knows if they have survived. Make no mistake, my young friend, we are valuable men. The two things which terrify the natives are horses and cannons. Captain Balboa is clever and that is why he has two guns. They are bigger than your falconets, they are the falcons. They fire a bigger ball and can fire it further. Our problem is gunpowder. Where we go, we cannot expect to find what we need to make it and so we have to take carts to carry it and the shot." He smiled, "We will use captured natives for that. Now you had better rest. It is good that you have nothing of value for if you had then these gutter rats would have it from you. As soon as you can I would get yourself a knife!"

Despite his warning, I felt better that Enrico was with me for he alone did not feel like an enemy. Perhaps it was the brotherhood of the gun.

When we were woken, and I had a rude one for the mocking began as soon as my eyes were open. The captain was eating elsewhere, and the slaves brought in our food. I learned many Spanish curses for the only words I heard were the curses or the mocking '*Conquistador*'! I developed a thick skin for I soon learned that they were only words and as one of the only two gunners on the expedition they dared not harm me for that would have incurred the wrath of Captain de Balboa. I even learned to smile on the inside, for it showed that I was superior to the others. Enrico and I were an elite.

Despite our elevated position, it did not bring us any relief from the labour of loading the ships. There were supplies and weapons to be taken aboard. Captain de Balboa was a knight and he had six other plated swordsmen with him. They were big men and professional soldiers. They had burgonet helmets while the other men, the harquebusiers and those with pikes and swords wore the morion helmet. As gunners, Enrico and I would be without any protection. There were six men who would act as servants for the expedition and serve the guns. As far as I could see they had no skill but all six looked as trustworthy as snakes and I did not like any of them. There would also be slaves to haul the guns which weighed more than five hundred pounds.

It took us a month to prepare the ships and then we sailed. The last thing we loaded were the two falcons we would be taking with us. They were in pieces and we would have to carry them like that until they were needed. There was the barrel, the trail and the wheels. When we needed to use them they would be assembled. I asked Enrico about that for it seemed wrong to me.

"We do not have enough animals to pull the guns. There will be natives who will be assigned to carry them. As for the assembly, that will be easy enough to achieve. Unlike the wheels on a ship's gun, these will have larger ones. I find them easier to fire. It may be that we do not need the falcons. If Captain Balboa has a horse, then that might be enough to cow the natives we discover."

Enrico was a kind man, and he took me under his wing. I never discovered the reason, but he ensured that the other men on the expedition did not take advantage of me. He was the chief gunner and, as with my father, would be rewarded with greater treasure than any of the other volunteers. As a virtual slave, I would have nothing!

The mocking from the others had not ceased but it had become bearable and seeing no reaction there was little venom in the words. The ships in which we sailed were unarmed. Enrico had told me that there was no need to mount guns on ships for there were no enemies. It explained our early success. Ships returning to Spain from Hispaniola were armed but that was because of pirates such as One-Eyed Peter who preyed on galleons close to the safety of Spain!

It was as we sailed south that I realised we would pass our island, the turtle. We were a fleet of fifteen ships, and I hoped that Edward and Jack would have the sense to hide the fishing boat and make themselves scarce when they saw the sails appear. No one else appeared interested in Turtle Island and I stood at the bow watching it as it grew larger. To my relief there was no fishing boat to be seen and no smoke rising from a fire but, as we drew closer, I saw that the pens for the animals had been destroyed and there was no sign of either the goats or the fowl. What had happened? It had just been weeks since I had been there but even the blockhouse we had made looked to have been partly damaged. I stared at it as we passed and continued to stare until it was a dot on the horizon. Had the treasure been taken? I hoped that Jack and Edward had dug it up and left the island with it, but I dismissed that idea. There was too much to be carried on the fishing boat. Over the next few months, I often thought of my two shipmates and the treasure of Turtle Island. I suppose I thought I might return one day and dig it up. It was a fantasy for it presupposed that I would survive this land and be able to have a ship which I could command. Neither seemed a likely prospect for Enrico had confirmed what Juan had told me. The jungles through which we travelled were men killers. More men died from the land than in battle. I realised that apart from the island I had not yet been ashore. My father and I, along with Jacob and the two boys had remained aboard the ship the whole time.

Once we passed Turtle Island we were on the last part of our voyage and Enrico began to offer me advice. The food we had eaten, he told me, would help to prepare me for the jungle. I did not like the food. It had too much garlic for my taste, but Enrico said that the insects did not like it. He suggested rubbing the cloves on my skin. He advised me to tie my hair back and then the cloth I used to tie it back could act as ear protection when we fired our guns. He had acquired better sandals for me too. We went barefoot on the ship, but we would need stronger footwear ashore. He also told me to rid myself of the hose which I gladly did. Finally, he found me a knife. I knew now, that despite their antipathy towards me the rest of the expedition would not harm me as I was a gunner. The knife would be needed when we were ashore.

"The captain will give you a weapon once we leave the ship. It will be a sword of some description. If nothing else, it will help you to clear a path through the jungle."

As we saw the mainland appear, one early morning I asked, "Enrico, what is it that Captain de Balboa hopes to achieve?" I pointed to the jungle which the closer we came to the shore looked increasingly impenetrable. "How can we cut a way through that and, if we do, what will we achieve?"

He lowered his voice, "The captain has been here before. It is why he was not punished for stowing away on the ship. Diego Velázquez de Cuéllar and Hernando Cortés are two of the most aggressive of the leaders and even now they are conquering Isla Juana. Captain Balboa and the Alcalde Mayor seek to make their own empire. That means we head south. Captain Balboa is convinced that there is another ocean as large as the one between here and Spain, but it lies far to the west; perhaps beyond the mainland. If he can find it then the route to the Indies may be shortened. It is why Columbus came here. The Portuguese and the Dutch have become rich thanks to their trade with the Indies but they have to navigate the stormy waters off Southern Africa."

"And what do you think?"

He smiled, "I could have stayed on the ship, but Captain de Balboa is a lucky man. I chose to come with him. He will make my fortune and then I can return to Spain as a rich man and I can raise a family."

That had been my father's dream, but One-Eyed Peter's ambition and greed had dashed that. I knew why Enrico was being kind to me. Apart from his kindly nature, he needed me to help us succeed and when we managed to find the gold then we could return home.

We landed at Nueva Andalucía and were met by the remnants of the men who had been left there to defend the colony. The soldier who had been given command was Francisco Pizarro whom I came to know well. That was when I was an experienced gunner, and my skills were in demand. The band of soldiers had been abandoned and they showed the effects of starvation, disease, and the attacks with poisoned weapons. Captain de Balboa was a persuasive man, and he had his own plans. He did not disembark the ships, but he went to speak with Pizarro, and he persuaded them to leave Nueva Andalucía and relocate further west. He told them that the land there would be more fertile and that we could make a better colony. I think that if I had been one of the men I would have jumped at the chance and they all did. There were seventy survivors, and they boarded our already overcrowded fleet and we headed further west to the place Enrico called the Isthmus of Darién.

Even I could see that this was a better place for a settlement and when I saw crops growing in the fields and that the jungle had been partly tamed, I understood why our captain had made his decision. While the new men who had arrived with Captain de Balboa headed inland, Francisco Pizarro and his weakened men began to build us defences. Enrico and I, along with the six labourers, began to unload first the guns and their carriages and finally the powder and the shot. The distant columns of smoke told us that there were natives in the area and both Enrico and Pizarro were convinced that we would be attacked.

My Spanish was almost perfect after speaking nothing but that since my ship had been sunk, however, instructing the labourers proved difficult. For they spoke a pidgin Spanish. Four of them were the result of liaisons between Spanish sailors and native women and none of the six had many skills. If they had then they would have been supplied with weapons. They could lift and carry and therein lay their purpose. Enrico had the same problem, and it took until dark for us to fit the wheels to the rack which was attached to a trail. Placing the gun on the rack was the easiest task. While they began the job of fetching the shot and powder we examined our guns. They looked identical but I knew from *Mary* and *Betty* that they would both act slightly differently when fired. We would only discover that when they were used in battle. Here there would be no test firing. By the time de Balboa and his men had returned we had most of the shot and powder ashore and covered by canvas. Pizarro's men had dug a ditch and begun to erect a palisade and I was already weary. The ships of the fleet lay at anchor and were an escape route if we should need it. Of course, Enrico and I along with the guns were expendable for, if disaster struck and we had to flee, they would not be easy to dismantle and take with us. We would have to be the rearguard and would, inevitably die. It gave us a vested interest in the plans of de Balboa.

The captain and Enrico knew each other, and Enrico was summoned to a meeting of the captains. He took me with him. De Balboa cocked an eye when he saw me but said nothing, "There is a large tribe not far from here. I know the chief for I met him when I was here a few years ago, he is called Cémaco and he commands more than five hundred men. They are fierce foes and use poison on their darts, arrows and spears." As we had less than one hundred and fifty, including the ships' crews, the odds were daunting.

Francisco Pizarro spoke. He was a thoughtful soldier and he spoke not from fear but to give Captain de Balboa some perspective. "Captain, my men and I lived from hand to mouth for more than fifty days. They are not cowards but nor are they in good condition. They will need to be given some protection."

De Balboa nodded, "I know and had Don Martín Fernández de Enciso given me more men and horses then I might have been able to spare them completely." He shrugged, "He wished you returned to Hispaniola. I see an opportunity here, Francisco." Nodding towards Enrico he said, "We have two guns and that will make the difference. Enrico, what can you do with your two guns?"

Enrico stroked his beard, "We have the ditch and the walls which Captain Francisco has built. We use those. If we angle the two guns, then their field of fire can protect the whole front. We might need to use our whole supply of balls, but we can clear the enemy."

De Balboa frowned, "And if we do so then the guns become useless."

I was young but as with Enrico, I had an interest in the matter. Without the guns I was unnecessary, "Captain, the beach has many stones, and we have canvas bags. If we fill the bags with the stones and put them in the barrels, then when they fire they will spread and do more damage to men. Of course, we would have to wait until the range was close, less than a hundred feet, but they would have a dramatic effect."

De Balboa looked at Enrico, "I have never used a weapon like that but when Tomas here and his father fired their guns, they used such ammunition and killed all the officers on the *'San Nicholas'*. It might work but we would have to reload quickly."

De Balboa was a decisive man and he nodded, "Then tomorrow do that and Francisco, you and your men will be in the centre behind the guns. They will be protected by the falcons and, in turn, can protect the gunners. I will place the rest of our men on the two flanks, echeloned back. We have ten harquebusiers, and I will have five on each flank. We will use pikemen to protect the swordsmen, the rodeleros."

With that, we were dismissed and as we left the Spanish gunner asked, "Will it work, Tomas?"

"Enrico, the balls we fire are large, but will the Indians come at us in neat ranks? I think not. We would waste our balls."

He put his arm around me, "You are clever, and your father taught you well. These cannons are new weapons, and they need young minds to bring out the best in them." Once back in the camp we had between the two guns he spoke to the six labourers. He told them what we intended and what they had to do. Four of them, being born of native mothers knew better than any of the dangers posed by poisoned weapons and their nods told me that we would need no inducements to make them work hard.

We were up before dawn and had already dragged the two guns to their positions. I had yet to name mine for I did not know her. Enrico had named his gun after his mother, *Isabella*. I just called mine, *My love*. Her name would come to me. Once we had them angled to give a wide field of fire our six labourers headed back to the beach with the canvas bags. Enrico and I had spent some of the previous night sewing them. The size was important for they would have to be the same shape as the balls we used, two and a half pounds. While they were away the other men began to hurriedly improve our defences and Enrico and I used some of the discarded, smaller logs, to make defensive walls around the guns. Gunners rarely stood and I was fearful of the poisoned missiles the natives might use.

We had priests with us, and we all knelt as they came along to bless us. They invoked the help of Santa Maria, the virgin of Antigua, and my prayers were as loud as any Spaniard.

Scouts were out and we had just twenty bags of stones and pebbles when the horn sounded. The natives were on their way. This was not a ship and we had a fire burning close by. The linstock was already glowing. I had Nuneo, Juan and Pedro assisting me. I had kept their instructions simple. While I loaded the gun Pedro would hold the linstock. Nuneo knew how to ram and dampen the barrel while Juan would fetch fresh charges and bags of stones. I had the gun aimed low for there was little point in aiming at heads. The intention was to make the natives part and send them towards the harquebusiers, crossbows and pikes on the flanks. The crossbows were slow and unwieldy to reload and to use but they had a long range. They would target the chiefs.

The five hundred or more natives who appeared from the land beyond the cultivated fields were fierce-looking warriors with decorated faces. Many carried wicked-looking clubs. Our soldiers had helmets to protect them. Enrico, myself and the labourers were vulnerable, and I wished that I had been given a sword. The only weapon I had for defence was the linstock!

Our leader tried to inspire us with words but the thought of a death by a poisoned weapon seemed inducement enough, "Men of Spain, today we fight our first battle together, but we have God and Santa Maria on our side not to mention the courage of men who are bringing civilisation to these barbarians. Fight hard and we shall prevail. God and King Carlos!"

There was no order to the native attack. Their chief, Cémaco, led them from the front and they ran at us. The crossbow bolts did little to slow them and their arrows descended from above. I did not look up, but I was terrified in case a poisoned missile gave me a long and lingering death. I heard them strike helmets. Paco, one of the labourers, fell screaming when an arrow hit his shoulder. I turned as he fell. It mattered not if the arrow was poisoned or not. The arrow wound was mortal. The others all made the sign of the cross. I looked down the barrel and held the linstock a handspan from the touch hole. Enrico and I had marked the range with a white stone. I could almost smell the natives as they reached it. I touched the hole and smoke and flame belched.

"Nuneo!" They were slow to react but Nuneo managed to put the dampened cloth into the barrel and it hissed. I saw that the gun had hit more than twenty warriors but the rest still came on. They were less than fifty feet from us by the time I managed to use the linstock. As Paco had died that was slightly quicker than Enrico and this time the natives were so close that the stones had an even greater effect.

Behind me, I heard Francisco Pizarro shout, "Pikemen forward!" Two walls of pikes appeared on either side of me. The pikemen had both helmets and leather brigandines. They had protection.

The belching flames from the guns made the natives wary now and they spread to the side. We reloaded but there was no target, for the natives had seen the effect of the gun.

"Pick up the trail and turn it!"

I saw an opportunity. If we opened fire, then the balls would fly down the length of the attacking Indians. I loaded the gun and put in a couple of larger stones that were lying nearby. There was a slight risk that a stray stone or two might come near to the pikemen but as they had ten feet long weapons it was unlikely. I touched the linstock. If the first rounds had caused damage then this last one took out thirty or forty men and some of them were the chiefs, Enrico told me that they were called a cacique.

Captain de Balboa raised his sword and shouted, "Attack!"

The pikemen raised their weapons as they stepped over the ditch and then advanced. The swordsmen, with their bucklers held before them, ran into the Indians. The enemy warriors were no cowards, but they had wood and stone weapons against steel and iron. It was a massacre and when the enemy right wing collapsed and Captain Pizarro led his men to attack the other flank, the battle was over. We had won!

Chapter 6

We had lost men but far fewer than might have been expected. Only Paco from the labourers had died and we would need to find another. We went amongst the Indians to make sure that they were dead and to search their bodies for treasure. None had purses but they all had some gold upon them. It was normally around their necks although one of their caciques had a golden coronet. I saw Enrico slip that into his satchel. I did not begrudge him the reward. I had four gold amulets studded with a jewel or two and I felt rich.

The bodies were piled by the labourers and set on fire as a warning to the rest of the tribes and to reduce the chance of disease. I went back to my gun. I had decided to name her *Dragon* for her fire seemed to me like dragon fire. I cleaned our *Dragon* and wondered if my decision to use the extra stones might have damaged her. I examined the barrel for cracks but there were none. I had no idea of her age. *Betty* had been a new gun, but her life had been cut short.

Captain Pizarro came to speak to me when he returned from the pursuit of the survivors. "I was surprised to see one so young working a gun, but you have not only skill but also intelligence. You won the battle today although I suspect that Captain Balboa will take the credit." I nodded for I knew not what to say, "You are English?"

"Yes, Captain."

He nodded, "I will keep my eye on you for I believe that you will be a useful man in the conquest of this country and," he smiled, "men say that you are called Conquistador!"

I shook my head, "When they wish to mock me, they do."

"Do not worry for I believe they have named you well."

He was right about our leader taking all the credit and Captain Vasco Núñez de Balboa wasted no time in writing letters to the King of Spain as well as Don Martín Fernández de Enciso to tell them that he claimed the land for Spain and he would be the one who built and ruled the city. It was a challenge to Don Martín Fernández de Enciso. The men had gold in their purses, and he had their support. Three ships sailed, one to Spain and the other two to Hispaniola. We needed more men.

Over the next couple of months, we built a town, Santa María la Antigua del Darién, and a quay to help unload the ships. Enrico and I, along with our labourers helped in the building. It was hard work for the heat and the humidity made it harder than it would have been even on a hot English summer's day. The sweat attracted biting insects and our bodies were soon covered in red angry bites. When stone arrived, along with more men eager to become rich, we built a fort, and the two guns were mounted on the walls. Almost as soon as we had defeated the natives, settlers arrived from Hispaniola. They were looking for the chance to become rich. Merchants arrived ready to rob what they could and sell back in Spain. Building and construction went on at a prodigious rate. To be fair to Captain Balboa, he was not idle, and he took men out each day to subjugate the natives whilst looking for gold. That there was gold was clear for even the meanest villagers had some gold about them.

When the ship returned from Spain, Captain de Balboa sent King Carlos his tenth share of the gold. He was no fool. By claiming it for himself he had denied Don Martín Fernández de Enciso his share and he needed the support of the king who had recently become the Holy Roman Emperor as well. De Bilbao knew the value of important men. I saw then the ambition of the man. It struck me that the men who led this conquest of the new world were little better than One-Eyed Peter. They were pirates who served themselves and would stab a fellow in the back as soon as look at him. De Balboa would build himself his own empire. Enrico told me of the Governor of Veragua, Nicuesa, who was a law unto himself and intimated to me that de Balboa had ambitions in that direction. Veragua lay many miles to the north and as there were no roads had to be reached by sea. I had learned that in this part of the world the sea was the road.

I found myself, despite the heat and hard work, surprisingly happy. Even though I had lost my father and friends and become a virtual slave since de Balboa had taken my tormentors to raid the Indians, my life was relatively pleasant. I ate well and slept under a roof. Enrico was kind and the labourers got on well with me. My skill with the falcon had proved pivotal. When the raiders came back to Santa María la Antigua del Darién it was with even more gold that they had found but, more importantly, they had heard through their captives of a powerful tribe who lived far to the south in the high mountains. There were rumours that the tribe possessed more gold than we had found thus far and our leader also heard more information of a huge blue sea to the west of us. The year ended with my life turned completely around. I was now part of a Spanish army carving out an empire. Who would have thought so just a year or two ago when I had been stealing wine from Frenchmen!

We stood guard each day on the guns and cleaned them. Once a week we test-fired them. I believe it was as a warning to the Indians for the boom could be heard for many miles around. I had a little money and I used it to buy a sword and an oiled cloak. Merchants had arrived to both steal and to sell! I was still treated like the labourers which meant I was given food and paid a pittance, but I was happy to bide my time and I kept my eyes open so that when we had to board a ship to fetch for the fort I was quite happy for my hands to take anything which took my fancy. I became an adept thief, not in the same class as Rob had been but getting better each day.

Christmas was celebrated well for the merchants who now lived in Santa María la Antigua del Darién had no wives to inhibit them and many paid for Indian girls to entertain them. De Balboa had a pack of hunting dogs brought over. They were savage beasts and they terrified me. He used them for hunting animals and Indians for he was a cruel man. I found myself talking with Enrico and Captain Pizarro who seemed to prefer our company to that of our Alcalde, Bilbao. He was interested in what Enrico had to say about the seas. He was keen to explore and like de Bilbao he had ambition, but I do not think that he was as ruthless. While de Bilbao and the merchants pleasured themselves, he sat and spoke of guns and exploring. I liked him.

"If I become a captain with a ship of my own, I would have you two serve me. What do you say?"

Enrico shook his head, "I have almost enough gold to return to Spain, Francisco. When we have our next expedition that will be my last and I shall sail home, but Tomas here is as good a gunner as I have seen."

I nodded, "And I would happily follow you, sir. But will the Alcalde let me go? I am little more than a slave and it is my impression of him that he would only let me go if there was something in it for him."

"You may be right and thus far I am just a minor captain but one day…"

On such a promise I hung my hopes.

Then, in the New Year, our peace was shattered. Word had reached the Governor of Veragua that de Bilbao had set himself up as Alcalde and, as Governor, he was coming to arrest de Bilbao. Fortunately for the lucky de Bilbao, a friendly ship brought word of the imminent arrival of the Governor. When he arrived, he found a mob waiting for him. De Bilbao had persuaded the merchants, settlers, and soldiers that Nicuesa would prevent them from profiting from the land and while de Bilbao watched from the town's walls the angry mob prevented the Governor from disembarking. They said that he had no power to rule them and he should leave. He begged in vain for the chance to land and when some of those on board the damaged vessel deserted him the Governor had no choice but to sail away. He cursed Santa Maria's people and swore he would bring down the wrath of the King upon them. Had I been de Bilbao then I might have been worried, but he was not and took the opportunity not only to raise men for another expedition but also claim the title of Governor of Veragua! The expedition, this time, would head along the coast, through the jungles to the northwest.

With the new men and supplies, he had obtained a falconet and he came to Enrico and me to tell us that he intended to head west, and he needed us to work the new gun. Enrico had been unwell since the New Year. He had the sweating sickness and whilst he appeared to have recovered, he did not relish a journey through the jungle. De Bilbao was less than happy but even that ruthless man could see Enrico might not survive such an expedition.

The old gunner waved a hand at me, "Take Tomas. He is as good a gunner as I have seen, and his three labourers work well with him."

De Bilbao looked contemptuously at me, "Conquistador?"

I said nothing and Enrico spoke up for me, "Remember the first battle? It was Tomas here who turned his gun and won it for you by firing down the line of Indians. You need a young man who thinks quickly and not this old relic." De Bilbao nodded and admitted defeat. "He will need a share of the profits for that is only right."

The Alcalde glared at me and then nodded, "I suppose you are right, and we need new blood if we are to make this colony succeed. There is a donkey for you to use to carry the gun." He jabbed a finger at me as though it was a sword, "I would not be held up by you. You had better not let me down."

I knew how to play this game and I bowed, "Thank you Excellency, I swear you will not regret this."

When he had gone, I thanked Enrico who shook his head, "I am going home with the gold that I have. This last illness made me think I was doomed to die, and I would die in Spain."

"Then you shall have half of whatever I am paid for without you I would have nothing." I felt that I owed him something and he did not object.

The problem we had with the falconet was the lack of balls. The ones for the falcon were too large. I had Nuneo and the others make up smaller bags of pebbles and harquebusier balls. I had seen the effect of the bags of balls on the Indians and deemed they were better than cannonballs. We would take just ten balls with us for that was all that came with the new gun. As I made that decision, I realised how much I had changed. We might not have fought for a long time, but I had become used to making decisions about the guns when Enrico was indisposed. We had plenty of powder and I ensured that my three labourers each had a machete. This blade was a handy weapon and could be used for cutting through the jungle. It was Enrico who advised me to take them. He also found a morion for me. The men who had died in the first attack had not enjoyed head protection.

I was both excited and nervous when the one hundred men of the expedition left Santa María la Antigua del Darién and headed into the jungle whilst following the coast. Francisco and his ten men accompanied my donkey and labourers. Francisco was, like de Balboa, a knight and he wore a breastplate and metal skirt. He carried a buckler and had a good sword. His men wore morions like me and they had leather brigandines. They not only had swords but also hand axes and machetes. They were well-armed, and I was pleased that they were guarding me. We had the only gun and with just one horse and a donkey, the falconet, as yet unnamed, might prove to be the difference between success and failure.

If I thought it had been hard building by the coast then the hacking through the jungle was harder. Insects and snakes were all around us and you stepped off the path at the risk of your life. We heard the sound of what turned out to be cats the size of wolfhounds. One man went into the jungle at night to empty his bowels. The scream and the roar told us that one of these beasts had taken him! As if they were not bad enough some of the men tried to frighten me with tales of the tribes. They said that some of them were cannibals. I was not afraid but I knew that the stories, while exaggerated and told to frighten me must have had some element of truth in them and I feared failure more than death for I wanted gold to give to Enrico.

The jungle was not as thick this close to the coast, but it was still oppressive and hot. I led the donkey with the falconet and the gun carriage aboard. One of my fears was that the wear and tear of assembly might result in damage to our gun. The carriage was lighter than I would have liked. Of course, I could always improvise. The barrel could be placed upon a flat surface and fired but reloading would take longer, and the accuracy would be in doubt. The labourers carried the powder, balls, and bags of shot. We travelled in the rear with the priests. The Spanish went everywhere with priests and whilst I am a God-fearing man the Spanish priests always terrified me. Each time they looked at me it was as though they were seeking sin and I knew that all men were sinful. They were with us not only to bless our enterprise but also to convert any Indians that we met. To that end, we had four captive and tamed Indians who would translate for us. I was just glad that de Bilbao's pack of hunting dogs were at the front. Enrico had said that they were trained to bring down Indians and animals but as they always growled when I passed them, I wondered if they might mistake me for an Indian. They would be used to pursue any Indians who fled!

After three days and camps which had seen me eaten alive by biting insects, the scouts reported that they had found a large village just inland from the coast. This tribe had not had contact with us, but the word must have spread amongst the tribes and when no emissary came to sue for peace then de Bilbao prepared for war. He sent for me and Francisco.

"English, I want you to assemble your gun tonight. Tomorrow we advance on their village and I want the gun ready to fire as soon as we sight the enemy. They have had a chance to speak with us and the fact that they have not means that they do not accept our authority. Francisco, I want you to command the men on the left and I will command the right. As soon as the village is sighted then the gun will fire, and we will attack from the flanks."

"Excellency, what if they attack my gun and my crew?"

He gave me his wolfish smile, "Conquistador, do not tell me you are afraid?" He laughed, "Fear not, my pack of dogs will be close by and if the Indians are foolish enough to attack you then they will be torn limb from limb. Besides, God will be with you for the priests and the supplies will also be with you!"

With that, we were dismissed, and I walked back with Francisco to our camp. He was more sympathetic, "Do not worry, as soon as your gun fires, the Indians will flee. They are brave warriors, but I saw the effect when they attacked at Santa María la Antigua del Darién and you fired your guns there. You, my friend, must ensure that your gun does not break down for if it does then the Indian numbers may well make a difference."

I liked my labourers and we worked well as a team. They were not as good as Ned and Hob had been but that was partly the language. With Hob and Ned, I had spoken the language of my birth and communication was easy. Although I could speak Spanish well the labourers had native mothers and their Spanish was not the Spanish I had learned from Juan and then Enrico. It was getting better and each day saw us communicating just a little better than the day before.

Now that the gun was assembled, I would be able to use the donkey to carry the bags with the powder, ball and shot. That night I took embers from the fire and put them in a pot which Pedro would carry the next day. I did not want a misfire. I also had an idea about heating balls to fire. I would have to have tongs made but it struck me that a heated ball passing through a wooden house such as the Indians made might ignite it and that would cause even more destruction. I think I had begun to change since his death, and I was becoming my father. To me being a gunner was a passion as much as a skill and I wanted to be the best that I could be.

With the dogs ahead of us we carefully hauled the falconet along the trail which was, mercifully, well-trodden and obstacle-free. I took great care to move any obstacle which might damage the carriage out of the way. The lines of soldiers spread out to the side and behind us, the priests intoned invocations to saints, the Virgin Mary and Jesus to help us destroy the enemy.

It was clear to me when we came upon the cultivated fields that the Indians had not heard of our gun. Perhaps they thought we were like Pizarro's band had been and just had swords and pikes. They did not flee but gathered before their village. There were more than five hundred of them and they presented a wall of shields backed by spears and clubs. They looked and sounded terrifying as they chanted, screamed, banged their shields and displayed garishly painted faces and bodies, but they would be no match for the discipline of the Spanish soldiers. As we loaded the gun, I reflected that they must have been a confident tribe who were used to facing their enemies in this way and winning. We had stopped beyond their bow range for we knew that all the tribes poisoned their missiles, but two or three hundred feet was their limited range. Next to us the dogs were baying, barking, and straining at the leash. They were keen to tear into human flesh. The Indians chanted and sang; it must have been their version of our priests' prayers.

Governor de Bilbao, he now insisted upon the title, came over to me, "English, you will begin this battle, fire and keep firing until we close with them."

"Yes, Excellency!"

I turned to Nuneo, "We will fire this ball first. If they attack us, then I want a bag of shot next and if not we continue with the balls."

"Yes, Master Gunner!"

The tribe was obligingly arrayed before their largest huts and I aimed the ball to hit them first and then carry on through the building. I was comfortable firing the falconet. I had learned how to fire when on *'Falcon'* firing **Betty**. I was more comfortable with the range and when I fired and the cannon cracked, I was already peering through the smoke to see its effect. One effect was to terrify the dogs and that pleased me. It made it less likely that they would risk coming close to the gun! The ball struck the line of warriors and hit one man in the chest. He was thrown to the ground as the ball passed through him to hit the next four men and then crack into the wall of the hut. There was heat in the ball and the hut began to burn. The Indians just stood, and I said, "Ball!"

To my left and right, I heard the command to move forward. I was now committed to firing balls for firing the shot risked hitting our own men. I made the slightest adjustment to the gun and fired again. The effect was almost the same for it was a different part of the Indians' line except that this time those who faced the gun began to move away. They did not come towards me but headed back into the village. Behind me, I heard the priests give thanks to God. It was my third ball that ended the battle. I hit the large hut and the building, which was already burning, was destroyed. The Indians threw themselves to the ground and abased themselves before our men. We had won. Three cannon balls had won the battle!

The chief was called Careta, and he was so traumatized by the cannon that he would not come close to it. When we hauled it into the village, he and his shaking leaders and holy men made sure that Governor Bilbao and the priests stood between us and him. He and his tribe happily accepted Christianity and were converted for, I think, they thought the cannon was made by our God! More than that they not only brought gold and silver to the Governor, but they also offered to provide men to help him to fight the other tribes. The caciques we met seemed as treacherous as de Bilbao and the other Spanish leaders!

De Bilbao was so pleased with the bloodless success that he gave me a large bag of gold. I gave him my heartfelt thanks, which they were because it meant that Enrico could go home. We were well fed, and we continued our journey towards the new sea after a week in which we collected more treasure. We headed deeper into the jungle. We now had two hundred Indians with us, and they took us along easier trails than the ones we had used before. They advised us on salves to stop the insects from biting and our journey was easier. Neither the Indians nor the dogs, however, would come close to the gun even when it was on the back of a donkey! The next tribe, whose cacique was called Ponca, simply fled to the mountains leaving their village and their treasure for us to take. I was not rewarded as well for I had done nothing. I did not mind.

Careta told us that the next tribe was the most dangerous for they had the most fertile land and the fiercest warriors. Governor de Balboa had already decided that this would be the last tribe we subjugated before he returned to Santa María la Antigua del Darién. He wished to send to the King of Spain his due and to ask for more men and ships. I was summoned.

"I want you and your gun ready to destroy this village tomorrow. The land has well tilled and open fields. I need them to see you and your gun."

I nodded. A year ago, I might have been terrified but now I was confident. As soon as dawn broke, we headed for the village and stopped, not at the edge of the jungle but a hundred feet closer to the village which lay in the distance. It was a large one and was more than a thousand feet away. De Bilbao came to me and said, "Can you hit the village?"

I looked at it. The tribe was gathering ready to do battle. I nodded, "Which hut?"

He laughed, "Perhaps you are growing into your name, Conquistador, for you are more arrogant. The largest one!"

I took aim and realised that I could hit the hut without hurting the men before it. I chose that method. It was not out of mercy, but I knew that the tribe would see it as magic. I fired and watched the ball arc. It struck the roof with a crack and the thatch there burst into flames. The effect was astounding. The tribe, supposedly the fiercest in the area, threw down their weapons and surrendered. Their chief, Comogre, also converted and when the treasure was brought, I received a healthy share. It was there that Governor Bilbao discovered that his dream of reaching the far sea might be realised. A month after we had arrived and while the Governor was still making his demands the chief's son, Panquiaco, who was less than happy that his father had submitted spoke and his words were translated, "If you are so hungry for gold that you leave your lands to cause strife in those of others, I shall show you a province where you can quell this hunger. The people are so rich that they eat and drink from plates and goblets made of gold, but you would need at least a thousand men to defeat the tribes living inland and those on the coast of the other sea."

That piqued de Balboa's interest. He took Panquiaco as a hostage and we returned to Santa María la Antigua del Darién. As we marched, Francisco showed his intimate knowledge of the workings of the Governor's mind, "We will not spend long in our city, Tomas, when we return here we shall come by sea and we will come with many more men. We have taken great quantities of gold but if Panquiaco is right then when we reach the far sea, what we have thus far will be a drop in the ocean. Our leader must be lucky!"

He dared say no more for although we were on friendly terms, he had no idea if I was a spy for de Bilbao. Nothing he had said was in any way critical of the Governor. When we reached Santa María la Antigua del Darién I saw that in our absence the city had grown and there were ships moored in the bay.

Chapter 7

Enrico had much to tell me when I joined him in the house we used on the island. The Governor of Hispaniola, de Enciso, had refused to allow any more settlers to come from his island. The ones who had arrived had come from Spain itself. Enrico was hopeful of finding a berth on one of the Spanish ships which would be returning to Spain. I gave Enrico half of my gold and he almost wept.

"I cannot take this! It is a king's ransom!"

I smiled, "There will be more." I told him what the son of the cacique had told me.

"Then I am happy for I feared to leave you here all alone." He leaned in and said, conspiratorially, "Stay with Captain Pizarro. He is a good man and can be trusted." By implication, de Bilbao could not.

"He is not a captain, Enrico."

"But he will be, that is why you should stay with him."

When Enrico went to ask de Bilbao permission to leave for Spain, even he was surprised at the response, "Of course, my old friend, and I will recompense you for your time here in the Indies. You can do me a favour too. I will give you a document which I would like given to the King along with his share of the treasure. I can trust you. You can also spread the word that I need shipbuilders for we will need ships if we are to conquer the other sea!"

And so, I lost my first friend in this new world. Had it not been for Enrico then I do not believe that I would have survived. I did not fear the bullies any longer for I had grown, and they had learned to respect my skill. We would never be friends, as I was with Enrico, but they would not harm me as it was not in their interest.

Enrico left me many of the things he would no longer need. His time as a gunner was over and he left me the tools of the trade as well as his spare sword and a helmet which was much better than mine. I had many things which had been lost when *'Falcon'* had sunk and I was grateful to the old gunner and I wrapped up the leather holdall, similar to an archer's gardyvyan. I had a feeling that I would need all three sooner rather than later. I bade farewell to Enrico just a week after we had landed. It was a sad parting for I had grown fond of him and he was the only real friend I had. He waved from the gunwale as the ship headed to Spain filled with gold, messages for the king and the news that the new world was even richer than had been first thought.

It was September when we set sail and I was the only gunner. After heading to our base close to the isthmus we left the labourers from Enrico's crew to man the guns at Santa María la Antigua del Darién. There were now enough soldiers there to be able to defend the place and the labourers knew how to load and fire the cannons. Francisco came with us and we sailed with one hundred and ninety men. He also had some natives, notably Panquiaco as well as the Governor's pack of dogs. We anchored close to the village of the cacique, Careta, and when we reached his village and the Governor told him of our plans, he happily supplied a thousand of his warriors. He also gave the Governor a warning that the cacique, Ponca, and his tribe had now returned to their village. We would have to pass through it to get to the sea which de Bilbao now called the South Sea. We were forewarned and it was good that we were. This time there was resistance. They were ready for us and we assembled the gun. They had moved from the village we had raided, and we were penned close to the jungle. The one thousand Indians swelled our numbers, but de Bilbao kept his Spaniards, and his dogs close to the gun.

He came to me, "I would like you to fire your little balls and cut a swathe through them."

I nodded, "We can do that, Excellency, but it means moving closer to them and my gunners have no protection against the darts and the arrows which they will undoubtedly send at us while we move the gun up."

He smiled, "That is simple enough." He called over the warrior who led the men from Careta's village and instructed him to have twenty Indians with shields mask our movements. The Indians were in awe of both the gun and de Bilbao and they did so happily. When four of them fell, writhing to the ground I was glad for de Bilbao's cold ruthlessness. The darts gave impetus to our work and we had the gun in position far quicker than I might normally have expected. As soon as we were ready, I had Nuneo tell the Indians to move. As they did so I aimed the gun at the centre of the line of warriors, just fifty feet from us. As soon as I saw them ready their weapons I fired, and the bag of tiny balls struck the first forty of them. The wall of Indians was simply demolished and that was because of the range. We had been so close that I saw, through the smoke, pieces of men cut and chopped from bodies. Those that were not killed instantly were maimed and wounded. At the same time, de Bilbao ordered the line of men to attack. The battle was one of the shortest we had fought. Ponca surrendered for two of his sons had been amongst those I had killed.

We had taken the treasure from the village on our first visit and this time we took some of their men to swell our numbers. De Bilbao sent Panquiaco back to his father for our route now went due west and would be over uncharted and unexplored land. We would use the Indians from the recently captured village. We had four days of hell. There was virtually no trail and we had to make our own. Two men died from snakebites and others suffered cuts that began to fester. I could see why no one had yet found this South Sea! Many suffered from the food that we ate for it was different from anything we had encountered before and the poor water. I had anticipated such a problem and my labourers and I had ale skins so that we did not need to risk the water. The guides from Ponca's village returned on the fourth day to tell de Bilbao of a large village that lay ahead. We followed the Chucunaque River and it was as we were descending down the slope towards the river that disaster struck. The donkey missed its footing, and fell as we were descending the trail and before we had unloaded the gun and carriage. I was lucky that I let go of the halter or else I might have been dragged with the animal and the falconet. The weight of the barrel and the steep slope broke the donkey's neck. Luckily, we had but a mile to carry the barrel and the carriage. Nothing was wasted and the animal was butchered. We would eat well after the battle, but we would now have to carry the gun. I rigged slings and had some of the Indians carry the gun.

The tribe was waiting for us, but I do not think that they had heard, yet, of our weapon. The jungle through which we had passed prohibited good communication. It was a large tribe but thanks to those of Careta's tribe who had survived we had parity of numbers. The Indians who had come with us told us that the way the tribes fought each other in this land followed a pattern. They arrayed before each other and shouted insults. Some had dances which they used others offered champions to fight. That was what the tribe of the village of Cuarecuá did. It suited us for it meant I could get to within just over one hundred feet and load with my grapeshot. The four harquebusiers we had left lined up next to me. The posturing and insults meant that they did not seem to notice us positioning the gun behind a very thin line of Indians.

The order was given, and the Indians simply stepped to the side. De Bilbao shouted, "Fire!" The falconet and the harquebus sent a wall of smoke and fire towards the Indians who were not yet ready to fight. They were in a ragged line but as they were just one hundred feet from us then the powder fuelled weapons did not miss. I quickly reloaded with another bag of balls. When the smoke cleared we saw that we had killed many men, but the tribe were brave to the point of being almost suicidal. They charged us and came directly for me. I managed to get off one hurried shot that struck the Indians when they were just twenty feet from me, and I killed so many that we had the chance to draw our weapons. It was at that point that de Bilbao let loose his dogs and they charged the enemy. The dogs would prove decisive but Nuneo, Juan and Pedro along with myself had little time to watch their terrible attack for the Indians came directly at us. Francisco Pizarro was close to us with his men and our flanks were guarded by pikes and swords, but the wild men threw themselves over the falconet attacking the gun as though it was alive. I think I survived because of that. I had yet to use my sword in anger. I swept it across the middle of the leading Indian who had burned his bare feet on the barrel of the falconet. Even though his guts were hanging out he still managed to strike at my head with his club. The morion saved me and the dying man fell at my feet. I brought my sword down on the back of the neck of the warrior who smashed one wheel of the gun carriage with his war club and Francisco skewered the Indian who tried to spear me.

Poor Juan stood no chance as he slashed with his machete at the bare-chested Indian whose stone-lined club ripped out his throat. The Indian was bleeding, but he still came at me. I picked up the linstock with my left hand and lunged at his face with the glowing end. As his eye was drawn to it, I hacked across his thigh. My hand jarred when I scraped along the thigh bone, but the cascading blood told me he was dying. It was then that two of de Bilbao's dogs ripped open the throat of Torecha, the cacique who ruled in the village of Cuarecuá. That was the end of the battle, but it was at a cost. Pedro was also dead and Nuneo had a wound that would need to be tended. Worse, the gun carriage was wrecked. We had the barrel and the shot but that was all for the gunpowder had been spilt and was now ruined.

It took half a day to bury our dead and tend to our wounded. It was Francisco who persuaded de Bilbao to rest for a while. We had less than twenty fit men and even the hardy Indians had suffered. I was invited to dine on donkey meat with them.

"Well, Master Gunner, can the falconet be repaired?"

I shook my head, "No and even if we could effect repairs there is no powder left."

He spat a piece of gristle into the fire, "Then what use are you to me?"

Pizarro spoke up for me, "Despite his youth he still killed Indians." He waved a hand around the village which looked more like a hospital. "We have but forty men left who can go on. I would advise that we rest here for some time to recover and then return home but I fear that you will wish to push on!"

De Bilbao's eyes flared with anger, "We are but a couple of days away from our prize! Of course, we push on!"

"Then you will need Tomas, will you not?"

I saw that he was defeated, "Then you, Conquistador," he spat the words out, "will come with me tomorrow when we find the South Sea!"

The next day, with the only healthy priest left to the expedition, Andrés de Vera, the forty-three Spaniards and two hundred Indians headed towards the mountains. We left my wounded Indians with the gun and the shot. One of Francisco's men, Alonso Martin borrowed a brigandine from one of the wounded men and I wore that. I felt like a soldier but as my battle had shown me, I had much to learn.

One advantage of climbing through the mountain passes was that the air was slightly cooler and the undergrowth less lush. De Bilbao must have had second sight for, at noon, as we reached the top of the mountain, there in the distance we could see the shining blue of an ocean. We had found the South Sea. Andrés de Vera began to chant the Te Deum and we all dropped to our knees. We had found the mystical sea. Were the riches of the Indies within our grasp? We made a pyramid of stones to mark the spot and some men carved crosses in the trunks of trees. Then we descended. Our goal was in sight but the smoke rising from the village below told us that we had another tribe to either subdue or persuade to join us.

The Indians we had with us were from Careta's tribe and they did not know the area. De Bilbao was in no mood to be thwarted this close to his goal and he was, as ever decisive and ruthless, "We will send three parties to find a trail to the sea. If the path is clearly impassable then return. The rest of us will camp here where the air is a little fresher and we will await your return. Francisco, you will lead one group. Alonso, you a second and Fernando, the third. Take three other men and four Indians. "

I was surprised when Alonso picked me. I later learned that Francisco had recommended me. With my ale skin and some salted and cooked donkey meat, we headed down through the jungle. Alonso was older than Francisco Pizarro and he was a clever man. He did not despise the Indians as de Balboa did and he chose four of the Indians who had been the most useful thus far. He let them lead hoping that their native instincts, as well as ability, would help us find the path. I brought up the rear and while I thought it was because I was the least useful, I later learned that it was a position of responsibility.

At first, I thought we had chosen the wrong path as we made slow progress. The Indians enjoyed using a metal machete to hack through the jungle. Their own tools were much less efficient. It soon became clear that far from being the wrong route it proved to be the perfect route for by the late afternoon we had found a trail and no cutting was involved. I suppose we could have gone back then for the Governor, but Alonso knew that there was a possibility that the path might take us somewhere completely different. When the sun began to set ahead of us and as we reached a small stream that bubbled down from the mountain tops Alonso chose to make a camp. We had seen Indian signs and we did not know the reaction there might be from the tribes in the area, but Alonso chose to have a fire going. We were grateful for it kept away some of the biting insects. We pooled our food to make a hunter's stew. One of the Spanish soldiers, Alvar, had a wineskin and he used that to enrich the stew. The Indians went to scout out the immediate area to check for danger and we four who remained sat and chatted.

"Tomas, are all the English like you?"

"What do you mean?"

Alonso shrugged, "You speak Spanish well and the language of the tribes better than most of the men who have lived their whole life here. We had heard that the English were an island, and each Englishman was the same. You only spoke English and you do not like to travel. Is that true?"

"I know that few Englishmen can speak other languages," I laughed, "however there are some folk in England, mainly in the north, whose English I do not understand."

Alonso laughed and Alvar nodded, "We have the same trouble, we call them the Catalans!"

"I was forced to learn Spanish and having learned one language then learning Indian seemed easy and I thought it might be useful. When

Governor Bilbao took me, I was little more than a slave and I have learned to do all that I can to stay alive and, perhaps, better myself."

The fourth Spaniard, Carlos, spat into the fire, "Do not feel offended, English, it is how he treats everyone he does not need something from. He will discard us as soon as we are no longer useful. Do you think that he will be concerned if only one of the three scouting parties returns? He will happily take the deaths of eight Spaniards for that is eight more men with whom he does not have to share his treasure. Now that you no longer have the gun then you will be like us and reliant on what you can steal!"

Alonso patted his friend on the back, "Carlos, you see everything as half empty, yet you are not far short of the mark in your assessment of our fearless leader." He stood to stir the pot, "Better, my friend that you follow Don Francisco."

"He is a knight?"

"That he is but Governor Bilbao chooses not to acknowledge the fact." He suddenly stopped, "All of this conversation is for here only, my friend. If de Bilbao hears a word of it then before we die, we shall slit your throat!"

I shook my head, "I have no reason to do that. I know that you are my crewmates now and I will respect your confidence."

The Indians came back and reported to Alonso. Thanks to my labourers I had a better knowledge of the local language and I helped to translate. I did not understand all that was said but I had enough wit to work it out.

As they ate, one of the Indians, Cacaro, spoke to me, "We do not know the tribes here, little warrior, but we have heard of two fierce tribes. One lives there." He pointed north, "and one lives there," he pointed south. If your people want more gold, then you will have to take it from them."

"Thank you. Who are their caciques?"

"Coquera and Tumaco."

I remembered the pearls we had found a lifetime ago when I had served on *'Falcon'*, "Are there any of the round, white precious stones?"

He nodded, "The tribes along the coast have many. They use them for trade."

Alonso had listened to the conversation and picked up some of the words. When the conversation ended, I told him what I had learned.

"You are useful, and I am pleased that Don Francisco suggested that you come with us!"

It was in the late afternoon of the next day when we finally reached the South Sea as Don Núñez de Bilbao came to name it. Alonso sent the Indians to see what they could find up and down the beach while we made a camp. We would stay by the beach. Alonso had an idea to find some means of viewing the shore from the sea. We had an axe and he contemplated chopping down a tree. That proved unnecessary as the Indians found a canoe. I wondered if that might bring trouble down upon us. Two of them returned from further up the beach and they were paddling an Indian canoe. When it arrived and the other Indians had returned Alonso pointed to the two largest Indians, "You two in the canoe. Tomas, you can come with me too. Carlos and Alvar make a camp and get a fire going. When I have ensured that there are no Indians close by, I will return and tomorrow we will leave to report to Governor de Bilbao."

When Alonso sat in the front and gestured for me to sit in the rear, I knew that he trusted me well enough to allow me to steer. I had been a gunner and not a sailor, however, I had watched One-Eyed Peter enough and sailed in the *'Falcon's'* small boat to have an idea what to do. I put my hand in the water, "The current is coming from the north and west. If we paddle north first, we will have an easier journey back, when we are tiring."

"We are in your hands, Tomas!"

I did not paddle us far from the shore; it was just enough to give us a good view ahead. The beach stretched uninterrupted for what seemed like miles. Alonso did not paddle all the time. He stared ahead sometimes with his hand shading his eyes. We spied, to the west, a group of islands. They were too far for us to investigate but the smoke we saw rising from them meant they were large enough to support settlements. After an hour or so he raised his hand and said, "We can head south now, Tomas. I see smoke which means there must be a village ahead."

We paddled south and when we passed our camp, I took us out to see a little more for I could tell that the tide had turned and was on its way in. This way we would be able to see further and it would not be hard to paddle back. This time we did not have long to paddle. We spied not only smoke but also, in the far distance a village which was close to the sea. I turned us around and we paddled back to our camp.

There was food cooking and Alvar and Carlos looked up expectantly. Alonso had the natives drag the boat up onto the sand and told the others what we had learned, "There is little danger from the north but the village to the south is uncomfortably close. When we have eaten, we will douse the fire for I would not draw native eyes to us, and we will keep a watch. I want one of us four on watch all night."

I did not regard the duty as a punishment, rather the opposite for it meant Alonso had accepted me as an equal and that made me swell with pride. I was given the easiest watch, the last one which meant I had an uninterrupted if shortened sleep. I heard nothing and as soon as I saw the first hint of light coming from the mountains, I roused the others. Alonso wasted no time on food. After we had made water, he had us break camp. Even that haste, however, was not enough. We had barely begun to move towards the trail when Cacaro shouted and pointed south. Twelve natives were running up the beach towards us.

Alonso was a good soldier and an experienced one, "Into the jungle and then stop. We will ambush them!"

Looking back, I can see it was the right decision. The natives would have bows and arrows and whilst our brigandines and helmets would protect us if the enemy had poisoned missiles we could be hurt. Our short-range weapons were superior to the tribesmen's.

As soon as we reached the trail, he split us into two. Alvar and Carlos hid on one side of the trail and Alonso and I on the other. He put the natives behind us to watch our backs. They just had a spear and a club each. It was our swords and daggers which were the deadlier weapons. I had my sword out and the shorter machete. My left hand was not as strong as my right, but I could use the weapon to block. I heard the natives shouting to each other. They all wore colourful garb decorated with the feathers of garish birds we had seen in the trees. It made them easier to see and I saw some run into the trail. Alonso had given no orders, but I knew that when I struck it would have to be decisive.

The trail was wide enough for three men abreast, but they came in twos. We were behind trees which meant that they would not see us. I had my sword ready behind me for I knew the blow I would use and as the first native ran into sight, I swung with all the strength I possessed. My father had taught me that a sword that was not sharp was not a weapon; it was an iron bar! My blade was honed sharp enough to use as a razor and my blow almost cut the native in two. Alvar also slew his Indian but before I could celebrate and strike again, I heard a cry from behind me. I whipped around as the two Indians protecting our backs were killed by the four natives who had sprung their own ambush. I barely had time to shout, "Ware behind!" before two spears were thrust at me. My sword easily deflected one, but the machete in my left hand merely took some of the sting from the strike. The fire-hardened spearhead gouged a wound down my leg. I lunged with my sword and the tip found the throat of one of the spearmen and my machete struck the hand of the second. His momentum brought him close to me and I headbutted him. The peak of the morion took his eye and as he dropped, I dragged the machete across his throat.

Alonso had three natives to contend with and although there were two bodies at his feet, I saw he had been wounded across the face. I stabbed one of his attackers in the back while Alonso slew a second. My machete scored a long wound down the third native's back and Alonso ended his life by almost decapitating him. He whirled to face more enemies but Alvar, Carlos and Cacaro had defeated them. Our other Indian lay dead. The Indians had all died in the ambush. Alonso had thought to protect them but, it seemed, their bodies had protected us.

Alonso, seeing that we had killed them all sheathed his sword, "I owe you a life, Tomas. One day I shall repay it." He looked down and saw that the natives we had killed each had some gold about them. "Take the gold from the ones you killed and then we run! If they sent twelve men to recover a boat, then they might send the whole tribe to seek vengeance upon us." They were fair men, and I took the gold from the four men I had killed. Two of them also had necklaces with pearls and one had a small emerald. I slipped them into my purse and within minutes of our victory we followed Cacaro up the trail. It had taken us two days to reach the sea, but we had begun that journey late in the day and we had camped. Fearful of pursuit we ran, and we just drank from our skins whilst on the run. When we reached the end of the trail proper and discovered where we had cut our way through the jungle we slowed, and both widened and marked the trail.

It was dark by the time we reached the camp our men had made. More men had arrived from Cuarecuá and the camp was a large one. Dogs barked as we approached, and harquebuses and swords were pointing at us as we stepped from the jungle.

Alonso gave a smile and bowed to Núñez de Bilbao as he said, "Excellency, we have found a trail. Tomorrow we can take you to your Mar del Sud! We have sailed on the new sea!"

Chapter 8

The priests were able to tend the wounds Alonso and I had suffered. Had they not, with the heat and the insects who knows what might have happened. As it was we were able to show de Bilbao the way to the sea but we were both uncomfortable and in pain.

The next day we set off towards the beach. The four of us led the twenty-two other men and de Bilbao back west. Francisco Pizarro was given the task of fetching the rest of our expedition from Cuarecuá and following our trail using Cacaro as their guide. De Bilbao was as excited as I had ever seen him, and he strode just behind Alonso and myself. He chattered like one of the exotic birds which seemed to inhabit these jungles. Despite their bright colours they proved hard to see in the thick canopy which shaded us from the sun and made the jungle trail feel like a bread oven!

"You saw Indians, Martin?"

Alonso did not turn to answer, "Yes, Excellency and they attacked us. Cacaro and the others seemed to think that there were two tribes. The one to the south is closer and they were the ones whom we fought. The other village is further north and there are islands not far from shore."

"Then we shall need boats!"

When we camped, at the small stream we had previously used, he continued to rattle off questions. Most of them we could not answer for he wanted to know of the treasure of the land. When it became clear that he had exhausted our knowledge he said, "Then when Francisco arrives with our men, we shall have to defeat these Indians and take captives. We must know where there is treasure."

The bodies from the skirmish lay where they had fallen. De Bilbao was unconcerned, but Alonso said to me, as we passed them, "We must bury the three who died with us. It does not do to dishonour fallen comrades. They were only Indians, but they died with us and we must honour their death."

De Bilbao took the standard of the Virgin Mary and drawing his sword he waded straight into the sea until the water covered the armour on his lower body. "I claim this sea, the Mar del Sur, and all the lands along it for King Carlos of Spain. As this is the day of San Miguel, I name this place, San Miguel! Praise be to God and the Virgin Mary for allowing me to discover this place and claim it for Spain!"

I saw that the other Spaniards had dropped to their knees and were holding their swords like crosses and I followed suit. I felt like a fraud for firstly, it was Alonso and the rest of us who had discovered the sea and secondly how could he claim as yet unknown lands for Spain?

When he waded back ashore, he had us begin to build a stockade. The bodies we had passed told him that there was danger. By the time the rest of the expedition joined us we had a wall and a ditch as well as one roofed, although wall-less building. Once the bulk of the men arrived, he used those who still sported wounds to guard our fort. The falconet had been carried but without powder she was useless. We placed her on the wall and de Bilbao instructed me to find the ingredients for gunpowder. I was not hopeful, but I bowed and nodded. We set off, along the beach and headed south to the village we had seen there. We knew from our own Indians that we had been observed but the tribe to the south must have been wary for they did not attack us. Instead, they waited and arrayed themselves for battle before their homes and families.

I naturally placed myself close to Alonso, Carlos and Alvar. I felt as close to them as I had to Enrico. We were on the left with Don Francisco. My time with Alonso and the others had given me an insight into the Spanish soldier of fortune. It was his men who had accorded him the title of Don. He came from a poor family but that just made him, in my eyes, even more admirable. He had achieved respect through his actions and that was no bad thing. He was ambitious and that was true of all the young men who had come west, and he sought both power and position, but I saw in him a natural nobility which was lacking in de Balboa.

The Indians we had with us were greater in number than the Spanish and I think that was what the enemy saw. We had neither gun nor horse but the metal we wore was completely new to them. They waited patiently as we advanced. We did have four harquebusier and they advanced just ahead of the rest of us. They rammed their stands in the soil and the sand and awaited the arrival of de Bilbao. They had enough powder for a couple of volleys and that was all. I think the natives were bemused by the four men who appeared just to have a long stick that smoked! The Governor stood silently for a moment and then shouted, "Prepare weapons!"

There was a collective hiss as swords were drawn. Alone out of the men with Francisco I had no shield. Instead, I used my machete again and prayed that the natives did not dip their weapons in poison.

"Open fire!" The four guns belched smoke and flame and the air was filled with the stink of gunpowder. Our supplies were almost gone, and I knew that we would have to either make more or forego such weapons! The effect of the four guns was minimal; just two men fell although another three were hit as the balls passed through unprotected flesh and into the bodies of those who were behind.

"Charge!"

We ran. The natives had received a shock and they hesitated. As I came to realise, hesitation could be fatal. In the moments that they stood and watched us, we had drawn thirty paces closer and when they released their weapons they did not aim well. Only a couple of our natives were hurt while the spears and arrows sent by Careta's men hit many of the natives. I was with the men of Francisco and while we were numerous, we were together and, it seemed to me, that was more important. Francisco himself wore a metal breastplate as did two other of his men. He seemed to draw the missiles of the tribe, but they bounced ineffectually from his helmet, shield, and armour. He also reached the natives a heartbeat ahead of Alonso and one of his other men, Diego. His sword slashed across three natives. One fell dead and the spurting blood on the other two did not bode well for them. I had my own battle. The native who faced me had some sort of wooden breastplate and he had a painted face with bright feathers in his hair. He also had a gold amulet around his neck. He had a small shield and a club. He roared and screamed at me as he raised his club to smash my skull. My helmet had saved me before, but I did not wish to test it a second time. I slashed at his club while it was in the air with my machete and the sharpened blade bit into the wood and held. As the warrior pulled back the head to free it from the blade I lunged almost blindly towards his middle and I felt the tip of my sword sink into soft unprotected flesh. As the club came free and he raised it again I pushed even harder and, grating off the bone, my sword angled up through his body. I saw the life go from his eyes. I pushed his body from my sword and saw that the natives were fleeing back to their village.

Pausing only to grab the gold amulet and slip it into my purse, I ran after Alonso and the others. De Bilbao had released his dogs and they were the ones who finally won the battle for us. After they had torn to pieces four warriors and the natives had thrown down their weapons, de Bilbao called them off. Three of the dogs had died in the battle and there were now just eight left, but they were still terrifying beasts. We discovered that the chief of the tribe, Coquera, had died and so de Bilbao appointed the dead cacique's son, Terraco, as the new chief but he first had the whole tribe converted and Terraco swear to hold the village for Spain. It was an indication of his ambition.

We had no wounds amongst our men and so we were amongst the first to search for gold and treasure. Although all that we found was supposed to go to Governor Bilbao, some of it found its way into our purses. He had the natives begin to construct boxes to carry the treasure away. We made the village our new home although we still maintained a presence at our fort. From Terraco we learned that the Indians to the north were the enemies of this tribe and that the chief there was called Tumaco. After a few days of rest and with a hundred of Terraco's men with us, we headed north towards the next village. The battle this time was over even more swiftly because Terraco's warriors took us by paths and trails to attack suddenly and swiftly from the land side. We did not even have to waste the last of our precious powder. Tumaco surrendered quickly and there was less slaughter and more treasure.

After the usual conversation and oath to become subjects of the King of Spain, de Bilbao discovered that the islands we had seen offshore were rich in pearls. The chief was a man called Terarequí. Using the native canoes, thirty of us, along with our leader, were paddled out to sea. The black storm clouds made it a difficult journey and the Spanish soldiers, myself included, spent the whole time baling water from them. Eventually, de Bilbao admitted defeat and after naming the islands, Archipiélago de las Perlas, and the largest island, Isla Rica, we returned to the village we now called Tumaco.

The men had all had enough of the expedition. The failed attempt to the islands was the last straw and whilst not mutinous, the mood was not happy. I think that Núñez de Bilbao himself wished to return for after the deputation asked him to head east once more, he agreed. We now had vast quantities of gold, silver and pearls. We had more than five hundred natives who were able to carry the boxes he had made and so we headed back over the mountain to Cuarecuá where we collected the falconet as well as Juan and the other wounded men. My last gunner was pleased to see me, and I was given four natives to carry the gun.

Of course, Governor de Bilbao was not going to take the easy route home and he chose to head due north. We had skirmishes and we had small battles but many of the natives had heard what we had done to other tribes and they submitted without bothering to fight. All were converted although the cynic in me wondered if, as soon as we left, they reverted to their own religion. We left no soldiers in the villages and I think the natives thought that our arrival and departure were like the natural disasters which visited their lands from time to time.

We had one major battle to fight. As we neared the coast a warrior chief, we learned from some of our new allies that his name was Tubanamá, had gathered the largest army we had yet seen and blocked our path to the sea. By now we were in a sorry state. Our clothes were little more than rags and many men had open sores caused by the undergrowth and insects. We had lost more men to disease, snakes, scorpions, and spiders than we had in battle and I knew that Governor de Bilbao was worried for he sent for me.

"Englishman, can your falconet fire?"

"If we had powder then aye." Juan had kept the gun clean while he had awaited our return and we had the linstock and rams. I knew that I could improvise ammunition from the stones, but I could do nothing without powder.

"The harquebusiers have gunpowder. I will have it sent to you. What about a carriage for the barrel?"

"I can improvise one."

"Then do so and quickly!"

The enemy were more than a thousand feet away and they were doing their usual posing and gesturing. Our warriors were doing the same and those actions would buy me enough time. I saw a group of rocks just two hundred feet closer to the enemy and it seemed perfect. Juan and my natives positioned the gun in a cleft in the rocks and when the powder arrived, I began to load the barrel. I had no bags in which to place the stones and so, with the one iron ball we had left I rammed them in the barrel. I knew that we risked ruining the falconet but the numbers of warriors who faced us told me that if we did not then we risked death. We had just finished, and I was ready with the linstock when Tubanamá raised his war club and the natives hurled themselves at us. I confess that the speed of their attack took me by surprise, but I held my nerve for Alonso and the others had been assigned to protect us and they had improvised pikes at the ready. One thing in our favour was that the gun had not been fired since our attack at Cuarecuá and it seemed the natives were unaware of its power. I fired the gun when they were just fifty feet from us. The crack made me jump back too and there was so much smoke, for the powder I had used was of poorer quality than my own and

I could barely see. When the pall of smoke began to clear I saw that I had cut through the heart of their elite warriors but rather than dismaying them it enraged them, and they filled the hole and came even harder. I drew my sword and machete.

Juan and I were protected to some extent by the gun and the rocks, but the agile Indians leapt in the air to try to fall upon us. Alonso's pikes speared many in the air. Two of them landed close to us. I had killed enough natives now and I had enough experience to know where to strike. Sadly for Juan, he did not. While I skewered my opponent, Juan had his skull shattered by the stone club wielded by the wild warrior above him. He had wounded the Indian but not stopped him. As the native screamed in victory I hacked across his neck. When the enemy chief was slain by Francisco the battle ended. As we took the treasure from the warriors we had killed I saw that the falconet would fire no more. I had overloaded the gun and the barrel had a crack. We left it on the rock where the rain would corrode it and the vegetation would cover it. The falconet would be buried but not by me.

After spending a couple of days collecting treasure and tending to wounds, we headed north and found ourselves in the territory we had first taken. We reached Santa Maria in the middle of January. The total worth of our treasure was 100,000 Castellanos. The amount was staggering. All the soldiers were also rich men. There was now a church and we all went to a service there, a service of thanks and to mourn our dead. My labourers had all been loyal and all had died. It was those men that I remembered.

As we came out Núñez de Bilbao called me over. Francisco Pizarro was with him, "Tomas the Englishman, known as Conquistador, I am mindful of your courage during our expedition and, as Governor of this land, I make you a free man. You are pardoned for the crimes of piracy and murder. Go with God!"

I had not murdered any, but I cared not. I could now, if I wished, return to England. I had more gold than I needed and perhaps, I could start a new life in my homeland!

Francisco asked me to serve with him, "You need a gunner?"

"I can see a time when I will need one and I know that you are thinking of returning to England. You are now a rich man and could do so. Your guns have saved us so many times that I am loath to lose you and you are a skilled warrior. I will pay you. It may not be much, but it will mean that you do not need to eat into your treasure. What say you, my young English friend? A better life than piracy eh?"

"A better life indeed." I liked the young Spanish knight, and I clasped his arm. I now had an employer and one who would soon need a gunner!

Master Gunner

Chapter 9

Castilla de Oro 1516

Pedro Arias Dávila had been appointed the new governor of Castilla de Oro almost a year since and de Bilbao fell out of favour while Francisco's star rose. The year I had spent with him had been productive. I now had a cannon that had been cast for me to my own specifications. It was a falconet. I had not yet fired it but Francisco's influence had ensured that I was not robbed and that the gun was ready when I asked. My decision to join Francisco Pizarro seemed a wise one. Yet it soon became clear that Francisco would not need a gunner as he set about helping the new governor to introduce the system called by the Spanish, repartimiento. It was a way to get the natives to continue to work, supposedly for themselves but pay a tax to the governor. As soon as it became clear that my talents would not be needed, I spoke to the knight, "I thank you for all that you have done for me, Francisco, but it is obvious to me that you will not be leading an army to the South Sea any time soon."

"But I will need you."

His voice told me that he was sincere but I knew that I could not simply sit and do nothing. I either needed to become a gunner again or return to England and I had used half of my treasure to pay for the gun which I hoped would make my fortune. "I am young, and I need to learn to be a better gunner. I have learned much already but this is a new profession and I intend to be the best. I need to find a war!"

It was Pedro Arias Dávila who gave me my answer. He was a shrewd man and he trusted Francisco. "You should go to Isla Juana. I can give you a letter of introduction if you wish. Diego Velázquez de Cuéllar was appointed Governor of New Spain for it was he conquered Isla Juana. He has an idea to sail west and conquer the lands there. He seeks gunners and soldiers."

Francisco nodded, eagerly, "And when I have completed my work for the Governor then, perhaps we can return to the South Sea. You and I know that there are riches there!"

The governor was not as confident as we were, "Let us first civilise these tribes before we risk our men on wilder ones as yet unknown."

Heeding their counsel, I took ship with my gun and headed for Isla Juana. It was one of the larger islands and, along with Hispaniola, was called New Spain. I landed in the capital, Santiago, aware that I would now have to spend my own savings! After renting a room and paying for the storage of my falconet, as yet unnamed, I went to present myself to the Governor. Francisco had taught me the right way to speak to nobles and the right clothes to wear. I was unrecognisable from the pirate who had been dragged in rags from the wreckage of *'Falcon'*. I had been given a good letter and it so impressed the Governor that he sent for the Mayor of the town, who had once been his clerk. It was then I met Hernán Cortés, although in those days he called himself Hernando. I thought, when I first met him, that he was a clerk for he did not have the frame of a warrior. It shows how wrong a man can be.

The two men seemed quite interested in how we had managed to overcome the fierce tribes we had encountered. I spent a happy hour telling them how we used a mixture of cannons and pikemen.

"And you have your own cannon?"

It was the mayor who interrogated me although the Governor did seem interested. "I have."

"From what I have heard, Englishman, despite your apparent youth you have great skill." The mayor tapped the letter the Governor had given him to read. "Francisco Pizarro himself says that he would have you as a master gunner."

"That is kind of him to say so." I could not see where this conversation was going.

The Governor said, "We have plans to colonise the mainland to the west. It is a land the Indians call Mexico." He gave a conspiratorial look at his former clerk, "There are many restless colonists here who wish to free themselves of our rules and when they are put in their place then we can begin to make an Empire for King Carlos." He nodded and patted his table, "I will hire you and your gun. You will be paid as a Captain of Gunners. There are more ships due to land here soon from Spain, and I do not doubt that there will be, amongst them, soldiers and gunners. Hernando here will hire the best, but I wish you to choose the gunners. There is no rush to this. We have no plans for this year and you can be selective. If Pizarro is correct then you are the man to pick the best. I envisage perhaps eight or ten guns."

I nodded, "And, as you say, this is not urgent but when we employ the gunners, we will need both guns and the labourers to serve them."

"As soon as the first gunners are hired then we shall hire the labourers,"

"And the guns?"

Hernando Cortés smiled, "And we will tax ships which land here an extra tax. One gun per ship!"

It was an interesting way of doing things. If I was one of the sea captains, I would not be happy about it but so long as I had guns, I was happy.

The Governor said, "From now on you deal with Hernando here. There is a convoy of ships due in next week. Be at the quay to meet them." He reached into a drawer and took out a small chest. He counted out eight gold pieces. "This will be your pay for the first three months. Hernando will see to the gunpowder and ball."

I was dismissed and the mayor left with me, "Where are you staying?"

"I took a room by the harbour. They have a building for my gun."

"You must stay with me. I would pick your brains and keep you close to me." I was flattered and I agreed. When I came to know the man, I saw that he had ulterior motives. He was more like de Bilbao than Francisco! Living under his roof I also saw that he also had an eye for women. He liked ladies but, it seemed to me, young and impressionable though I was, that he liked anything that wore a dress. All of that was for the future and I was just excited to be given such an elevated position so early.

When the two of us went to see the arrival of the ships, I saw, because Hernando pointed him out to me, one of the disgruntled knights who wished to be freed from the official yoke; Hernández de Córdoba. He led the rebellious colonists. Hernando Cortés was always smiling even when, as I discovered later on, he was not smiling inside. Hernández was the opposite and I rarely saw him smile. He had a permanently angry face. The two men acknowledged each other and then assiduously avoided any eye contact at all. It became clear that we were all there for the same purpose. Hernández sought colonists he wished to take to the mainland, the land they called Mexico, and he needed protection from the natives. There were many soldiers who had served Spain in the European wars and now sought to profit from the new, rich colonies of the west.

I knew what I was looking for. I wanted those who had blackened fingers from working with gunpowder. No matter how much you washed it became ingrained in the skin. I was not worried about age, Enrico had been old but, in a perfect world the ones I hired would be like me, young. I did not want to have to constantly prove myself. I was still young but my experiences in the jungle heading to the South Sea and my father's training had given me skills beyond my years and, as Enrico had often told me, I had some God-given talent. I was a natural gunner.

Hernández and Hernando both sought those who carried weapons, a helmet and had the scarred looks of veterans. There would not be many pikemen for their weapons would be too cumbersome to transport but swords and good daggers would be in evidence. As for harquebuses…they were in such demand in the old world that we would be lucky if any chose to bring their weapons to this new one. Hernando had a jingling bag of coins and he spied the first two soldiers as they came down the gangplank, somewhat unsteadily after weeks at sea. They each carried the cabacet helmet which looks similar to the morion one I had been given. Their swords were good ones with the curved hilt favoured by many. Across their backs, they carried their bucklers. They both wore brigandines and carried the rest of their gear over their backs.

Hernando pounced on them as they reached the stone quay.

"I am Hernando Cortés, the mayor of this town, and I am here both to welcome you and to offer you employment." His smile became broader, "Unless, of course, you are rich men who have come here to enjoy the pleasant clime and the beautiful native girls."

His smile always worked, and the men smiled back and one said, as he nodded, "We had come here for work but we thought to head further south where we hear Don de Bilbao is taking gold and pearls as though they were the husks of wheat."

"If I tell you that this young man who is next to me was with de Bilbao then you will see that he has chosen the route which is more profitable."

The one who had not spoken said, "But he is barely a boy." He smiled at me, "No offence!"

I did not need to answer as the mayor did it for me, "And a master gunner who so cowed the natives that in some battles he fired but three rounds and they surrendered."

The two looked at me with new respect and I had to admire the silver tongue of the mayor. He took out two gold pieces and proffered them.

The two men smiled and, after exchanging a glance, one said, "We accept."

Hernando pointed to a wooden stall where two natives were selling ale, "Go and refresh yourselves and we will join you when we have secured more men."

While we had been talking Hernández de Córdoba had pounced but without the lure of coins, the man he had accosted had shaken his head and headed into the town. I saw the mayor note the man, he would seek him out later. The next man who descended was huge and with a morion helmet and a breastplate over his back he looked perfect. Before Hernández de Córdoba could speak to him Hernando stepped forward, "I am the mayor of this town and I am seeking men to work for me."

The man grinned, "I am Jesus Martinez and if that is gold in the purse then I am your man, but I am not cheap. I have never been defeated in battle and I have killed more than twenty men."

That was the first time I saw the smile leave, not Hernando's mouth but his eyes, "You know we do not fight civilised men but barbarians who have stone weapons?"

The man snorted, "If they are men then when I meet them, they die."

Hernando said, "I fear you will be too expensive for me, try Hernández de Córdoba, I am sure he would need your obvious skills."

The man was taken aback. I suspect he had seen Hernando offer money to the two other soldiers and thought to take more than the two coins. His face darkened so much that I could not help the smile which crept across my face. It was a mistake, "You will both regret this but you, boy, sooner!" He turned and stormed off to Hernández de Córdoba.

I was curious why he had been rejected, "What was wrong with him?"

"A troublemaker. He will not need his armour fighting natives, you know that. I want more pliable men."

The ship had emptied of passengers and we headed down to the next one. The convoy had tied up in an orderly fashion and that suited us as it meant we could see more men. We found another three on the next two ships but no gunners and then I spied a man and his son. The man had blackened fingers and he carried a linstock. It was my time to pounce, "You are a gunner?"

The man nodded, "Fernando Bolivar." He looked around, "Where is your master?"

I knew that I coloured, it was involuntary, but I just nodded, "I know I look young, but I have been a gunner these last five years and I am the master gunner of the mayor here, Hernando Cortés."

The mayor beamed, "He is right and believe me the words he speaks are true. He has shown himself to be skilful."

"I have my own gun, a falconet and I can hit the rudder of a galleon at five hundred feet and disable it," I said and was about to turn away for I did not want to have to keep justifying myself.

The man shook his head, "I believe you for your hands show that you are a gunner. This is my son, Jose, and I will accept your offer although I have no gun."

"And I am Thomas Penkridge, born in England. My father was a gunner."

His face broke into a smile, "Then I am doubly happy to join you. I would have my son train as a gunner, but I thought him too young."

I laughed, "You can never be too young."

Hernando handed him a coin and said, "Join those others."

We found no more gunners, but we did manage to employ two more swordsmen. We gathered up our warriors and headed to the barracks which had been built recently by the Governor in anticipation of our success. In contrast, the erstwhile rebel, Hernández had found but two. The one we had rejected and another. The new men we had chosen were happy with their accommodation but as I had no idea when we would be setting off on our attempt to claim more land for Spain, I was unable to answer all their questions. Having had a long voyage from Spain they would need time to recover. That evening as I ate with Hernando, we tended to eat early as he had a string of ladies he liked to visit, I raised the question of guns.

"We will need guns and before we order them to be made, I need to know the targets."

Hernando paused in his chewing, "Why, what difference does it make what the size of the gun is? The natives will be terrified of them as soon as they are fired."

"Most are, I agree but some still came on even though the guns were killing them. They are not fast to reload and if the natives run quickly then they can overcome the gunners!

Realisation dawned, "Ah."

"Do they live in wooden buildings or do they build in stone?"

He wiped his mouth, "Thoughtful questions to which I do not have the answers. The foundry we have cannot produce big guns. I will have to either commandeer even more from the ships or send to Spain."

"Do not forget powder and ball although sacks of small stones are very effective. Do I have your permission to have another four falconets made? They are lighter to transport and are quite effective."

"I will have to speak to the Governor, but I think so."

Over the next month, we found many more soldiers for word spread that the mayor and Governor were seeking them. I found but three more gunners and none of them were as good as Fernando who had spent much time with me at the foundry where we supervised the manufacture of the falconets. His son was almost twelve and keen to become a gunner. He was like my shadow for I was the living proof that he could become a gunner. Unlike me, however, his mother still lived. Jose was the eldest and his mother hoped to join us with Fernando's other children.

Life was good until one night, as I was heading back with Fernando and Jose from the foundry we came across Jesus Martinez. He was drunk and he was not alone. Had I seen him earlier I would have avoided the encounter, but I was telling Fernando and Jose how I had been forced to fire a gun using the cleft of a rock as a trail. The swordsman and two others just loomed up out of the dark.

"The little English rat, who laughed at me! Your Mayor is not here to protect you now, little one and I sail to Mexico on the morrow. What say I give my sword a little practice?" He drew his weapon.

"If I caused you offence, I am sorry. I will not fight you!"

"A coward to boot! Typical of the English!" He was drunk but he had quick hands. His sword lunged at my face so fast that had I not been stone-cold sober I might have ended like One-Eyed Peter and lost an eye. As it was, I spun around, and his sword trimmed a lock of hair from my head.

The other two with him kept their swords sheathed as Fernando said, "Three against one would be murder!".

I drew my own and slipped my dagger into my left hand. He was angry that he had not taken my eye. His lunge had been for that sole purpose and he now saw a youth with a shorter sword who was making a fool of him. He had begun the fight and he could not walk away. Now he would kill me and not worry about the consequences. He was taller and broader than I was, and he swung the sword with its edge aimed at my neck. I brought up my own sword, but I barely stopped the blade and I had to step back. That, in its own way, helped me for as I stepped back, he began to overbalance and as I flicked at his sword the tip of my weapon tore the sleeve of his doublet. He roared with rage as though I cheated somehow and drawn blood. He grabbed his sword in two hands and raised it to smash down on my head. I had barely survived a glancing blow; a two handed one would surely kill me. I held up my dagger and sword to make a cross. Perhaps God was watching me for I managed to hold him as all three hilts locked. He still wore his helmet and he grinned. I knew he would head butt me and I would be badly injured. I did the only thing I could, I brought my knee up with all the force I could muster and drove it into his groin. I had once seen Rob do that in a fight when we were in Falmouth. I connected well and heard the intake of breath. His sword dropped as he fell backwards.

One of his companions said, "That is as good as you can hope, Englishman. Now go before the watch comes. We will take him back to our camp."

The other said, "It is good that we leave tomorrow for this one bears a grudge, and he would kill you. Next time he would not give you a chance."

I needed no further urging and hurried back to Hernando's. "You did well Tomas, but you were lucky. You need a better sword."

"Aye, I know."

I felt obliged to tell Hernando of the incident. He smiled, "Then I am glad I did not employ him. So Córdoba leaves tomorrow? The Governor of Isla Juana will not be pleased. Still, it will give us better news of the mainland." He looked like he had finished and then said, "Our friend, Francisco Pizarro, will be here within the week. He is bringing de Balboa. The Governor has tired of his plotting. The man will be tried for treason!"

The next day the news was all about the ships which had sailed to the mainland. There were soldiers on board the ships, but they had taken no cannons and nor did the ships have anything larger than a couple of harquebuses. I hoped, despite my encounter with Jesus, that they would fare well, but I doubted it. I learned, as we ate that night that others had been west and found jungle and stone buildings that appeared to be made to a pyramid design. The tribes did not sound as primitive as those close to the South Sea. I began to wonder if falconets would be big enough for from the description of these structures they were soundly made with a huge base and then rising into the sky, becoming progressively narrower. Of course, those early accounts could have been an exaggeration. It would be better to await the return of this newer one.

When I saw the former Governor of Veragua, Vasco Núñez de Balboa, I could not believe the change in the man. I had never liked him, but I had admired him. Now he looked like a shrunken version of his former self, whilst my friend, Francisco, looked every inch the knight. His new role seemed to suit him. I was invited to dine with the Governor of Isla Juana, Francisco, and Hernando. I knew that I was in elevated company and I dressed accordingly. There were ladies there too. I had become used to speaking to Spanish nobles, but Spanish ladies were something else. I saw Hernando flirting with the Governor Velázquez's sister-in-law, Catalina Juarez. That the lady was taken with the handsome mayor was understandable, but I feared that Hernando would treat her like many of the other women he had met; use and then discard her. He had a voracious appetite. However, it allowed me to speak to Francisco, who gave me the news that another expedition had crossed to the mainland, this time further north than the one with the pyramids. Juan de Grijalva had with him more than one hundred and seventy men but, once again, no cannons.

Francisco smiled at me, "Tomas, had they sought my advice I would have said to recruit you!"

"Kind of you to say so."

"When do you leave for your expedition?"

I shrugged, "I fear that the Governor of Isla Juana is not as enthusiastic about the idea, unlike our expedition, the men who have sailed west, thus far do not seem to have found treasures such as we did."

He leaned into me to speak quietly, "I have reports of people who live in the South Sea, many weeks south of where we first saw it and they are so rich that they have gold pieces embedded in their ears. Some have gold in their ears big enough to eat off!"

I laughed at the idea and it attracted the attention of others. "Sorry!" I turned back to Francisco, "I cannot understand why would they do that? I can see that they might put gold on their heads and around their necks, but their ears?"

He shrugged, "It is what I have heard. Until we have facilities on the South Sea coast, then it will remain a dream. It took us long enough to cut through the small patch of the jungle but to do so for what amounts to months, perhaps even a year, just to build ships would be foolish!"

The rest of the evening we spoke of those who had been with us. I was sad that few remained. A very small number had returned to Spain, but most had succumbed to the jungle, battle, or disease! I realised that as much as I wanted to return to England a rich man, and I was far from that yet, I wanted to return alive and perhaps I should do what my father and One-Eyed Peter had not, I should return now. I had enough to get me home and to hire men to serve my guns. I had skills that could be used aboard English ships.

Francisco's visit was all too short, and he left the unfortunate de Bilbao languishing in jail awaiting his sentence of execution to be carried out. It was shortly after this time that some men who had led an expedition to the west returned. This was not Córdoba's but the captain, Juan de Grijalva. He brought the Governor of Isla Juana the news that he had found a land that was contested by natives but was rich in gold and silver. He said it was called Yucatán. He had returned to find more men, guns, and powder. When I heard the news, I contemplated offering my services. However, when I mentioned it to him, Hernando curtailed that idea. He invited de Grijalva to his home and he not only extracted much information, but he also hired three of de Grijalva's men. I never had the chance to offer my services.

I suppose I should have been flattered that Hernando Cortés was so keen for my skills, but I was not. He sent for me to tell me that the guns we already had would be augmented so that we had eleven. I had eight gunners and that was manageable. "Now, my friend, we just need the powder and the ships from our Governor, and we sail west."

"To Yucatán?"

"Perhaps but as there are two expeditions there already, I thought to sail further north. I now have some men who sailed with de Grijalva and we can avoid encroaching on land already claimed." He wanted the glory for himself.

As we headed for the Governor's residence, I thought that Hernando Cortés had it all. He had arrived with nothing in this new Empire and was now one of the three most powerful men in this land. I saw the other side when we were ushered into the presence of the Governor. This was the one time when Hernando's smile left his face.

Before he could even ask permission, the Governor jabbed an accusing finger at him, "You have abused your position, mayor! My sister in law's honour has been put in jeopardy by you and your actions!"

Hernando was a quick-thinking man and that day I saw the signs. "Governor Velázquez, nothing could be further from the truth! I was merely trying to find the right time and place to ask for her hand in marriage! I am sorry that my duties and preparing for this expedition, which we both want, have put it from my mind."

It was as blatant a lie as I had ever heard, and I am not sure that the Governor believed it. He put the mayor to the test, "Then before you leave on this expedition you shall be married. One month from now!"

The smile returned, "And that cannot be soon enough for me. And the expedition? We can have the ships and the powder?"

"When you have spent a week as man and wife then we shall see."

As we left Hernando said to me, "I am sorry that you had to see that, Tomas. Still, a man has to do all that is necessary if he has a dream and I have one."

"A dream?"

"Tomas, I like you. You are honest and brave and so I will confide in you. I would have an empire on the mainland. Not like here with little islands and land that a man has to fight for but a larger land where someone with good men and cannons can control thousands of natives and reap the reward!"

I decided then that I would give Hernando his expedition and if God willing, I survived then I would take whatever treasure I had and return to England.

A week before the wedding Hernández de Córdoba returned with a handful of survivors from his expedition to Yucatán. There were just two ships left and they had been forced to sail to La Florida first. He died three days after he arrived in Santiago. I saw nothing of the man who had tried to kill me. He could be anywhere, but the odds were that he was dead. What de Córdoba did tell Governor Velázquez before he died was that there was a huge amount of treasure but the warriors who lived there were fierce, well organised and good fighters!

I did not see much of Hernando who had a wedding and an expedition to organise. I was busy with my own part. I had powder, ball, and guns to load on the ship which had been assigned to us. I confess that Fernando Bolivar had made my life much easier. He had been with me when we had found gunners and it was his belief in me that allowed me to lead for they took their cue from him. I had hessian bags packed as well as lead balls and pebbles; I remembered how effective they had been in the fighting with the southern Indians. I also bought seasoned slaves to work the guns and we spent the two weeks before we were due to sail going through the drills we would need. The falconets would be carried in pieces and they would have to assemble them on land. We had no horses yet and no likelihood of getting any. Until we did then the slaves would have to carry them.

It was after the wedding, which I attended, that disaster struck. The day after the marriage Catalina ran to her brother-in-law. She felt she had been duped by Hernando and that there was neither love nor affection in their marriage, already! I knew this because he came to the quay where we were loading the ship and told me. "Tomas, I fear that Governor Velázquez may revoke our charter and forbid us to sail. I have spoken to the other captains and they are ready to cast off as soon as I return. Your falconets and falcon are most important for this expedition. Are they loaded?"

"They are all aboard but dare we risk the wrath of the Governor? Look what happened to de Bilbao!"

That cavalier smile reappeared, "I will go to pour oil on these troubled waters. Be ready!"

I just had my chest to board. I bought some fruit and wine from the quayside and then strode aboard. I had got to know the captain and he smiled, "We leave when the mayor returns."

"Good the tide will be right. And do we know where we shall sail, Englishman?"

I was now known as Englishman for the insulting Conquistador had long been forgotten. I shook my head, "I know not but as we have yet to find horses, I am guessing we will sail somewhere else before we head west."

He nodded, "Aye, well, that will give me the chance to see how we sail with this extra weight."

Fernando and Jose were at the bow of the ship. Fernando was smoking a pipe. I had seen natives smoking the brown leaves which grew over here but the only one I knew who smoked was Fernando. "So we go?"

"We go."

"I had hoped that Maria and my family would be here by now but..." He tapped the clay bowl on his hand and scattered the ash in the water, "I have spoken to the priest and when she comes, he has money to give to her. Pray God that we return."

I nodded, "Amen to that, my friend!"

Chapter 10

Trinidad, Isla Juana 1519

We had disobeyed the Governor and sailed for this new land that promised riches. Hernando was gambling that he would find this new land filled with gold and treasure and that his success would bring forgiveness. I was not so sure, and I wondered how I would fare. The Governor had commissioned the expedition and he had hired us. Would he see me as a conspirator?

We stopped at the port of Trinidad on the southern side of the island to board more soldiers and, crucially, horses. This was another example of the sharpness of Hernando's mind. He had anticipated something like this and as the Governor knew we would not leave without horses and a full complement he had arranged for us to pick them up at Trinidad. It was there I met one of the captains who would lead us. Alonso de Ávila was almost fifty and yet he had the energy of a much younger man. Like Hernando, he had come to this new land to become rich and powerful. I suppose we were all the same, but I do not think that I was quite as ruthless as either of the two men who led us. The de Alvarado brothers had also been to the mainland before and they were on our leader's ship.

I was not sailing on Hernando's ship and so I was not privy to his planning. I was with Captain Pedro on his carrack. We were overcrowded but my guns and powder were safe below deck and my gunners, having been the first aboard had the luxury of a cabin. The rest endured the deck. The need to regroup each morning after becoming separated in the dark meant that our voyage west was slow. I did not mind as it helped me to get to know the slaves and my gunners better. Fernando had become my lieutenant. He was the most experienced gunner we had aboard and had forgotten more about guns than most knew. I think he was happy with the position because of Jose. Jose was wherever I was, and I knew he would be a gunner. I would encourage him for my father had done so with me just eight short years ago. He would be the little brother I never had.

I came to know Captain Pedro well, too. He was young to be a captain, I took him to be about thirty, but he seemed skilled and he was popular with his crew. He had not been in the Indies as long as I had, only coming out six years earlier. He had never sailed the southern waters, but he knew the northern part of the sea quite well. He had been with Ponce de Leon when he had discovered La Florida.

"There is nothing there, English! Jungle, trees, and pretty flowers but no gold and no silver. I can never see men like us living there. It is best left to the natives."

"And do you know this place, Yucatán, to which we sail?"

"I was with him there when we named the River Grijalva."

"Then why are you not leading this fleet?"

He smiled, "Mine is not the largest ship and the brothers, de Alvarado, were eager to tell our leader where to find the treasure." He shook his head, "They are ambitious men." I could tell from the tone of his voice that he did not like them.

"Are not all such leaders?" I was thinking of the former Governor, de Bilbao.

Shaking his head he said, "Captain Juan de Grijalva was not such a man. When we found the natives, he did not have to fight them, not at first. It was only later when we tried to venture inland that the Indians attacked us. Even then he did not prosecute the battle for he knew we might be defeated. We had neither horses nor guns such as yours. It is why I am happy you are aboard. Your powder might be dangerous, but your cannons will guarantee we win, and I will be rich. I came here with Captain de Ponce to become rich. I hope to have a home and a wife in the fullness of time, and I would leave the sea and become a landowner. I have some land on Hispaniola but not enough slaves to work it. I hope that we will make enough this time for me to return home, get more ships and when I have made my fortune leave the sea. She can be a savage mistress and this little sea has storms and winds which make ships disappear. That is not to mention the pirates who now seek to take our ships when we near home waters. I think, young Tomas, that I will need gunners such as you one day."

"Then you think that we will succeed?"

He laughed, "Our Captain-General has shown that he is willing to bring down the wrath of a Governor on his own head. I do not think he will fear the Indians that we meet." Cortés had begun to use the title of Captain-General. It was, like most of the expedition, not sanctioned by either Isla Juana or the crown but it was a title and we cared not that it was not legal.

I learned much from Captain Pedro who seemed to like me. He was a contrast to, Francisco Pizarro apart, the other conquistadors I had met. I did not count Fernando or my other gunners as conquistadors, for as gunners we just followed orders. We would not be the ones plotting and planning to carve out an empire. We were more like Captain Pedro. We wanted enough treasure to be comfortable. In my case that would be back in England. I was flattered that Captain Pedro thought to employ one such as me. He questioned me at length, as we sailed west, about where one would find such gunners. I was not of much help as we had struggled to find gunners. I, once again, thanked my father for giving me, in a couple of short years the skills to become a gunner. I had realised from what Francisco said, that I must have some natural ability, given by God for I seemed to know things without being taught.

When we hove to off the river then I knew Captain Pedro had been right about the skills of the captains in the fleet. Our fleet of eleven ships had all survived. With five hundred men and thirteen horses, not to mention the eleven guns, we were one of the smallest expeditions ever sent to conquer a new land. The other, smaller expeditions had been there to scout but the Captain-General was intent on conquest and that was clear from the start. Along with the ship carrying the horses we were not at the fore. Four of our ships headed into the river and the native town which lay there. We watched from a distance and I expected smoke from the harquebuses Cortés had with him, but we were signalled to sail into the river and there we took on food from the Indians as well as freshwater. Juan de Grijalva, it seemed, had managed to make friends here. I began to wonder if my guns might be needed after all.

We did not go ashore but, on the second day, I saw a native canoe push off from the opposite shore to the town. A man, I later learned was a Franciscan priest who had been shipwrecked, landed, and was taken to Captain-General Cortés. This man would prove to be invaluable. His named was Geronimo de Aguilar. We had taken on enough supplies for us to continue to explore and, the next day, I expected us to set sail either upriver or further along the coast to seek this city of stone. As I rose at dawn and made water a terrifying sight greeted me and the men on watch, more than two thousand Indians appeared close to our ships. We had less than a hundred men ashore and as they attacked Cortés and the men with him, I was convinced that our expedition would be over before it began for the cannons were still in the hold and the horses had yet to be landed. It was then that Pedro de Alvarado showed his skill. He landed his one hundred men, and they came to the aid of our beleaguered men. The two hundred drove the natives away and we were left wondering, aboard our ships, what was happening? It was late in the day when Hernando Cortés returned with the men assigned to guard him. His breastplate was bloody but, as ever, he was smiling. We were summoned ashore and the cannons and horses were landed. We had taken Potonchán which was the name of the town where Cortés had been entertained! I had been a bystander and was relatively safe aboard Captain Pedro's ship but all that was about to change.

I was summoned to Cortés' side as he had some minor wounds tended to by priests. He gestured to Geronimo de Aguilar who was at his side, "We are lucky, Tomas, and God has sent us a sign that we are to bring Christianity to this pagan land. This is Geronimo de Aguilar who is a priest, shipwrecked here some years ago. He can speak their language and it was he who warned us that the Mayan Indians planned to attack. We had short notice or else I would have had your guns. We were lucky and we did not lose many men but we have too few to begin with. Land your guns for we shall need them. The Indians have fled inland and are headed for somewhere they call Centia. I have claimed this land for King Carlos and Spain so that we now act legally!"

He said the words loudly for he was making sure that all his leaders, the three de Alvarado brothers, Gonzalo, Pedro and Gomez, Alonso de Ávila and the others all heard them. He was trying to undermine the Governor who had forbidden us to come.

"I want the horses and cannons ready to follow us. The ships can control the town and tomorrow we will make three columns and seek this, Centia. Be ready to follow us!"

I knew that we could have the guns ready for we had practised so much that my slaves knew how to do this blindfold, but the horses had been at sea. Admittedly it had not been a voyage of weeks but, even so, I would have rested them. It took the rest of the afternoon to bring the guns, powder, and ball ashore. The priest, de Aguilar, who watched while the guns were landed, told me that the land through which we travelled was a cultivated plain and that there were roads. I decided to risk using the wheels we had made for the cannons as pulling them would be easier than carrying them. It was late when we finished, and we slept by our guns with guards sent by Hernando to protect us.

The three columns left at dawn and we rose to begin to prepare to follow them. Gonzalo de Alvarado was left to command the column. The Alvarado brothers were seasoned warriors and amongst the toughest men I had ever met. Gonzalo was a younger brother of Pedro, but he had more experience than some men much older than he was. He had men mount the horses but placed them at the rear behind the cannons. The men on foot preceded us. I was excited to be leading my team of gunners for the first time but also nervous. Would the carriages hold up under the rough treatment they were going to receive? When we fought would my gunners and my cannons do all that was expected of them? Would the Indians have poisoned weapons? My mind was so full of questions and fears that I did not notice the sounds of battle. It was Jose who alerted me.

"Captain Tomas, do you not hear the fighting?"

I looked up and heard the shouts and then the loud crack as a harquebus was fired.

Captain Gonzalo rode up, "Master Gunner, bring your guns at the run. We have the battle to win! Clear the way for the guns and the horses!"

His brother, Gomez, commanding the rest quickly had the road cleared and, grabbing one of the ropes which hauled the guns I shouted, "Gunners! We run to war!"

The falcon moved far more easily than I had expected. As we ran, I turned to ensure that the powder and shot in their carts were keeping pace with us. I smiled as I saw Jose had taken it upon himself to help the slaves pulling them. We had melded into one force and that pleased me.

Captain Gonzalo said, as he passed me, "Engage the Indians and I will take my horsemen around the rear!"

I was horrified at the sight which befell me. The whole savannah was covered in warriors with plumed heads and their faces covered with ochre. They were pressing on all sides of Captains Cortés and de Ávila who led their column. There appeared to be three hundred Indians for every Spaniard. I began to fear for my life for I had never fought against such odds. It was then I remembered that I was in command. When we reached the rear rank of our men, it was just two men deep, I shouted, "I want the guns spaced so that there are ten feet between each gun. Load the guns with the sacks of stones. Aim at the bellies of the Indians! When I give the command then fire and keep firing the bags of stones until I tell you to cease!" While my crew did as I ordered I shouted to Captain de Ávila, "Captain, when I give the command have your men fall back behind our guns. We are ready to fire!"

It says much that the Captain, as he slashed his sword across the neck of a half-naked Indian, replied calmly, "Aye, English! Be ready men to unleash the fire of the dragon to tear into these savages!"

I looked down the line and saw that every gun captain held his linstock ready. I looked down the barrel and saw it was aligned correctly, "Fall back!" The space I had left made it easy for our men to, gratefully, run to take a position behind us. The Indians looked shocked when they saw the barrels of our guns, and I shouted, "Fire!" A line of smoke almost fifty paces wide and with belching flames obscured the Indians. "Reload and keep firing!" I did as the other captains did and ensured that the barrel was still aimed correctly. We fired again and again!

Suddenly the whole Indian army, even those who had not been fired upon, hurled themselves to the ground. I shouted, "Cease fire!" And, as the smoke cleared saw that it was not our guns which had cowed the Mayans but the thirteen horsemen. I was told later by our Franciscan translator, Geronimo de Aguilar, that they had never seen a horse before, and they thought that the man and horse was a new creature. We had won! The battle of Centia was a great victory for Hernando Cortés. He was not a soldier, but he knew how to employ soldiers and let them do what they did best. The order was given, after we had collected our wounded, to head back to Potonchán for we were exposed upon a plain and Potonchán had our freshly erected defences.

The horsemen led and we, the gunners, followed. The cannons and carriages had fared well. Gonzalo de Alvarado, Cortés, de Ávila, and Geronimo de Aguilar rode and walked next to me at the head of my guns.

"Captain Gonzalo, that was a brilliant and brave move!" Cortés was both relieved and exulted by the victory.

"Thank you, Captain-General but I must give thanks where it is due, Father de Aguilar told me that the Mayans had never seen a horse and I gambled. It paid off."

Captain de Ávila patted me on the back, "And I never thought that our young Master Gunner would be so cool, calm and collected under fire. You sited your guns perfectly and showed no fear. I had thought when the Captain-General appointed you that he had made a mistake. My apologies. You have my respect!"

I smiled and shook my head, "If I had been in your position then I, too, might have thought the same."

Captain-General Cortés was laughing as he said, "We all did well and have good reason to be pleased with ourselves. We had more than seventy men wounded, and some two-dozen killed but we slaughtered many times that number."

Father de Aguilar said, "You will know if you have succeeded, Captain-General, if the Indians come bearing gifts. That is their sign that they have been defeated."

None of the Indians had come close to my guns. The nearest bodies had been more than fifty paces away. My gunners were all impressed by the bags of pebbles I had used. They had not seen them before. Perhaps my time as a pirate had not been wasted. Before we left to return to our fortified camp we searched the dead and found gold and silver on the warriors we had killed. It seemed that the Mayans took the precious metal to be a way of keeping a warrior from being killed. It had not saved them from our falcons and falconets.

Some of the wounds suffered by the soldiers were horrific. Those who had breastplates had been saved from death by their armour, but their faces, hands and legs had been hacked and chopped by crude yet effective weapons. Luckily, none seemed to have been poisoned and for that I was grateful. It took longer to return to the city as we had to cater for the wounded, and we had been forced by the urgency of the situation to hurry.

My gunners and I slept aboard the ship. The city was already crowded and the ship, which had a good berth, was a better choice. The wounds and the dead brought more flies but the sea seemed to keep them away. There was something about the gentle rocking motion when you were tied up which helped sleep. The next day the Indians brought offerings. We now knew this was their way and confirmed that we had won. We had a perilous foothold in this land. There was not only food, gold, animals, and animal skins but also twenty young women. Cortés was a clever man and he had one eye on Spain. He had all the women converted to Christianity as a symbol of Spanish rule and he claimed the land for Spain in the name of King Carlos and in his own name. That was the first time I heard him use the name Hernán. The only reason I could see for him to do so was that there were many men call Hernando, but he was the only Hernán. A cynic might say he was trying to cause confusion as Hernando Cortés had been forbidden by Governor Velázquez to sail to this new land! Perhaps the name of Hernán might not be recognised!

The twenty young women were comely, and one caught the eye of the Captain-General immediately. Malintzin was young and incredibly beautiful. She was christened, Marina, as that was as close to her Indian name as the priests could manage. I had seen some of the women our Captain-General liked when in Isla Juana and she was exactly the type he liked. She became known as La Malinche. Within the day she was taken to the quarters of Cortés and was with him as a permanent concubine. She did not seem to object, and she was treated well. Some of the other women were also taken as bedmates by other leaders.

We had lost men and needed more. Whilst we were safe where we were for the Indians accepted us as their overlords, we knew that there was an empire to the west which had conquered all the tribes and that they had a city in the middle of a lake. We would not take on such an empire with what we had. Half of the ships, including Captain Pedro's, would be sailing back to Spain with treasure for the king and to request more men to join us. The other half would bring more men from Isla Juana. As we took our chests and bags from his ship, he confided in me that he had secured enough trading goods of high value to enable him to return to Spain a rich man. I suspect that some of the gold and silver captured from the city would also find its way into the Captain's possession. I did not mind for he would do what my father and One-Eyed Peter had planned. He would get out of this dangerous world when he chose. He was a man with a plan and in the short time I had come to know him I believed that he would succeed. I hoped so.

We headed up the coast to a place we named Villa Rica de la Vera Cruz. It was not far from Potonchán and a better anchorage. When he founded the city he did so formally and in the name of King Carlos. It was the final severing of ties with the Governor. Our ships had sailed not to Santiago or the other town used by the Governor, Baracoa, but Trinidad. La Malinche proved pivotal in the way our campaign would be handled. She could speak the language of the Aztec who were the overlords of all the tribes. They were the rulers of this vast empire and we learned, through La Malinche, that their city was called Tenochtitlán and their tlatoani, or king was Moctezuma II. While we waited for the return of the ships with more men, horses and guns, the Captain-General sent some of the tribe we had conquered, the Totonac, to find those who could take messages to the Aztec ruler. The Totonac ruler, Tlacochcalcatl, promised thousands of warriors to help us for he wished to free himself from the yoke of the Aztecs. I knew all this because my action at the battle of Centia, whilst not as dramatic as that of the horsemen had shown all that I was a leader. I was privy to the councils of war held by the Captain-General. When Geronimo Aguilar translated the words of Tlacochcalcatl, I could not help but think that the Totonacs were merely exchanging one master for another.

The word came back that Moctezuma refused to speak to the Captain-General so that when our ships arrived, he made his mind up to march the two hundred miles to Tenochtitlán. That he was disappointed at the paucity of the reinforcements was clear. We had gained only two horses and four cannons. Leaving one hundred men to guard Villa Rica de la Vera Cruz and with six hundred Spanish soldiers, fifteen horses, fifteen cannons and almost a thousand Totonac warriors not to mention others who would act as servants, our army headed to Tenochtitlán. However, before we did so and to the anger and annoyance of the captains, he scuttled the ships which had brought back the reinforcements from Isla Juana. We were stranded in this land and we would either win or we would perish. There would be no halfway! I was pleased that Captain Pedro's was not amongst the ships which had been scuttled. He would be safely on his way back to Spain and I prayed that he would avoid the pirates and realise his dream.

We left the coast in the middle of August and headed inland knowing that we had many enemies ahead of us and few friends behind. The Captain-General was a gambler, and he was gambling not only with his own life but the lives of all those he led.

Chapter 11

We did not travel quickly through this new land where everyone ahead of us was a potential enemy. It was not the guns that slowed us up but the fact that there were women, priests, and carts we had made to haul the supplies we would need. We were able to take food from the locals, although, at first, in the land of the Totonac, it was freely given, but men liked beer and wine. We had gunpowder to transport as well as spare weapons. At first, we travelled through the jungle but, fortunately, it was not like the jungle through which we had hacked to get to the South Sea. There were roads that served the Aztec Empire. That alone told me that we would have to fight to take this land. When I had been with de Bilbao the tribes we had met all fought each other. There was no unity. The Aztecs, it seemed, were as Imperial as the Spanish. I did not think this would be easy. This was not like travelling through the jungle of Panama. The Aztecs built good roads and kept them maintained. The buildings were stone and the Indians were all clad better than those we had met in the thick jungles far to the south. The Aztec civilisation also had tended fields and there appeared to be little danger from wild animals. While that made our life easier I could not help but think that the Aztecs might prove to be more of a match for us.

I had my own battle with the recently arrived four gunners who had come with the four guns which had joined us from the scuttled ships. They resented me. Two days into the march one of them, Pedro Gonzalez openly challenged my authority. He was a big man, and he had a savage-looking scar on his face. It had been the result of a bar fight. Although he had won and killed his opponent with a knife, he had a hatred of all Englishmen as the man he had killed had been English. There was only one way he would accept my authority and that would be if I either dismissed him and sent him back to Vera Cruz or beat him. I chose the latter. I did not wish to do so but there were three other gunners. If I dismissed him then they would see that as a weakness.

The challenge came one evening. It had been a hard day of marching and we had had to repair one of the trails on a gun which meant we were the last ones into camp, and we were on the very edge of the village we had taken over on a flat piece of ground which lay a hundred paces from the main camp. The slaves we had were good men and they set to preparing food while I had the gunners check all the other guns. The truculent Pedro stood with his hand on his sword hilt and his feet in a fighting stance.

"You, English, are a piece of shit and I will no longer follow your orders. I say we have a vote and choose a new captain!"

The other three new gunners were standing close to him and I saw this for what it was, a challenge to my authority. Fernando said, easily, "That is not the way it works over here, Pedro, and besides, you would lose the vote. The rest of us have seen how clever our Master Gunner is. He helped to defeat the Totonacs and we would follow him. Do not do this for he is a friend of the Captain-General!"

Pedro laughed, "Aye and when the Governor sends an army to fight this traitor then that will mean nothing! If you cowards will not support me then," he drew his sword and dagger, "I will take his title by force of arms!"

Had I sent Jose for help then I might have avoided the fight, but I remembered my first days as a Spanish gunner when I had been called Conquistador. Those who had called me that were now all dead, most of them in the jungles to the south. Such hatred could never be converted. I drew my own weapons. Fighting for my life was not something new but this was a big man. I took comfort from the fact that the other man I had fought had been a swordsman, Jesus Martinez, and he had not defeated me. The other slight advantage I had was that I was leaner and had fought, I think, more recently. Perhaps I was clutching for hope but as he came towards me, I tried to remember every other fight in which I had been involved. I was glad that Fernando had made me buy a new and better sword. As our blades clashed and rang out, mine held but I saw his buckle a little. He tried to gut me with his dagger, but I had fast hands and I blocked the blow with my own dagger. He must not have noticed the fact that his sword was no longer straight for he brought the sword from on high to take advantage of his height. I turned the blade of my own sword so that his edge struck the flat of mine. The buckle worsened and was more noticeable, and I saw fear in his eyes. I could not take any chances with such a dangerous opponent who wanted to kill me and so I tried to stab him under his right arm. He was slower than I was, and his dagger barely stopped mine, my blade scraped down his side and drew blood. It was my turn to swing and I brought my blade towards his left side, this time with the sharpened edge aimed at him. His dagger had just blocked mine and it did not stop, completely, the swing. I wounded him again. He was now bleeding from both sides and he took a step back.

113

"I have drawn blood twice and you are hurt. End this now!"

In answer, he roared and swinging both weapons ran at me. It was a mistake for he exacerbated the wounds and blood flowed. He would be weaker. He also made it easy for me as I dropped to one knee and made a cross with my dagger and sword. He could not stop himself and as his blades scraped off mine, he began to fall forward. As blood dripped on me, I rose, and his legs flew into the air. Normally, when a man landed like that, he would be winded but as he fell we all heard a crack and watched the light leave his eyes. Two of my gunners moved the body and saw the reason, there was a huge rock and the back of his head had hit it. Bits of bone and brains lay beneath it.

Whipping round to the other three I glared at them and my voice was filled with venom, "You have three choices: face me sword to sword, leave or," I paused as I heard the sound of men coming to our camp, "swear to obey every command that I give!"

The three were terrified and dropping to their knees, clutching, and then kissing their crosses they all intoned, "We swear!"

It was Pedro de Alvarado who arrived with armed men wielding drawn swords. He took in the scene and shook his head, "Master Gunner, you must come to the Captain-General and give an account of yourself."

Sheathing my weapons I nodded, "Bury him!"

Captain-General Cortés was seated next to La Malinche who was feeding him tasty morsels. The other captains also had some Indians feeding them as they sat around a huge table. His smile, the mask he wore constantly, briefly left his face, "You are the cause for my dinner being disturbed?"

Before Captain Alvarado could speak, I said, "One of my gunners challenged my authority; we fought, and he cracked his skull when he fell. He is dead."

"That is not good Tomas. We are now short of one gunner."

I shook my head, "We are not, Jose, Fernando's son can command a gun. I was not much older when I started."

"Even so I do not wish this to reoccur."

I nodded and then said, "Captain-General, when he insulted me, he said that Governor Velázquez was raising an army to come and punish us."

I saw his mind thinking for his eyes flickered and then he nodded, "To be expected. Then when he comes, we shall fight him and, by that time I hope to have a native army at my back." I saw the nods and smiles from the captains. We were undefeated and they were confident. "Do not let me down again, eh Tomas?"

"No, Captain-General."

As I went back to my camp Father de Aguilar came with me, "Would you like to confess to me, Englishman?" I shrugged. "I have to see to the body of the man you slew, and I can hear your confession then."

"I did nothing wrong, Father de Aguilar. Ask the men for he began the fight and, had he won, then he would have needed to confess. All that I did was to defend myself."

The priest shook his head, "Confession is never wasted. You English, I can see that your beliefs are not as strong as ours." He made the sign of the cross over me, "I will bless you in any case."

The gunner was buried by all of us and Father de Aguilar said words over the grave. When we left, I wondered if this would be the only gunner who would remain in this new land.

The first tribe who challenged us were the Otomis. More than three thousand of them awaited us where the land began to climb to the highlands. They were dressed and arrayed like the Totonac but did not seem overly afraid of the men on horses. Captain-General Cortés was reluctant to risk another charge and so he had my guns placed along our whole front. I wondered at the wisdom of such an act for the last time, when we had been closer together, we had cleared a large swathe of Indians. In addition, I would have to rely on my gunners to do what they had to without my orders. I had to agree but I placed the three new gunners close to me and Jose on the far side of them. We had more than forty harquebusiers and they were also spread across the front. As the two sides lined up, I went to the gunners and told them what to do. "When I give the command then we fire ball. We keep firing until they are one hundred paces from us and then change to bags of stones. Listen for my command." I was in the centre while Fernando was on the extreme right. When I reached him, I counselled, "Keep weapons close by for this battle may see them close with us."

The Indians outnumbered us and I did not think that Cortés would attack first. He did not. The Otomis moved forward, and they ran. I shouted, "Fire!" as I put my linstock to the touch hole. My falconet fired first but a pall of smoke enveloped us. I could not see the enemy well enough to gauge the range, but we fired ball after ball at the shadows which came closer and closer until I heard the harquebusiers open fire. They would not waste their powder and so I shouted, "Bags of balls!" I loaded the first bag and we fired. Shadows and shapes appeared through the fog of powder and we knew they were the Indians. We could now hear the screams and see the bodies of the Indians falling but they were brave men, and they came on.

Behind me, I heard Pedro Alvarado as he gave his commands, "Pikemen and swordsmen, advance!"

It was none too soon. We had cleared the front ranks but there were so many who were racing towards us that we would only manage one more volley before they were on us. There was simply too much space between guns. As I fired the last volley, I drew my sword and shouted, "Defend yourselves!" I barely managed to drag my sword across the fabric armour of the Otomis warrior who had used the wall of dead to spring in the air. Had my sword not been razor-sharp then the padded garment might well have lessened the effect of the strike. As it was, he tumbled behind me, guts and entrails falling from his stomach. The wall of pikes and swords hit the now demoralised Otomis and within a few minutes, they had fled.

This time we had far fewer dead and wounded amongst our army although we lost eight of the slaves who had worked the guns. The Otomis, just like the Totonac accepted the defeat and promised to be our allies. As we had killed more than two-thirds of their army, they would not be able to supply warriors to help but the victory put heart into the army. The dead before us yielded gold, pearls, silver, and other precious jewels. Although we had to compete with the rest of the army in the salvage operation my men and I all managed to secure purses of treasure. Of course, with our ships scuttled there was little likelihood of my making it back to Isla Juana, let alone England!

Pedro de Alvarado procured twenty Otomis for me to train as men to transport the guns and were a replacement for the dead Totonacs. They would not be slaves and they were fearful of the cannons, but they were not the major problem. We could not speak their language. I had to use sign language and we began, as August turned to September, to learn each other's language. I know that all the leaders were trying to speak the local language but with so many variations and dialects, it was going to be a hard task. I suppose I was luckier than most having had to learn Spanish first.

The Otomis warned us that the next tribe we would face would offer a sterner test than they had. The Tlaxcalteca had never been conquered by the Aztecs and had been allowed to be independent just so long as

116

they caused no trouble. We knew that they spoke the same language as the Otomis, Nahuatl, and so we might be able to use words before we used force.

We did not have far to go to see the truth of this thesis and we headed to Texiuhuitlan, their largest city which sat astride the road we would be forced to use. They fought us three times. The first time they sent just two thousand men and they were defeated easily when they charged us. The second time, when we were closer to their capital, they brought four thousand men but the fact that we had a slope and sides protected by hills meant that they were defeated. It was when we were near their capital that they brought the largest army I had seen thus far. There were, I guessed, ten thousand warriors. So far, we had not slain large numbers for they had seen how effective our guns were.

The Captain-General conferred with his leaders and this time devised an interesting plan. I was one of the leaders. I had explained to the Captain-General the benefits of having the guns altogether and he agreed. Accordingly, he placed pikemen to our right and we were interspersed with the harquebusiers. The swordsmen were to our left and behind them were the fifteen horsemen. All wore plate and had protection for both their legs, saddles, and horses' heads. This time they would be used. The crossbowmen would be placed in a thin screen before the pikes and swords. Their job would be to release one volley each and then run back to the protection of our main line. It would be a pinprick but even if they just hit forty or so that would be forty or so less that we would have to fight. We would be reliant on gunpowder weapons to cause the casualties. The Tlaxcalans put their best warriors in the centre. Obviously, the survivors of the earlier two battles had warned them of their efficacy. Perhaps they thought their best warriors would be able to overcome such weapons.

Once again, the Indians began the fight and they raced at us wielding a variety of weapons. We had learned to identify their generals and their standards. Each tribe had a slightly different insignia, but they were all so different from the bulk of their warriors that we targeted them. Some of the harquebusier were proud of their accuracy. Admittedly it was only once the enemy had closed to within fifty paces, but it was far more accurate than our bags of balls which killed and wounded indiscriminately.

My guns were closer together and I could control them better. Jose had survived his first battle and this time was next to me and his father as we both wished to coach him. We opened fire when the Indians were four hundred paces from us. The Tlaxcalans had chosen a hard, summer dried plain for the battle as it suited their speed. It also suited me and when I fired my first ball, I made it hit the ground so that it was like a stone skimmed on an English pond; it bounced up and after ploughing through men, hit the ground again and continued to bounce through successive ranks. After my first ball, both Fernando and Jose saw what I had done and emulated me. We changed to bags of stone shot after that for the Tlaxcalans were fast and were closing with us.

Suddenly I heard a trumpet from our left and I knew what the signal presaged. The swordsmen broke ranks and the fifteen horsemen charged the left side of the Tlaxcalan army. It was like the first time we had used that weapon. The Indians stopped and prostrated themselves to the ground. They had not even closed with the pikemen and we lost not a single man. We had slaughtered, with our guns, more than five hundred and as we and the harquebusiers had done the actual killing, we plundered the bodies and reaped a rich reward. Soon I would need a chest for my treasure.

We had an even better result when the Captain-General spoke with their leaders. The Tlaxcalans were so impressed by us that they offered their soldiers, they had an army of more than twenty-five thousand and they supplied more than two thousand warriors to help us. This time, when we left their land, we had those as scouts and knowing the land they were able to warn us that, as we neared the Aztec capital, an army from the Cholula tribe were awaiting us.

I was impressed by the way Captain-General Hernán Cortés was conducting this war. It was in contrast to the predictable way Governor de Bilbao had blundered towards the coast. He sent emissaries from the Tlaxcalans to explain to the Cholulans that we meant them no harm and our intention was to get to Tenochtitlán for we wished to speak to Moctezuma. Perhaps the Tlaxcalans told them how we had defeated their army for they quickly not only agreed to allow us to pass through their land but gave us another one thousand warriors. I had no idea of the size of the Aztec army, but we now had a potent force heading towards their city on the lake.

We were now a good team. Even the three gunners who had been threatened by me now seemed to accept me as a leader. The Indians we had with us were also a revelation. Unlike the slaves we had originally, they regarded working the cannons as an honour. They seemed to think

118

that my gunners and I were some kinds of wizards. They understood fire but the hurling of stones through the use of fire was a mystery. We gave them Spanish names, which they seemed to accept. I could speak a large number of words from the Nahuatl language, but my gunners could manage only a few and the names of the Indians were, to them unpronounceable. The Indians seemed to accept that. La Malinche had been a good model for them.

One problem we had, with the whole army, was the carnal needs of the men. Luckily the Indians seemed to turn a blind eye to it and when La Malinche showed signs that she was with child and that it was the Captain General's, then others began to take women from the villages through which we passed as sleeping companions. Fernando and I were the exceptions. Fernando had a wife and I had never enjoyed the company of a woman and, if truth be told, I was a little fearful of it. Had I begun younger then I might not have seen it as a problem but even when I was offered a companion I refused.

Pedro de Alvarado spoke to me, quietly, after I had refused a woman for a second time. He and I got on for he liked the way I used guns. He had commented on the way I had bounced balls for he had never seen the like. "Tomas, why do you refuse women? If it is that you prefer the company of men, there is no shame in that. There are men in this army who are like that. They stay hidden but there is no shame."

I shook my head, "No, Captain Alvarado, I like women, at least I think I do, but I do not like this taking of a woman. Do you think the men who take women will want them to return to Isla Juana or Spain?"

He laughed, "I certainly will not for my wife would not approve!" he smiled, "You have honour, Tomas and that is no bad thing. I shall spread the word. You choose to take a woman when you are ready."

I doubted that I would ever be ready but at least the strange looks and comments ceased.

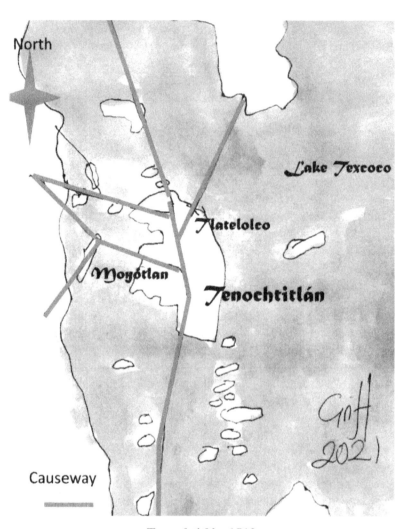

North

Lake Texcoco

Tlateloco

Moyotlan

Tenochtitlán

Causeway

Tenochtitlán 1519

Conquistador

Chapter 12

Tenochtitlán November 1519

The army which reached the Aztec capital was large and ensured that
we did not have to battle to gain entry. We were met by Aztec officials
who greeted us warmly as ambassadors. They halted us at the edge of the
huge lake upon which the city was built. I saw little of it at first as the
horsemen prevented a clear sight of it. The Captain-General, leaders, our
horsemen and the Spanish part of the army were to be admitted. Orders
came for me to leave my guns and gunners with the bulk of our army, the
Indians, while I was to accompany the Captain-General. Leaving
Fernando with our precious weapons and the Indians and slaves we had
brought I hurried to catch up with the others.

I walked across causeways built over the lake. These were not little
bridges, the causeway we used was more than a couple of miles long. It
was a piece of engineering that astounded me for it suggested that these
Aztecs were superior to us. I had never seen anything remotely like it.
The surface was solidly made and well maintained. In the distance I saw
stone buildings rising high into the sky. They were too far away to see
clearly but they were far higher than the odd two story building I had
seen in Falmouth and Totnes. They looked high from a distance and I
knew that they would be even higher close up. As well as ambassadors
there were soldiers and the ones who escorted us outnumbered us by
more than two to one. If our position changed from guests to enemies it
would not go well for us. I hurried to catch up with the other captains,
all of whom rode horses.

Ahead I could now see the buildings rising from the water and I had
never seen such a magnificent city. Huge stone buildings climbed, it
seemed, to the skies and there were so many of them that they appeared
to go on and on into the distance. How could we even think that we could
conquer such an Empire? The causeway did have bridges so that canoes
could pass beneath it and I saw other causeways heading to the east and
west. When we passed over them I realised that the bridges were hinged.
That would allow larger boats to pass through or make it hard for an

attacker to assault the city. These were an ingenious people. The closer we came to the heart of the Aztec Empire the more imposing it appeared. I had never been to London but from what my father told me even that city was nothing compared with this. Once we entered the gates, the streets, which were wide, straight and paved, were lined with magnificently dressed warriors. If this was a trap, then we would all be slaughtered for we were seriously outnumbered, and my guns were miles to the south.

I hurried my way through the pikemen and swordsmen to reach Father de Aguilar and La Malinche. The Captain-General had taken one of the horses to ride and with the other knights and captains, in full armour, made an imposing sight. Even the Franciscan priest seemed in awe.

"Father, how can the Captain-General even think about conquering such a place?"

The priest turned, "I know, Englishman, that your beliefs are not as strong as we Spanish but even you must realise that these Aztecs, the Mexicas, make human sacrifices." He pointed to the pyramid that appeared to ascend to heaven. The steps leading to its top were speckled with red. "That is the blood of human sacrifice and it is our duty to show these heathens the way to God. I can see now that when I was shipwrecked here there was a divine purpose to it. I was sent to be the guide to help the Captain-General to get here and now I must begin to convert them!"

"How big is this city? I can see no end to it."

The priest turned to La Malinche and asked her something. She replied and he said, "There are sixteen sections to it, and it is divided into two halves. The main part, here in the south is Tenochtitlán, while the northern part is Tlatelolco." He pointed, "See, they have aqueducts such as they have in the Holy City of Rome! Surely that is a sign that we are here to convert them." He was a fervent Christian, and nothing could dissuade him from his mission to make these Indians into Christians.

We had reached the main square and I saw a party descend the stairs of a large palatial looking building. It was clear from his dress that the one in the centre was Moctezuma. The Captain-General dismounted although the rest of the knights stayed mounted. He waved forward La Malinche and Father de Aguilar, and I was left to wait by the rump of the horse of Pedro de Alvarado.

The knight looked down at me, "I wish we had more horses, Englishman, for as good as your guns are, it is the sight of us on horses which inspire fear. Look at the faces of those fierce warriors." The warriors were all dressed magnificently and whilst they did not have weapons, save a dagger, that they were warriors was clear but behind the warriors and their king were half-naked men who all glared fiercely at us. Their upper bodies were stained with black dye and they had painted faces. I later learned that these were the priests and there were more than five thousand of them in the city! Along with the Emperor, they ruled this empire. From a distance, they were imposing but when we were invited to sit and dine in the great square with the king and an equal number of warriors to our army, I saw the priests close up and they were even more frightening! They had filed teeth and they had mutilated their own ears. Their hair was matted with blood, the blood of the human sacrifices they had made, and their eyes were all bloodshot! The food was magnificent, but I could not enjoy it for I feared the priests who did not dine with us but glowered and glared at us from the steps of their temple.

I was honoured to be seated near to the Alvarado brothers. We got on well for we shared common experiences and, I think, we all trusted each other's martial skills. The Captain-General was with the Aztec king who looked to be a man in his fifties. He did not look like a warrior. La Malinche and Father de Aguilar translated the words and Cortés passed the choice titbits down to us. In that way, we learned that the Aztec king welcomed us as his guests in his kingdom. He had promised the Captain-General gold and silver although he said that they had little. I confess that when we retired to the huge hall they had put at our disposal, I wished that I had stayed with my guns for I feared that we would all become human sacrifices in the night. My fears were unfounded not least because Pedro de Alvarado kept sentries around the hall all night! The feting and feasting continued for many days and despite the words of the officials, the treasure we received was an enormous amount. There was so much, in fact, that Pedro de Alvarado had men moved from one of the largest rooms we had been given and guards watched it all day and all night.

We were allowed to wander the city freely although I still suspected treachery and I made sure that I was with Fernando and Jose when we explored. The Empire must have been a rich one for I saw neither paupers nor beggars in the city. I had never been to a large city, but I had

123

been told that every one had the poor begging on street corners. Even Santiago was heavily populated by the poor. Some were forced to beg through circumstances, but others saw it as a way to exist for they were lazy. The people we saw were not lazy, at least not in the normal sense of the word. Those who appeared not to work were the very rich; I suppose they were like the lords of the manor in England whose ancestors had carved out their own piece of land and profited from it. So too with these Aztecs who had conquered and subjugated all the neighbouring tribes. They exacted tribute from them and therein lay their riches. Their Empire was protected, I could see, by a large army. In the city we were vastly outnumbered by the Imperial Army but, it seems, we were tolerated. After a couple of days, I returned to the camp with my gunners and my guns, outside the city, although we had completely free access to it and the Aztecs who guarded the causeway did not hinder our movement.

One night as Fernando, Jose and I sat and ate the food which was served to us we spoke of what we might do with our treasure. We knew we would all share in the profits and whilst we would get a fraction of that taken by our Captain-General we would be rich men. Fernando had already decided his future, "I know not about Jose but now that my wife is here in this new land, I will cease to be a warrior and I will farm. There are slaves to work the fields and the land seems fertile. I cannot believe that the Indians on Isla Juana have cleared so little land! They seem to enjoy just gathering the bounty that nature provides."

Jose shook his head. The boy had become almost a man in the time we had fought our way here. War does that; it kills or makes you stronger. "I would be like Captain Tomas. I would be a gunner and I would continue to explore this land. We have barely touched it and yet the treasure we have taken is staggering. There is nothing we cannot do. These Indians cannot stand against us!"

I knew that Jose was wrong but that was because these were the first Indians we had seen and our victories had been relatively easy, "Jose, I fought the Indians in the Isthmus when we went to the South Sea. There were fierce, fearless warriors who faced us, and we barely escaped with our lives. We have not fought these Aztecs. We fought the tribes they subjugated; think about that. I agree that we have not yet begun to take all that there is to take but, for me, I have enough." I had made sure that my own treasure, taken from the battlefield was safe. I was still counting on the pay from the Captain-General, but I was sure I had enough and this time I would not bury it for it to be lost.

"Then you will not carry on once we have conquered these lands?"

"No, Jose, my father and my shipmates gambled one shipload of treasure too many. I will return to England. I think you are right, both of you, for you but I yearn for the green fields of England and ale from a tavern. I will have enough to buy a small manor and I will be able to live comfortably. I may well take some slaves back too for the Indians work hard but once the Captain-General allows us to sail back to Isla Juana then I will quit this land."

"Allows us?"

"Do not forget, Fernando, that Cortés defied the Governor. We are the Captain-General's army and until he has the written support of the king then he cannot allow one of us to leave. Why else did he burn our boats?" I had revealed problems that neither of them had thought about.

I suppose that it was Christmas when things changed. Our priests had tried, unsuccessfully, to convert the natives. A few hundred of the Tlaxcalans had become Christians but the cynic in me suspected that they were being pragmatic and had not abandoned their pagan beliefs. The ones who did so were accorded privileges. The first I knew that there was trouble was one night when Pedro de Alvarado and ten of his men arrived, on foot, at our camp. That was unusual and I knew that there was danger for they were in their armour and had helmets and shields.

"Englishman, there is trouble. I need you to bring four of your guns with us into the city. We need to be able to cut down any Indians who try to attack us. You will need to be quiet for we have to do so surreptitiously."

I had wondered when the populace would tire of our presence and I nodded. I had campaigned enough to understand how to adapt. "We can use the four smaller falconets which can be easily carried and if we use the bags of stones then we can clear large areas." I was not thinking of the Indians as people but as wheat to be harvested. That was one effect of being a conquistador. They were no longer people, they had become just targets."

"Good. We will wait for you."

I knew my gunners and the crews. The Indians who worked the guns seemed loyal to us and I chose the ones I considered the best. I roused the men I needed and asked them to gather their war gear. Fernando and Jose were two of the gunners and Raphael, the fourth. I left old Pedro in charge of the rest for he was a reliable soul. We waited for the Indians to come, they first had to make slings for the barrels. The trails and wheels, powder and stone bags were easier to carry. I spoke quietly to Captain de Alvarado who had just brought another twenty swordsmen as escorts.

"What has happened?"

He lowered his voice, "I trust you, Tomas, and so I will confide in you. Some of our men, on the coast, were killed by Aztecs. The Captain-General feels that this is just the beginning of more treachery. We intend to take the Emperor prisoner and hold him hostage to ensure the rest behave themselves."

I said nothing but I realised the implications of such an action. The Captain-General was claiming the whole Empire! We had not yet fought the Aztec army and this could be the single action that precipitated such a fight.

Getting into the city was not as easy for Captain de Alvarado as his journey out. Perhaps the priests and warriors had got word of what we intended. We had just crossed the longest causeway when a hundred or so priests and warriors suddenly appeared before us. There was no chance of using the guns, but Captain de Alvarado was a bold leader.

"Draw weapons! Tomas, guard your guns and follow closely!"

I drew my sword and my dagger. I now had a sword that was longer, sharper, and altogether superior to any I had used when I had fought with de Bilbao. I turned to the other three gunners. "Stay with your gun and defend yourselves!"

I saw the fear on Fernando's face and knew it was not for himself but for his son.

"Charge them! For King Carlos, God and Spain!" Captain Alvarado led the charge and his men fanned out in an arrow shape behind him.

I nodded to my Indians, "Whatever happens keep the guns moving. Even if we fall get the guns to the rest of the army!" I led my gunners, and we ran after the mailed men. Those carrying the guns knew they could expect no mercy from the Aztecs and needed no urging. The Aztecs favoured edged clubs and wooden shields. They might not hurt a man in armour with a helmet, but the Indians had no protection at all. In the dark, I could see that these were their Jaguar warriors and were an elite unit. Their headgear was the head of a jaguar and while it looked frightening it did little to prevent damage from an edged weapon. The shields used by our men were superior and their helmets, lined and padded, would withstand the weapons the Aztecs used. My gunners and I had little to protect us. Although we wore helmets and the leather brigandine I used might stop an arrow, a club would still break a limb.

Spanish swords slashed and stabbed the Aztecs, but these were fanatics and even the priests, armed with just a dagger, hurled themselves at the swordsmen. I saw one priest, his entrails hanging down, who was still trying to claw and bite the Spanish swordsman who had laid him open. We were making progress, but the enemy numbers meant that we had taken casualties and soon we slowed. I no longer had the luxury of being a spectator. When a Spanish swordsman was speared just in front of me two warriors leapt through the gap and seeing a conquistador with no armour thought that they had an easy victim. One of the two was a Jaguar warrior while the other wore just a kyrtle and carried a wooden spear. The Jaguar warrior was the danger and I just kept an eye on the spearman as the club was raised to smash down on my morion. Even as I lifted the sword to block the blow of the edged club the spear was rammed at my chest. I barely managed to flick the head of the spear away. I had stopped the blow of the club and I was close enough to the Jaguar warrior to see the doubt on his face. My sword had not only a hilt but a round piece of metal that afforded some protection. As the warrior raised his club for a second strike and while we were close enough, I punched at his face with the hilt of my sword. The guard struck his eye, and the round metal broke his nose. He could not help but reel back and I whirled as the spearman tried to take advantage. This time the spear raked my cheek and I tasted salty blood. The fear that it was poisoned passed briefly through my head before I was able to slash my sword across his neck. Bright blood spurted and showered the warrior, spearman, and me. The warrior was angry, and his eye hung down. I was no physician but even I knew that his judgement would be affected and so I waited for his next swing. His lack of one eye meant that he missed me and I was able to ram my dagger into his throat. I twisted and pulled. Although he had a gold necklace this was not the time for looting!

Although we were winning, we were now moving at a crawl as we headed to the sanctuary of the rest of the men in the main square. I could not afford to look around and see if we had lost either men or guns. As we moved ever closer to the square, I saw that there were fewer swordsmen in front of me. I was close behind Captain Alvarado. The men who had fallen had been well protected, but the sheer weight of numbers meant that some men died, and I knew that I had less chance of survival than the professional soldiers. My dream of a happy home in England could end here on the causeway leading to the heart of Tenochtitlán!

Captain Alvarado encouraged us with his words, "Not far and my brother has pikes and harquebuses waiting. Keep heart!"

At that point a priest leapt into the air, using the dead body of one of his own chiefs to do so. He landed behind Captain Alvarado and I saw the dagger raised to stab our leader in the back. The priest had no armour and I lunged up and under his right arm. The tip came out of the opposite shoulder as the dagger fell. Miraculously the priest had still enough life to turn and spit at me, his sharpened teeth, blackened face and matted hair making him look like some sort of hellhound. The Captain turned and nodded his thanks just as a second priest, eager to avenge his companion hurled himself at me. He landed on my chest but, luckily, I held on to my weapons although the air was knocked from me. As he straddled me, he raised his wickedly jagged dagger to end my life. His knees had pinned my arms and I did the only thing I could do. It was a move I had often used in Devon when I had played, roughly, with the other boys from the village. I brought my knee up between his legs to throw him from me. The look of surprise on his face told me that it had worked, and he sailed over me. I had enough breath to leap to my feet and I slashed my sword across his throat. I was now at the back, but I saw that the cannons, powder, wheels, wedges, and trails were just behind Captain Alvarado. I ran to catch up as stones were hurled at me. More men had come to join the priests and Jaguar warriors but the causeway, designed to protect the city now limited their effect. I turned and swashed my sword at half-naked men who had spears and daggers. It made them pull back when the edge tore open the chest of one of them! I had pushed my luck enough and I raced after the others. Behind me, I heard wild shouts and blood-curdling screams. I did not need to turn around to know that it was one of the priests urging on the Aztecs to slaughter us.

I heard Pedro de Alvarado shout, "For the love of God, give us aid!"

Ahead of me, I saw the shadow of the city and its walls. The number of Aztecs who chased us made me wonder if the whole populace had risen. Were the gates barred and held against us?

Then I saw, to my relief, the gates open and I heard Gonzalo de Alvarado shout, "Get to the side!"

I knew what he intended. He had the harquebusiers ready and they filled the gate. Some of the Indians carrying the guns and our equipment seemed to freeze and so I added my voice, speaking their own language this time, "Get to the side for our men will open fire!" Perhaps it was the familiarity of my voice of command which worked for they all leapt to one side and as I threw myself unceremoniously to the ground the harquebusiers opened fire.

As soon as they did Captain Gonzalo shouted, "Pikemen, charge!" The men with pikes, the same weapon we had used on the ship, raced from the city to smash into the already demoralised Aztecs.

Captain Pedro de Alvarado also did not wish to push our luck and he ordered a retreat within the city. As the gates slammed shut, I almost wept with relief. Captain Pedro came to clap me about the shoulder, "You saved my life back there and I shall not forget it!" He held out his hand and, after sheathing my sword, I clasped it.

"Nor I for I was sure that we were dead men!"

He nodded, "Perhaps we were remiss not to bring in your guns sooner."

I looked over my shoulder. "We had brought but four. Should we have brought the rest? As soon as the thought entered my head, I dismissed it. We would not have managed to bring the precious guns. I had chosen the best men and we had barely made it. We had been lucky for it had just been eight of the swordsmen who had perished. We had to work out the exact number the next day for the Aztec priests displayed their butchered bodies which had been dismembered. It was a lesson to us all.

We wasted no time, despite the harrowing journey and the lateness of the hour, it was almost dawn, and we set the guns up in the square each one covering one side. I had the Indians make barriers before and around the guns. The harquebusiers also made similar barriers while the gaps were protected by pikemen. The swordsmen were placed around the Imperial Palace. Emperor Moctezuma was now our prisoner and the Captain-General had shown his colours. We were gambling and I prayed that it was not a foolish one.

It was noon before I had my wounded tended to and stitched. Few of my men had escaped injury for with the Indians had been boys hurling stones from slingshots. Mine appeared to be the most serious; it was certainly the most noticeable and I would have a scar. My beard had been shaved to enable the priest to tend to it and I took solace that the new growth would hide it. As I went to lie down and snatch an hour or two of sleep, I chuckled to myself. It was not as though there were any ladies who would likely notice the angry red line which ran from just below my eye to my chin and the other soldiers each had their own scars. War in the Indies was both deadly and dangerous!

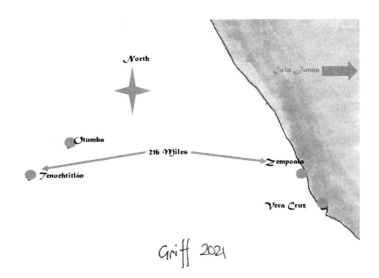

Aztec Empire 1519

Chapter 13

The threat to their Emperor appeared to keep the Aztecs in line for both the office and the man were revered. The priests were the other powerful entity and we had bloodied their noses too so that, for the time being, they behaved themselves. We estimated that more than one hundred priests had been slain in the running battle. That meant there were just four thousand nine hundred left! The attack had made both Fernando and his son eager to return to Isla Juana. In Jose's case, it was just to see his mother before he embarked on a life of war. He had seen how close we had come to death. They had been behind me and seen the savagery of the priests at close hand. When I had fallen behind, they had feared the worst and my survival made them both think of their own mortality. Fernando just wished to be away from war. He had his bag of treasure and he wanted to be able to spend it on his family. We moved the rest of the guns, gunners, powder and supplies to the stronghold we had made in the main square. We would be able to defend ourselves.

When I spoke to Geronimo de Aguilar as he tended my wounds, he explained why so many Aztecs wore gold. "It all begins with the Emperor. He has vast quantities of gold given to him as tribute from the tribes. He gives it to his leaders and they, in turn, use the gold to reward their men. They wear the gold in battle so that others can see their courage. The more gold they wear, then the greater their courage, or so they believe."

I nodded for it made sense and explained why every warrior we saw had some gold or silver on them and that they wore it so openly. In contrast, our soldiers hid their gold.

The Captain-General seemed to be emboldened by the event. That was probably because he had not been in danger and with the Emperor cowed, he decided to celebrate Christmas. He had married La Malinche and some of the other young women given to us after our first victory had taken up with his leaders. Now he decided that the rest would be married off. The young women had all been baptised and he deemed it a fitting celebration of Christmas to have them married. He came to me with Pedro de Alvarado, "Tomas, you were such a hero at the battle of the causeway that I would like to reward you. You shall marry one of the girls on Christmas Day. I am giving a dowry of a hundred gold pieces to each of the grooms!"

I shook my head, "I am not yet ready to take a wife."

He laughed, "Nonsense, you have needs, we all have needs!"

I of all people knew just how much of a need the Captain-General had! "No, Captain-General, when I marry it will be because I have chosen the mother of my children and it will be an English woman!"

The familiar smile left his face and he glared at me, "Tomas, this is not a request it is an order. My other leaders have all chosen their women. There is one left for you, Katerina, and you shall marry her. If you prefer the company of men that is something between you and your conscience, but all of my leaders shall be married and that is final!" He turned and left.

Captain Pedro smiled, "This means nothing, Tomas. When we return to Spain then the women will be left behind. It is a gesture, a symbol if you will. La Malinche is about to give birth and our leader sees that as a sign from God that we are meant to be here. Our seed will be planted in the women of this land and they will all become Christian. The bloodletting of those barbaric priests will end. You see that is a good thing, do you not?"

I nodded, "I suppose so but it does not sit right with me!"

He laughed, "You English! I like you, Tomas, for you are unlike any other of the warriors we have!" He simply did not understand me.

Fernando was philosophical about the whole thing, "You gain a hundred gold pieces and from what I have seen as soon as the captive girls were given to us they resigned themselves to their new life."

He proved to be right. Katerina, when I met her was small and a little dumpy, but she was more than happy to be married. As I came to learn she thought it an honour to be married to the Captain of the Guns and one whose scar marked him as a great warrior! I do believe that she loved me. I liked her and she was pleasant company, but I did not love her.

The wedding was a grand affair and took place in the main square with the Emperor in attendance. Geronimo de Aguilar officiated, and he gave me some comfort, when I confessed on the night before the wedding and told him that I was not happy about the ceremony. He told me that I was doing God's work and the women were more than happy for the union. It was, however, cold comfort for it did not fit in with my plans. I wanted to go home a rich man and I wished to choose an English bride. Were my plans, like One-Eyed Peter and my father's being thwarted? Would I ever get home?

The Captain-General had chambers prepared for the newlywed couples and it was there I had a surprise. Katerina was, perhaps, fifteen years old, but she had been trained in the art of love. I later learned that the twenty captives we were given had been chosen from an early age and given the training. Katerina taught me the art of love and by the morning the doubts which had assailed me the day before appeared to be gone. I woke with a smile on my face wondering at the experience I had enjoyed during the night. Katerina proved to be as dutiful a wife as one could hope for and my food was prepared, clothes cleaned and all that I needed provided by my new bride. I could not speak her language when we first met but in the two months after the wedding, we quickly learned the words of the other's language. It was once we could communicate that I discovered her joy at the marriage. She told me that one of the reasons she had been chosen was that the rest of her family had either been killed or taken as slaves in a raid by a neighbouring clan. She had survived because her two-year-old body had been protected by the corpse of an elder brother. The next thirteen years had been her training to be a wife and now she felt fulfilled. I still felt unhappy that I was married, unwillingly, but comforted by the joy of Katerina and, to be honest, each night was a pleasure. Even though we slept close to Fernando and the other gunners, Katerina had no inhibitions and after the first embarrassment, I found that I could shut out the presence of the others.

In March the increasing plumpness of Katerina was explained when she told me she was with child. La Malinche's baby had been stillborn and that had worried me that, perhaps, we were not meant to cohabit with the Indians. My fears made my joy a little more muted than the others who had married at the same time. The Captain-General gave us a house in which we could live once he discovered Katerina was pregnant and I was there when the messenger reached us from Vera Cruz in April. Gonzalo de Sandoval had been left to guard the port with one hundred men. He sent us the news that the Governor of Cuba had sent General Pánfilo de Narváez with one thousand men and guns to bring back Captain-General Cortés in chains to Isla Juana!

I was summoned with the other leaders to a meeting with our charismatic leader. He looked bemused rather than daunted. "The Governor, it seems, still disapproves of our action!" I hid my smile. It was his action but by calling it our action we were complicit in the rejection of the Governor's authority. "Vera Cruz will hold out. I propose to take two hundred and fifty men to deal with this threat of the

Governor's army. Captain Pedro de Alvarado will remain here with two hundred men. We will leave all the guns except for one. Tomas, you will accompany us! We will use two of the horses to transport the gun. We leave before dawn!" He smiled, "You will have a short time to say your farewells!"

I was touched by the tears shed by Katerina. She appeared to have genuine affection for me and, I confess, I was beginning to have feelings for her. I was just unsure how she would take to England. When I had spoken with Captain Pedro and he had said that Katerina would just be for this land I had known that when I left to return to England, I would be honour bound to take Katerina. It was where I saw me raising a family, but I was unsure how she would take it. England and this land they called Mexico were so different that just as I could not see myself living for the rest of my life here so I could not see her being happy in England.

Fernando agreed to watch over her. He was worried about me, "Tomas, these are not savages that you fight; they are Spaniards like us and will not be cowed by horses or guns! There is more than four times your number and they have horses, guns, and cannons too. You have to win for defeat would mean your death!"

I nodded, "I know and if there was any other way or if I had a choice then I would not be going but we have cast the die and win or lose we are the men of Hernán Cortés."

He made the sign of the cross, "Aye, you are right, and I just pray, for the sake of both of our families that we have made the right decision."

We virtually ran, as we hurried back to the coast. Messengers had arrived to tell us that the enemy soldiers were waiting for us on the coast at Zempoala. We had a thousand Tlaxcalans with us, but they were of dubious quality. We had defeated them easily and we knew that they would not attack either cannons or horses. Their main use would be as scouts and to, perhaps, terrify General Pánfilo de Narváez who would not have faced these fierce-looking warriors. I thought it a vain hope and as we had but one falcon with us my prospects of survival were slim. The enemy would simply aim all their guns at mine, and I would last but a few balls. My men were optimistic. I had chosen the best of the native gunners and they seemed to think that I could do anything. I knew I could not but, as we headed ever east towards the coast, I took solace from the closer affinity we developed on the march. When we had to fight, we would be so much closer.

We had Gonzalo de Alvarado with us although I would have preferred his brother, Pedro. It seemed, however, that our Captain-General would make the strategic decisions and I was not sure how that would turn out. We fought our way across a hot and stormy land in May, towards the coast. The air was heavy and oppressive. It felt as though I was wearing plate armour. It was hard to breathe and I was just grateful that we did not have to carry the gun and the poor horses were the ones who endured that task. The rain added another worry for me. It was bad enough that gunpowder, during a long journey, sometimes separated into its component parts and required mixing again before it could be used, but if the powder became wet then it would not fire. We had done our best to protect the precious powder with oiled cloaks, but I was not sure that it would be in a condition for us to use it when we reached Zempoala.

As we neared the coast and while the rain abated briefly, I sought out the Captain-General. He was in conference with Captain Gonzalo. He beamed when he saw me, "Ah, Tomas, all goes well with the gun?"

I had learned that false confidence was not what was needed and the reckless Captain-General required truth and honesty. I shook my head, "The powder will be too wet to use and even if we were to dry it then, in the rain we would not be able to use the linstock."

His face fell and I saw a smile on Gonzalo's face. With a rueful shake of his head, Hernán Cortés said, "And that is no surprise for Captain Gonzalo has just said the same thing, but I hoped my lucky talisman would bring me good news."

"We have but one gun with us; how would that win the battle for us?"

The smile returned telling me that he already had a plan in place, "We were going to make a night attack. I have sent a rider to Gonzalo de Sandoval in Vera Cruz to tell him that we plan to attack on the night of the 27th of May. He is to bring as many native warriors as he can and attack the enemy in the rear. Your confirmation of Captain Gonzalo's opinion seems to dash that hope."

"Do not forget, Captain-General, that if I cannot fire my gun then they cannot fire their many guns. Surely their guns are the danger and if nature negates them then that helps us."

His smile spread, "Just so! Just so!"

Captain Gonzalo nodded, "The two elements our Indians fear, Captain-General, are the horses and the guns. If nature takes out the guns, then if we can eliminate the cavalry we should win."

"Then we pray for the rain to continue and we will use our men to remove the threat of their cavalry."

Captain Gonzalo stroked his beard, "At night they will be tethered. I will lead the men who will capture the horses." He looked at me.

Captain-General Hernán Cortés also looked at me, "And you will be with the men taking on the guns. You need to secure them so that we can use them."

I saw the wisdom of the plan and the flaw, "Then I must be given the authority to order the men I lead. I am no swordsman, but I know gunners. We need the gunners alive or else we have no one to fire the guns."

Captain Gonzalo backed me up, "My brother trusts this Englishman, Captain-General, the men will follow him. I would put Hernando Salazar to lead the men. He also fought when de Bilbao went to the South Seas. He knows Tomas."

So it was decided. I, along with Hernando Salazar, who thankfully remembered me, led thirty men armed with swords and pikes. We and Captain Gonzalo would precipitate the attack. The Captain would take on the enemy horses and I the guns. Once we had stormed the night camp then the Captain-General would unleash his Indians and the rest of the men. We would have to hope that the forces from Vera Cruz had received our message and were in a position to close the jaws of the trap.

My Indian gunners were disappointed that they would not be with me. As I left our camp during the evening of the 26th they begged to be allowed to come with me. I had chosen good men. Shaking my head I said, "You need to put the gun together and keep the powder dry. If this attack fails, then when I return, I will need the gun ready to fire." I knew that the gun would not be fired as torrential rain had returned and was falling so hard that it made for poor visibility. I wanted my gunners safe.

Following two Indian guides, Captain Gonzalo and I made for the camp of General Pánfilo de Narváez. We knew, from our scouts, that the horse lines and the guns were close together and well-guarded, but the general sent by Governor Velázquez had not prepared defences against an attack. He had placed his weapons ready for battle and with clear lines of fire. Hernando Salazar led ten of the best swordsmen and I tucked in behind them. They were good men ahead of me for they were rodeleros.

I had impressed upon them the need to keep the gunners alive. I saw that the eleven of them had all adopted the lighter, padded protection used by the Indians. This was not the country for plate. I still trusted in my leather brigandine. I had padded it, close to my chest, with my spare hose and a shirt. The attack on the causeway had shown me that I needed all the protection I could get.

I had my sword and dagger drawn. I knew how effective two weapons could be and the many fights in which I had participated had given me the confidence to wield them well. The enemy general had helped us by clearing a good field of fire for his guns. The rain also aided us for it allowed us to close with them, unseen. I knew that, to our left, Captain Gonzalo was also sneaking through the rain which thundered down to soak all to the skin. The greatest danger we had was to slip and that the noise of the fall would alert their sentries. The sound of the rain as it crashed down to the ground made even that likelihood slim. Even so, I watched my feet as I followed Hernando.

The guns and the earthworks which were thrown before them appeared to be just shadows, but I recognised the barrels of guns that were larger than my falcons. We needed those guns! Inevitably it was a slip that alerted the enemy. It was to our left and was one of the men with Captain Gonzalo. It was a knight whose armour rattled as he crashed to the ground.

I heard the cry from just paces before me, "Stand to!"

Hernando Salazar had fought many battles and he responded, "Charge!" We ran.

I knew that the gunners would not be standing watch. They would have a camp that was close to the guns but protected from the rain. They would also sleep close to the precious powder. The first men we met could be attacked with impunity. They were the adventurers who had joined this expedition for profit. They would fight hard and if I struck, I would have to do so with commitment. I heard the clash of steel and saw Hernando's arm and sword sweep down to bite into the neck of the first sentry. I followed him as he clambered over the sodden mud into the earthworks. I used the barrel of the bombard to help me over. The enemy camp was roused, and, behind me, I heard the trumpets as Captain-General Cortés, ordered the rest of our men to attack. A battle at night was confusing. The Indians who would join us would find it hard to discriminate between friend and foe. I was glad that I knew enough words of their language to attempt to dissuade them from ending my life.

I did not think that the men brought to fight us would have learned the language yet.

The first men who reached us to throw us back beyond their defences were half-naked men armed with spears, pikes, and swords. They were clearly not gunners. The pike which was thrust at my head might have terrified the boy who had first sailed to sea with his father, but I had faced Aztec priests and Jaguar warriors. I used the cross piece of my sword to fend off the deadly pike while I rammed the dagger up into the ribs of the Spaniard. He tumbled behind me. When I heard the trumpet from ahead then I knew that the men from Vera Cruz had arrived as the five blasts were the signal our Captain-General had demanded. From behind me, I heard the blood-curdling cries of the Indians as they raced ahead of the rest of our men to leap into the fray. The effect on the enemy defenders was nothing short of miraculous. They saw the warriors who, even in the dark and the wet, were colourful and terrifying coming to slaughter them and they hurled down their weapons and implored us, fellow Spaniards, to save them.

Even before Hernando gave the order I had shouted, "You five, with me!" I led the five men to the gunners. I had spied the improvised tent made by pegging out oiled cloaks and I ran to clearly terrified men. I shouted, "I am Captain Thomas, Captain-General Cortés' master gunner. Surrender and you shall live!"

The first Indian raced towards us, his already bloodied war club raised, and his shield held before him. He had the wild look of a warrior with blood lust in his veins. I shouted, in Tlaxcalan, "We are with Captain-General Cortés." He raised his club and then realisation set in as he recognised me.

"You are the one who makes fire!" He turned to those following him and shouted, "Follow me!" They hurtled off towards the rest of General Pánfilo de Narváez's army who were fleeing for their lives."

One of the gunners, a greybeard nodded and said, "You might be young boy, but we will surrender to you! What did you say to the savage?"

"That we are on their side!"

A younger gunner, a little older than me said, "Are there more like that?"

I laughed, "Believe it or not there are far worse at Tenochtitlán. You are safe now but know this, I will command these guns and you now serve, Captain-General Cortés."

The old gunner nodded, "We have little choice and, it seems, we were ill led. We will follow you!"

When General Pánfilo de Narváez was wounded, losing an eye, then the battle ended and the army which had been sent to capture us quickly and pragmatically decided to join our army. Our paltry numbers were now swollen by almost a thousand men! The Captain-General had gambled once more and won!

Chapter 14

We had barely begun to march back to Tenochtitlán when a messenger arrived to give us news which clearly disturbed the Captain-General. "My lord, Captain Alvarado has sent me. The Aztecs planned a human sacrifice at the Fiesta of Huitzilopochtli. When the captain tried to intervene, we were attacked. We were forced to kill many priests and nobles. The city is quiet now!"

The frown on his face told me that the Captain-General did not believe the story, but Captain Gonzalo defended his brother, "Pedro would not have slaughtered men unnecessarily, Captain-General. He must have feared for the lives of his men."

"Then the sooner we get back the sooner we can restore good relations with the Emperor." He stared at the messenger, "The Emperor is unharmed?"

"He is and the captain has him safely secured."

"Then we make haste and return as soon as possible! Victory is almost in sight!"

The extra guns, powder, and men meant a slower journey back. We had taken no treasure this time and we had lost men so the mood was more sombre than one would have expected after such a victory. For my part, I was just pleased to be heading home. I found that I had missed Katerina. Was I becoming attached to her? Perhaps the thought of a son or daughter had created a bond.

We did not reach Tenochtitlán until the middle of June. The Captain-General went directly to Captain Pedro while I went to see my wife and my gunners. There I learned the truth of the massacre. The feast had been held with Captain Pedro's permission but when he saw the gold with which the Aztecs adorned themselves, he ordered the warriors and priests to be surrounded and the harquebusiers and falconets simply scythed through them.

"I did not enjoy it, Tomas, and I would leave now if that is possible." I could tell that it had affected Fernando and Jose for both were unhappy at the prospect of remaining.

As much as I wanted to leave as well, I knew that Captain-General Cortés would not allow it. Shaking my head I said, "When calm and good relations are restored then I will seek permission. I had hoped for more treasure, but I fear that the cost of such treasure is a price I am not willing to pay."

For the next two weeks, I spent as much time with Katerina as I was able. I had to work with my new gunners to weld them all into an effective fighting force. I knew that this was necessary as there was an air of unrest in the city; we had been tolerated before, perhaps even welcomed by some but now there was hatred in the eyes of the Aztecs. The time I spent with Katerina was well spent. She seemed to glow, and the smile never left her face and made my time in our home a relief after the tension of the city.

I spent little time with the Captain-General who was almost permanently locked away with the Alvarado brothers and the Emperor. I was asked for reports on the state of the guns and the men. My original gunners were the ones in whom I had complete faith. The new ones, the ones who had surrendered were more of a mixed bag. The old gunner, Philip, was sound but some of the others had rarely fought in a battle and certainly not against the Indians. I was not sure how they would fare if we had to fight and, increasingly, it looked like we would. The mood in the city became ugly; a combination of the massacre of so many of their nobles and priests combined with an Emperor who was a prisoner was just enough to begin to turn the whole populace against us. The fear of the horses and our cannons had lessened with familiarity. Father Aguilar had told me, once, that the Aztecs had a god who appeared to ride a horse. When they had first seen our knights in shining armour mounted on horses they had thought that, perhaps, we were gods come down to earth. Now they knew differently and even though our numbers were swollen by the men sent to defeat us, we were still vastly outnumbered. If it was not for the Tlaxcalan allies we might already have been defeated.

I spent all my spare time with my wife, Fernando, and Jose. For Fernando, Katerina represented all that he desired, his own wife and family. He understood pregnancy and was able to help me understand the changes in Katerina. Jose just enjoyed our company and so they ate with us and after we had eaten, we would sit and talk in the cool of the evening after the unbearable heat of the day.

"When the baby is born, Tomas, perhaps you ought to ask the Captain-General if you can go to the coast."

I shook my head, "He would not allow it. He sees me as his master gunner and something of a lucky talisman. So long as there are guns, and we win then I will have to stay here. You could return. I will speak to him on your behalf if you like. We now have more gunners, and it should be possible."

His face brightened, "You would do that? I have more than enough gold now that we have been paid."

One result of the massacre was that however much the Captain-General might have disapproved of Captain Pedro's action, we had taken advantage of the gold he had accrued. The three of us had satchels made of deer hide. Our Indians were skilled and had sewn them for Fernando and Jose. Katerina had made mine while I had been in the east fighting. They fitted around our bodies and beneath our clothes. If we had to battle again then we would wear them. They would add extra protection to our bodies and if we had to leave for a further expedition, they were quick and easy to take. There was a rumour that our leaders were planning to head further north where, it was rumoured, there were gold mines. My exclusion from the inner court of Captain-General Hernán Cortés meant that I now heard only rumours. The four guns which had originally been in the square were now augmented by the rest and the centre of Tenochtitlán was tightly protected by our cannons.

"Would Captain Pedro not back you if you asked the Captain-General for permission to leave?"

I frowned and Katerina, seeing it, stroked my head. I changed the frown to a smile and kissed the back of her hand. "I am no longer sure that I know Captain Pedro. His massacre when we were away seemed not only reckless but unnecessary. He could have waited until we returned and then we could have simply demanded the gold." Since I had heard of the killing, I wondered at the motives of the senior Alvarado brother. Was he trying to usurp the Captain-General? The men we had left in the city were all loyal to the Captain. Who knew if the gold they gave to the Captain-General when we returned was all that they had taken? I was suspicious.

The Aztecs became more vociferous in their objections to our presence. Orders came from the Captain-General for us not to move around the city alone and to remain armed. Some of the locals were killed by our soldiers who were attacked when walking in a distant part of the city. Perhaps they were some of the new men trying to find gold, who knows. Whatever the reason it was a spark and showed the feelings of the Aztecs. The Emperor, it seemed, was no longer adored in quite the same way. I kept my gunners alert and had them make sure that there was a fire kept burning by each gun so that a linstock could be quickly lighted and a gun fired. I impressed upon them the need to keep the gunpowder mixed so that there would be no misfires. We needed our weapons to be ready at a moment's notice. We were running short of bags of stones and small balls. We only had ten left for each gun. The lack of river pebbles was a problem I had not anticipated. Had we not hurried back west so quickly I might have had my Indians collect them from the beaches. Hindsight is a wonderful thing! Not all of our guns faced the square, many of the newer ones controlled key junctions in the city and I was kept busy from dawn until dusk checking on the cannons and the men.

Katerina was much larger by the time June drew to a close. She had never been the slimmest of women and now she struggled to move. The heat in the city was oppressive and if it was not for the lake water which helped create a breeze, would have been unbearable. I had walked, with Fernando, and Philip, around the gun emplacements. They were strategically located to protect the main square. Patrols of pikemen and rodeleros ensured that the roads close to the square were kept safe. As for the rest of the huge city…

I was roused, in the early hours of the 1st of July by one of Captain Pedro de Alvarado's lieutenants, Rodolfo, "Captain Tomas, you are ordered to rouse your men and stand by your guns!"

"Why?"

"The Emperor has been murdered and it is feared that the people may rise. Having the guns manned is a precaution, that is all!"

He left and as I was dressing, I woke Katerina, "Pack some things, it may be nothing, but the Emperor has been killed and there may be trouble."

"What things?"

"Food, drink, a few clothes; stay here and if we have to leave then I will come for you."

She hugged me, "I trust in you, Tomas. You are a good man, and we will be safe while you live!"

I kissed her and forced myself to hurry out. I woke Fernando, Jose, and Philip. I told them what I knew. Jose asked, "Murdered? By whom?"

"I do not know, and it really matters not. If he is dead, then who will the people look to?"

Fernando saw what I meant and said, "The priests!"

I nodded, "And they hate us. They may well have killed him to make the people rise. I know this is hard, but you must tell the gunners to be ruthless. We are outnumbered and we cannot afford to be sentimental. Any who attack us, men, women, even children must die!"

I knew I had changed since I had left Devon and I was not sure I liked this new Thomas.

Even as we raced for the guns, we heard the almost bestial screams coming from all around us. Those who led us had tried to keep the death a secret, but the word had still got out and there was a sound like a swarm of buzzing wasps punctuated by roars and screams. We would have to fight.

My original men were close to the main square and I saw, as we arrived in the first light of dawn, that every soldier we had was armed and ready to fight. We had almost fifteen hundred men and a few thousand Tlaxcalans, but the Aztec army alone dwarfed those numbers by ten to one. When one added the population of the largest city any of us had ever seen then the odds did not look good. In addition, the horses would be of less use in the city and the Captain-General would be reliant on our cannons.

I heard the cannons placed further out from the square open fire and saw clouds of smoke rising in the air. The revolution had begun!

"Load with ball and bags of stones. Be ready to fire as soon as you see them!" My gunners shouted their acknowledgement. Jose and Fernando were close to me and Jose gave me a wave and a grin!

The first thing I did was to order all the cannons to be turned around. They had been placed, originally, to cover the square from the steps above but the square was now filled with pikemen and rodeleros and in the centre were the priests and the women. I felt my stomach turn as I realised that I had left Katerina in our home. I dared not go back for her and I prayed, with all my heart that God would watch over one who had recently joined his flock. I had little time to do anything about it as with a flash of bright colour the Aztecs, led by the frightening priests flooded from every street and passageway to hurl themselves at us. We could see nothing but a sea of barbaric humanity carrying a variety of weapons. This was no time to conserve either powder or ball and I put the linstock to the touch hole as soon as it was a range of three hundred paces. The ball scythed through the crowd but more filled the spaces. All around me the other gunners and harquebusiers were firing as fast as they could. When the heads of the gunners who had been further out at the junctions were waved atop spears then I knew that we would lose. I would not go down without a fight and my men and I worked so relentlessly that we touched the bare red-hot metal and barely flinched.

The Captain-General saw what was happening, and the trumpet sounded retreat. We would have to leave the guns! I shouted, "Put the powder near the guns, leave a trail and light it! God speed!" I knew not if any heard my words, but my Indians did, and they placed the barrels of powder while I laid a trail. The Aztecs were almost upon us as I lit the powder which fizzled, popped, and then raced to the powder. I was forty paces away when it exploded, and the explosion knocked me from my feet. The pieces of metal and balls we had left cut a swath through the Aztecs and bought us time. I saw a dead harquebusier.

I spied Fernando and Jose, "I must go to Katerina. Save yourselves!"

Fernando shook his head, "We live or die together!" With drawn swords, we ran, not after the fleeing army which headed for the shorter, northern causeway, but down a narrow street, south, towards our home. We did not escape unscathed but the mob we met was a relatively small one. There were but three of us, however, the mob was just made up of men and women who had grabbed the nearest weapon they could, a hoe, a meat cleaver, a kitchen knife. Katerina's life was at stake and we chopped, slashed, and hacked our way through them leaving a street full of dead and wounded. They were the last enemies we found on the way to my home for we had passed the main line of Aztecs who were now in full flight after the main army. I had seen some of our soldiers returning to their barracks to retrieve their treasure. I knew it would cost them their lives and that they would be hunted by the Aztecs. We were also seeking a treasure, but this was a human one, my wife and unborn child. We did not need to collect our gold as the three of us had ours strapped beneath our brigandines. As we ran to our home, we passed the butchered bodies of our army. Men had been almost torn apart. We found one falcon surrounded by its slaughtered crew. The cannon was intact and the powder, ball and linstock were still in place. The Aztecs had feared its power!

Miraculously we reached our home without incident and Katerina was there, cowering beneath a table. I embraced her, "Come, we can still escape." She squeezed me tightly and I held her firmly. While we lived then we had hope.

She had gathered food and a couple of skins of ale. We grabbed those and Jose found a leather bag in which he put other items we might need, flint, whetstone, and the like.

Fernando said, "Which way?"

There were two causeways leading north. I guessed that the Captain-General would use the shorter one which led to Tepeyacac. There was a longer one that led northwest, crossing the island of Coltonco. There was a road and a bridge that headed west. "The southern causeway is too long and exposed. We go either to the west one or the northwest one."

"Then we risk running into the Aztecs!"

I nodded, "It cannot be helped and whichever way we run there will be danger and, perhaps, death. I do not think that they will be in the mood for prisoners. We will go back the way we came for the square may have emptied now!"

Fernando nodded, "We trust your judgement and to God!" We all made the sign of the cross.

It was when we reached the abandoned gun that the party of Eagle Warriors spotted us. They were heading from the square and scuppered my plans to return that way.

"Quick, Jose, fill the barrel with balls and Fernando, pile the powder barrels around it. Katerina, run back the way we came!"

I did not even look to see if she had obeyed but began to lay a trail of powder, picking up the linstock as I did so. I blew on it to make it hotter. Aztec warriors can run fast, and we had not completed the task when I realised they would catch us! "You two run after Katerina and I will follow!"

They cared for Katerina and obeyed. I lit the trail of powder which, I knew, was too short and then threw the linstock at the leading warrior who was just ten feet from me. Perhaps he thought it was a magic device for he turned and ducked. It allowed me to run after Jose and Fernando. This time the explosion hit all three of us. Katerina had obeyed me, and I saw her peering from around a building as the smoke started to clear and, coughing, the three of us rose. I turned around and saw that the confined space where the gun had been made the explosion more concentrated and it had completely wiped out the warriors. Grabbing Katerina's arm I led us west. My original plan was now in tatters. We would have to skirt the main square and make our way west until we could turn and head north.

We did not run but I used Jose to scout out the intersections and see if they were clear then we followed. It was not speedy, but it kept us safe.

My wife's condition meant we could not move quickly in any case. Katerina kept as close to me as she could. There was terror on her face as we passed bodies in the streets. As we passed the bodies of an Aztec and Spanish priest, entwined in death, she murmured, "Tomas, I am afraid I will slow you up. Leave me and I will take my chances."

Shaking my head I said, "Katerina, we will all stay together, and I will not leave you!"

"But I need to make water and the baby makes me slow."

"Make water when you must and if we have to go slowly then so be it!" She nodded and we continued but I made the pace slower. Jose, who led, realised this and he made a more comfortable pace for my pregnant wife. It was a slow journey.

As the sun reached its zenith, I estimated that we were halfway to the west side of the city and the area known as Moyotlan. There we saw a woman tending to a wounded Aztec and, even worse, she saw us. She did not raise the alarm but continued to tend to the man; I assumed it was her husband. When we reached the next intersection, I restrained Jose, "Head north! She will report that we went west. They may not think that we would be foolish enough to follow the rest of our men."

He nodded and we went as fast as Katerina would allow, north. As we passed open areas, I saw the lake to our left and had a better idea of where we were. The woman tending her man had been a warning and we moved even more cautiously. The afternoon wore on and we had still evaded the Aztecs. We could hear fighting, but it was to our right and seemed far away. It was late afternoon when we reached the western causeway which, eventually, led to Tlacopan. We heard the noise of battle from ahead and any hopes we had of using it were ended when we spied some of our comrades trying to fight their way to safety. Aztecs were before and behind them. They would die. I waved Jose to continue north, ignoring the causeway which led to the west. We heard the clash of weapons and the cries of the dead and dying but the buildings gradually masked it.

It was dark when we crossed from Tenochtitlán to Tlatelolco, which was the northern part of the island city complex. It was a small victory, but we had yet to reach the causeway. We had been forced to stop many times to avoid being seen and Katerina was struggling to continue. She needed rest but she did not complain however I could see that she was suffering. I had never been to Tlatelolco which was less grand than the southern part, Tenochtitlán. The streets were narrower and the houses meaner. There were also more people about. There was a second western causeway at Nonoalco, but it was guarded and none of us was in any condition for a fight. We kept going until we spied the great causeway which went north and west. This too was guarded but there were just six men, we could see their shadows and their fire. After what we had seen then the odds of two to one seemed acceptable. We found an empty house close by. The gaping door was a good indicator that it was unoccupied. It was very small and stank of animals, but it was shelter. We ducked inside and, after ensuring that the nearest Aztecs were the six men guarding the causeway then I spoke, albeit quietly, "We eat now and drink. Katerina, you will stay here. The three of us will take off our helmets and sneak up on the six guards. I am guessing that they will be as tired as us. We kill them as silently as we can and then head across the causeway." The sounds of fighting from the northeast had long since ceased and the last warriors we had seen had been the ones on the western causeway.

I put my arm around Katerina, "You have done well and if we can make the causeway then we have a chance."

"I am afraid, Tomas. The baby!"

"We trust in God. If we make it out, then I promise we shall leave this land. Our leader has gambled once too often, and we have lost! We will make a new life in Isla Juana!"

She hugged me and tears ran down her cheeks, "Good!"

I took off my helmet and nodded to the other two. I slipped out first and flattened myself against the wall of the dwelling. In the distance, I could hear wailing. I wondered if it was the woman who had been tending her husband. When the other two joined me I edged along the wall. As soon as I could smell the Aztecs, I stopped. They had a fire burning to keep away the insects that lived by the water and they also smelled of the food they ate; it was different from ours. I moved my head so that I could see beyond the edge of the rude dwelling. I saw the Aztecs who were twenty paces from the building, and I did not think that they were looking in our direction.

I pulled my head back and nodded to Fernando and Jose. I began to slide along the rough wall to the end of the building. I hoped that we were just shadows for the six Aztecs soon came into view. They had not moved but we could hear the murmur of their conversation. When I reached the end it was time for a decision. I turned and gestured to the other two with my sword. I stepped from the building and ran towards the six men. We were lucky that the fire spoiled the night vision of the three men squatting on the far side of the flames for the first they knew of the attack was when my sword hacked into the neck of one of the Aztecs whose back was to me and my dagger plunged into the shoulder of a second. Jose's sword ran through a third and his falling body scattered ashes from the fire into the faces of the other three. My sword slashed sideways across the naked chest of one as Jose and Fernando slew the other two. It had all happened in moments and there was now stillness and the smell of burning flesh from the body on the fire.

I gestured to the other two to dispose of the bodies and I hurried back to Katerina. I took her hand and led her from the stinking room into the fresher air. I smiled and whispered, "All is well, and the causeway is clear."

After donning my helmet and picking up Jose and Fernando's I slipped my hooded cloak over her head and about her shoulders. I hurried her to the causeway where my companions had disposed of the bodies although there was still the smell of singed hair and burning flesh in the air. The causeway headed into the blackness of Lake Texcoco. As we hurried along it, I could hear nothing and yet I knew that our army must still be fleeing and, I assumed, fighting. Perhaps our journey had taken longer than I had thought. This was not the main causeway and was not as well made as the one which I suspected the main army had used. That they had used it became clear when Jose spied something bobbing in the water to the east of us. He waded in the shallow water to haul it in for we were not sure if it was alive or dead. It was the naked body of a priest, a Catholic priest, and it had been mutilated. That spurred us on.

The silence ended just a short time later. Katerina had been forced to stop by stomach cramps and we had taken advantage of the halt to eat and drink something. We were less than a third of the way along the causeway and approaching the island of Coltonco, where we could see the shapes of fishermen's dwellings when we heard cries from behind us.

Jose said, "They have discovered that their sentries are gone. We will need to run!"

Katerina rose and nodded. I held her arm as we moved quickly towards the fishermen's houses. It was not a run but a fast walk. Katerina could move no faster. I glanced behind and saw that warriors were chasing us. There was a chance, a slim one admittedly, that we might be able to lose them on the island and head west but that depended upon the fishermen being asleep. The noise of the warriors behind meant that was unlikely.

Jose and Fernando were twenty paces ahead of Katerina and me. They were not trying to outrun us but were just being prepared to deal with any danger. That danger manifested itself as they stepped from the causeway onto the island for half a dozen fishermen emerged from their homes. In their hands, they carried fish spears. Jose and Fernando did the only thing they could, they slashed and stabbed with their swords. I let go of Katerina's arm, "Keep running north! I will try to hold them up." She nodded and waddled off as fast as her condition would allow.

The sound of the fishermen dying brought others from their huts and a barbed fish spear was jabbed at my face. I flicked it away with my sword and ripped my dagger across the man's stomach. Although we had forced back the fishermen nearest us others were emerging from the huts ahead and I saw that Katerina was in danger for she was close enough for the three Aztecs chasing us to catch her. I slashed and swashed to clear a path and then ran towards her. I do not think that the three men who ran at her with spears even knew that she was a woman. They plunged their spears into her body. She had nothing with which she could defend herself and I heard her screams as she fell. I had a fury in me that made me oblivious to all. I fell upon the three and chopped my sword into the head of one while my dagger tore across the throat of a second and I headbutted the third. The peak of the helmet drew blood and my sword finished him off.

I knelt by Katerina. She was dead and it was my fault. I should have stayed by her side. I kissed her head as Jose shouted, "Tomas, we must run. The Aztecs!"

I turned and saw that the rest of the Aztec warriors were almost at the island.

Fernando said, "You can do no more for her. Let us not waste three more lives."

He was right and I rose. I took the cross I had given her from her neck. It was my only reminder of her. As I stood, I saw that there were, perhaps a dozen warriors. If the fishermen joined them then we would be well outnumbered. Sheathing my weapons to make running easier, we ran north along the causeway. It was now a foot race and we were exhausted already. When there appears to be no hope then a man can find strength he did not know he possessed. I remembered the first days of my incarceration after my father and the others had died. I had discovered that no matter how low you felt there were hidden reserves upon which you can call and so the three of us ran. Behind us, we heard the pounding of bare feet on the causeway. I did not risk turning to see how close they were for I could judge that by their voices. I knew enough of the language to pick up some of the words and that helped.

We could see the northern shore as a darker patch above the lake when Fernando said, "One of those spears cut me. I must stop."

That he had run for more than a mile with the wound showed his courage and fortitude, "Jose, turn and charge them. They will not expect that."

I whirled around and drew my weapons. The Aztecs had also spread out and four were ahead of the rest, but they were less than twenty paces behind us. I did not falter but ran directly at them. Even as I slew one a second hit at my head with his club. The helmet saved my life and I gutted him with my dagger. Jose was next to me and we had slain all four before the rest arrived. The delay allowed Fernando, wounded though he was, to slip between us. I pushed my left shoulder to touch his right. We would live or die together. The spear which was thrown hit me square in the chest. The sharpened spearhead penetrated my leather brigandine but did not tear into my flesh. The leather satchel and my gold stopped it! The warrior who had thrown it looked in horror as I ripped the spear from my brigandine and hurled it back at him. It caught his shoulder and blood spurted. We were fighting for our lives and I was fighting for vengeance. My wife and unborn child lay dead and I wanted to extract punishment on every Aztec I saw. The warriors did not help themselves as they hurled themselves at us, often getting in each other's way. Even so, stone edged blades raked across my arms. My legs were speared but to give attention or even thought to the wounds would have resulted in my death. I sliced, stabbed, slashed, and hacked until there were none before us. The fishermen were still there but they had waited a hundred paces from us. When they saw the dead warriors they turned and fled back down the causeway.

I looked up at the sky to the east and saw the first faint light of approaching dawn. "We have time. Let us tend to our wounds and then continue north." I pointed, "We have but a few miles to go."

Jose and I had minor wounds, but Fernando had a savage slash along his thigh. It would need to be stitched but we had neither needles nor thread. Instead, we cleaned the wound, as we had with our own, with the beer. It was a poor substitute for vinegar, but it would clean it. Then I took my spare shirt from beneath my brigandine and made it into bandages. I tied it tightly around the leg. Jose went to the Aztecs and hacked a spear into a manageable walking stick. He also took the gold and silver from the corpses. It was unspoken but we had all had enough of this land.

When we set off to walk it was almost dawn and we saw that we were closer to the land than we had thought. We trudged off the causeway and then went along the Aztec road which headed northwest. Hopefully, we would find the rest of our comrades. If they had survived.

Chapter 15

We did not find the rest of the army until the evening of the next day, and, in fact, it was only the fires of the camps which helped us to find it. We had taken so long to reach it as we hid whenever we suspected there were Aztecs close by. Although some might have been allies it would not do to make our lives hang in the balance on that assumption. Fernando's wound also slowed us although he did not complain and would not allow us to help him. I saw the pain etched on his face and the sweat as he took each step. We eked out our meagre rations and even when we spied and smelled the campfires, we still had enough for another day.

The sentries were both alert and suspicious, and I was glad that they were armed only with swords and pikes. Had they had harquebusiers then they might have opened fire first and asked questions later. As it was, as soon as they spied us, we were surrounded by a mob of armed soldiers. I was recognised and while Fernando and Jose found the nearest campfire I was taken to the Captain-General. Gone was the confident smile. He and the de Alvarado brothers were seated, brooding around a fire with the other lieutenants and captains. I saw that Alonso de Ávila was still alive. He was a tough old warrior. I confess that I was surprised by the warmth of my welcome.

The Captain-General beamed, "Tomas, you truly are Conquistador! You have managed to arrive a day after the last survivor and, so far as I can tell, you are the only gunner."

I shook my head, partly because I was sad that all the others had died but also because I wanted him to know that Fernando and Jose still lived. "There are three of us, but my wife is dead."

The reaction from all of them added to my determination to leave this army. The Captain-General shrugged and said, dismissively, "Luckily she was just an Indian and if you need another then when we reach Tlaxcala you shall have the first choice for it was your guns that enabled so many to escape!"

Captain Gonzalo shook his head, "The nine hundred men of the rearguard would dispute that, Captain-General!"

"They did their job, and we shall honour their memory when this is over." As Pedro de Alvarado poured me a beaker of wine Hernán Cortés asked, "And how did you escape?"

I told him how we had returned for Katerina and used the abandoned gun to affect our escape. I concluded with her death, "And then the pursuit stopped, and we are here. What is happening now?"

It was Pedro de Alvarado who answered, "We have five hundred men left and perhaps three hundred Tlaxcalans. We have just five harquebusiers and precious little ammunition for them. More importantly, we have no cannons. In fact, our one advantage is that we still have horses. Our scouts tell us that an army of forty thousand is heading here to wipe us off the face of the earth."

I nodded and took the enormity of the odds in, "And exactly where is here, Captain?"

Hernán Cortés answered, "Otumba. The Tlaxcalans are raising more men to come to our aid but as the Aztecs are due here by morning it is unlikely that they will reach us in time. We will have to fight with what we have."

"And then?"

Pedro de Alvarado laughed and clapped me on the back, "I like you, Englishman! You think that we can survive?"

I emptied the beaker and nodded towards Hernán Cortés, "The Captain-General thinks so and while we live then there is hope!"

The grin on the face of Hernán Cortés was from ear to ear, "And you will bring us good luck! When we defeat these Aztecs then we will raise another army, return to Tenochtitlán and this time we will be ruthless!" He smiled at his captains, "We will use our horses and charge them as El Cid might have done. We go for the leaders and their war chiefs."

I stood, "I have no guns to fire. Where do I fight?"

Captain Gonzalo de Alvarado smiled, "With me, for you have shown that you can fight and that is what we shall need fighters."

"Then I shall join my last two gunners."

One of the priests who had survived was tending to Fernando's wounds. I saw that the priest had a sword hanging from his belt and he had a helmet with him. The flight from the Aztec city had changed us all. Jose had found us somewhere to sit close to his father and I joined him. He handed me some food and I ate while I watched the priest stitch Fernando's leg. The stitches were small and that took time. Fernando bore it all stoically. When he had finished Fernando fished out a piece of gold, "Thank you, father."

The priest bit the gold and said, "Most of the treasure of this army was left behind. You are fortunate. I thank you."

Some of the others sitting around the campfire looked curiously at Fernando. We would have to watch out for theft but that would be after the battle. Until then life would be more important than gold. Fernando joined us, his leg stretched out and the pain on his face now apparent. I told them what would be happening. "Fernando, we all have wounds but yours is the worst. When we fight you stand behind Jose and me; guard our backs." He looked as though he was going to object. "You know that with the numbers we shall fight Jose and I will need someone to be the eyes in the backs of our heads. That will be you. I am still the captain. Obey." He nodded. "Have you the whetstone, Jose?"

"Aye."

He took the stone from the bag of supplies he had carried from Tenochtitlán and handed it to me. I began to sharpen the sword. Fernando drank deeply from the ale skin. He spoke to no one in particular, "The dream is over then." We knew that he meant the dream of the Captain-General.

I shook my head. I knew the man far better than either Fernando or his son, "He has tasted the river of gold and he wants more. This is a setback. If we survive tomorrow, then he will raise more men and try again. We lost many men in the last days, more than we have left but the Aztecs also lost many of their elite warriors. Tomorrow will see them throw the best that they have at us." I handed the stone back to Jose and lay down. "I will sleep and pray that my dreams are not haunted by Katerina."

Fernando put his hand on my shoulder, "I am sorry, my friend, we have not spoken of this. I cannot conceive of the pain you must be feeling. If I had lost my wife and a child who had yet to be born then I know not how I would feel."

I shook my head, "Feel? It is too raw to feel. There is a numbness in my head and my heart. We had no time even to bury her. I have been thinking only of survival. When we reach land which is civilised then I will be able to mourn. Now, I am too weary to do anything other than try to sleep."

Perhaps God took pity on me for it was as though I was unconscious. I slept and nothing entered my dream world.

I was woken by the noise of the camp rousing and I heard, from the dim recesses of sleep, the call to arms. It was not yet dawn, but all were awake.

A rodelero put his arm out to help me to my feet, "Captain Gonzalo sent me. You three shall follow me." He saw Fernando rise, stiffly, "Can he fight?"

Fernando laughed, "As the alternative is to sit and wait for death to come then aye, I can fight!" We followed as quickly as we could. As we arrived, I saw the horsemen were already mounted. They had, and I know not whence they had brought them, lances! There were just twenty of them and they were led by the Captain-General and some of the other leaders: Gonzalo de Sandoval, Pedro de Alvarado, Cristóbal de Olid, Juan de Salamanca, and Alonso de Ávila.

Men were forming lines and we stood in the second rank behind a handful of men with pikes. The others in the front rank were rodeleros. Hernán Cortés raised his lance and shouted, "Our Indian scouts have told us that there are forty thousand Aztecs approaching and they are led by Matlatzincatl, the new Emperor of the Aztecs. He is the head we must remove. You soldiers have shown that you have great courage. We are here to fight another day because our rearguard sacrificed itself for us. Let us honour them by taking revenge on these savages! If we are marked to die let us do so by killing as many of these heathens as we can and then God will welcome us into heaven as the heroes we truly are!"

There was a cheer, of sorts, but the Spanish soldiers all gripped their weapons a little more tightly, most made the sign of the cross and, in their eyes was determination. I think I was more impressed by the Tlaxcalans for they still stood with us. They had not deserted our army and while the presence of some of their families explained it, I still believe that it showed how much they hated the Aztecs.

I turned to Jose and clasped his right arm, "It has been an honour to fight alongside you!"

"And I thank you, Captain Tomas, for you have given me the chance to become a gunner."

I nodded and faced Fernando who stood just behind us. I clasped his forearm, "And you, Fernando, if your son and I fall promise me that you will get back to Isla Juana and your wife."

He gave a sad little smile, "If you and Jose are dead then I will not be far behind you, but I swear that if I can I shall get back to my family."

I turned to face the front again as father and son embraced.

"They come!" The Spanish voice which shouted the warning came from one of our horsemen. I drew my sword and dagger. Both were sharp enough to shave with. The men who had pikes before us had small shields strapped to their forearms and the rodeleros had slightly larger bucklers. Many of them still had their armour and even those who had discarded it wore padded jerkins. We had stuffed our spare hose and shirts beneath our brigandines so that, with the satchels of treasure and spare clothes, we looked overweight. I cared not what we looked like; I wanted as much protection as I could get.

At first, all that I could see was a shadow that moved from the south. It was as the sun suddenly flared into the sky, lighting the colours of the warriors, that we saw the horror that we faced. The horizon, as far as the eye could tell, was filled with Aztecs. It was then I saw that you could recognise the war chiefs for they were the ones wearing the bright headdresses. Perhaps the Captain-General's plan might succeed. We did not need to kill the whole army, an impossible task in any case, but if we decimated their leaders then they might lose heart. I just prayed that there were few Aztec priests amongst the warriors!

Our horsemen showed that they had the courage and were not cowards for they charged into the heart of the advancing savages. Their lances speared the Aztecs before the warriors could use their clubs and axes. Then our attention shifted from observing our horsemen to fighting for our lives. I was so grateful to the pikes before us as the Aztecs hurled themselves at them as they were a barrier to the obsidian headed clubs and axes the warriors used. The Aztecs seemed to have a complete disregard for their own lives and just wanted to get as close to us as they could. The pikes hewed down the first wave of Aztecs and it was only then that I realised that the Aztecs were not using slings and, so far, they had not used either arrows or spears. I wondered why and then, as the second wave closed with our pikes and the rodeleros I lifted my sword for I knew that soon I would be needed when the first of the pikemen was laid low by a blow from an obsidian edged maquahuitl which dented the soldier's helmet. The Jaguar warrior screamed as the soldier fell. As luck would have it, he occupied the space before me and I stepped into it. It was not out of bravery or any sense of false heroics. If I did not, then our line would be breached, and we would all die.

It was the same warrior who had clubbed the pikeman and as he raised his maquahuitl I knew what he intended; the same blow which had felled the pikeman. That made it easier for me and I lunged at the Aztec's throat. My sword was a better weapon in the melee than a pike and the warrior fell gurgling blood from his throat to lie at my feet. The death settled me for I had killed one of the better Aztec warriors and when the next warrior reached me wearing a loincloth, carrying a hide shield, and wielding a wooden club then I felt much more confident. As the club came down towards me, I blocked it with the blade of my dagger while I lunged at the shield with my sword. The tip went through and as my dagger sliced off three fingers of the Aztec's hand, my sword found his chest. All along our line we were having similar success and it came to me, the Aztecs were trying to render us unconscious, they wanted us for human sacrifice. That was why there had been neither arrows nor stones!

It was one thing to hope that they were trying to render a man unconscious, but it did not help you to fight any better or to slay more enemies. It was like trying to hold back the sea and when the pikeman to my right fell then Jose stepped into the gap, picking up the dead man's weapon as he did so. He swung the head in an arc and caught an Aztec in the throat. The blood gushed and splashed over us. I used my dagger and sword as a cross to block the blow from the large war club which descended towards me. I brought my knee up into the groin of the Aztec and when I connected, he could not help but involuntarily double up. I rammed my dagger into his neck.

The ground was now slippery and slick with blood, bodies, and writhing men. I think I was luckier than most for I had been a sailor and I moved my feet further apart to give a better balance. The pikeman to my left was unlucky and he slipped. The Aztec who clubbed him had but a moment to celebrate his victory as my sword hacked across his stomach. He looked in horror as a mass of what appeared to be a nest of snakes slipped out. Fernando stepped into the gap. I knew that we now had a very thin line. The next man who fell would not be replaced. We had been pushed back eight or ten feet from where we had begun. It was a flat battleground and there was room for us to move backwards, but it was alarming. Men who had been wounded were being tended to by priests and they were closer now.

I saw the war chief dressed in Jaguar skins as he waved his men forward. He had a feathered standard behind his back. and he ran with his men towards us. Perhaps they thought that our lack of armour made us weaker, or it may have been that he was a clever man who had seen that our line was the thinnest at this point. Whatever the reason he ran at me with a shield and maquahuitl. He was a war chief for he had a feathered standard attached to his body and that meant he had earned his title. He was a big man and ran at me confidently. He held his shield away from his body and I knew, as he made straight for me, that a sword through the shield would not work as well as it had the first time. He held his maquahuitl above and behind him. He would strike to hit me across the side of the face and head. He was unconcerned with prisoners and sought my death and the breaking of our line. One thing being a gunner had taught me was timing. Firing a falconet at the perfect time, when the ship was on the up roll could, if well aimed, shatter a mast. The chief had made himself the point of an arrow and that gave me confidence. Jose and Fernando were not the war chief's target, I was. They would not be hurt by the swing and whatever I did would affect only me. As he neared me and started the swing, I raised my dagger as though to block the strike and then dropped to one knee. My sword was below his shield and I drove up as the maquahuitl struck air. My sword found flesh and I pushed as I began to rise. The blade slid between bones and continued up. My hand became wet, with what I knew not but as the maquahuitl fell then I assumed I had been successful. I continued to drive up and his body became limp. His feet lifted off the ground when I became erect and as I tipped my sword down so his body slid from my sword.

The warriors who had followed him stopped and stared at the body. The blood was beneath him and it was as though he had no wound that could be seen. His feathered standard was shattered, and his men just stared. Captain Gonzalo was five men down and he shouted, "Push them back!"

We ran at the stationary Aztecs who seemed mesmerized by their dead chief. We struck first. Jose's pike was rammed into the stomach of one and then he swung it from on high to take a second in the neck. I stabbed my opponent in the guts with my dagger and, as he fell, lunged at the man behind him. All along our part of the line, the Aztecs were being slain and suddenly, without any word of warning, the warband turned and fled. It was a minor victory for there were still thousands of Aztecs before us, but it gave us respite.

"Reform the line and recover weapons. Move the wounded and stand firm!" Captain Gonzalo raised his sword to me in salute.

I sheathed my weapons and picked up a pike. Fernando did the same. Jose had shown us that it gave us a better chance of survival. I saw that our horsemen were deep inside the Aztec lines. It seemed that they were almost immortal for despite the sea of savages around them they all looked to have survived and even more surprisingly, their lances were intact. That was the only time we had for another war chief rallied his men and they came at us again. My mouth was so dry that I felt I was in a desert, but we had no opportunity to drink. The battle was far from over.

This war chief was neither an Eagle nor a Jaguar warrior. That did not make him any less an opponent, but it gave me some comfort for he would have looked up to the Jaguar war chief I had just slain. The Jaguar and Eagle warriors were the equal of our knights. At the same time, I knew that the warriors would seek me out for I had killed a Jaguar war chief. We were all weary and lifting the pike was an effort, but I knew, as did all the others that we had to fight until we dropped and hoped that others would live and stop us from being taken as prisoners for sacrifice.

This time the Aztec warband, there had to be four hundred or more of them, came in a straight line or as close to straight as they could manage while they negotiated the dead. It was fortunate that they wished us alive for they used shorter weapons rather than long spears. We had a wall of pikes once more. The spike on the end could keep the Indians at bay while a blow from the axe head would be fatal. The screams from the Aztecs showed that this warband was not dismayed by the dead Jaguar war chief for they followed their own. This time the war chief did not come for me but made for the plated knight, Captain Gonzalo.

Once more the Aztecs showed themselves to be fearless and reckless. The pike was a good weapon to keep an enemy at bay, but these warriors seemed to think that they would be faster than the man wielding the pike. They were wrong and I soon learned to use the edge of the axe head to sweep across the naked middles of the warriors. It was an effective way to stop them although one Aztec managed to swing his club at my head even though his entrails hung from his eviscerated stomach. Had the blow landed full on then I might have been hurt but he was dying, and it merely made my head ring as it smashed into my morion. It was a warning to me, and I held the pike, even though it made my arms ache, further from my body. Fernando was not so lucky and the blow which hit his helmet knocked him, thankfully, backwards and I took a half step to the left where I was able to close the gap to the rodelero who stood there. I risked a similar wound if I turned and so I kept my face to the front. The rodelero had a blade that had bent slightly and was a little notched. As I stabbed into the face of an Aztec who lunged at me with a maquahuitl I shouted, "My sword is sharp. Take it!"

He nodded and after plunging his own sword into the earth drew my sword, "Thank you, Englishman! I am in your debt." With a better weapon, his strokes became smoother and two Aztecs died within a handful of blows.

I was so weary now that I could barely hold the pike with its heavy head. The Aztecs came on relentlessly and I knew that it was a case of when and not if we would all fall. The Captain-General and his men still remained whole and their horses ploughed through the Aztecs with apparent impunity but still, the enemy came. I heard a wail to my right as the edge of a maquahuitl bit into my right leg. I brought down the axe head and sliced through the arm of the Aztec and then I rammed the spike up under his chin and into his skull. I saw why there was a wail. Captain Gonzalo had slain the war chief and his bodyguard. This time the warband fled back as one. These were not the Jaguar warriors. It was also at that point that Juan de Salamanca thrust his lance through the Aztec leader, Matlatzincatl. The wail we had heard was echoed across the field and the Aztecs began to flee. They were not helped by the wall of bodies around their leader and the horsemen, although their horses were tired, continued to slay the Aztecs.

Captain Gonzalo shouted, "Advance! Let us end it here!"

Jose and I turned; Fernando was sitting up and a priest was bandaging his head, "Go! I am alive!"

We advanced and somehow found energy I did not know I possessed. Perhaps it was the thought that if we could slay more then we might, indeed, make it back to the coast.

It was dark by the time we reached our camp. We had chased the Aztecs for almost two miles but then we were too tired to continue. As we headed back, we all took to robbing the Aztec dead. All had some gold about their person and in my case, this was my passage back to England. Fernando had taken all from those who had died where we had fought and the three of us had a tidy haul to add to the gold already in our satchels. It was dark and we secreted our cache without prying eyes observing us. As the servants and Tlaxcalan women began to prepare food we tended to our own wounds. The cut on my leg was not serious but it would hurt and if it became infected then could be dangerous. I took some vinegar to clean it.

The rodelero who had been next to me returned to hand me my sword, "I thank you again." He smiled, "Another rodelero laughed when he told me that your nickname was Conquistador. I think he was wrong to laugh for you have the blood of a conquering warrior in your veins. I know that you are a gunner and yet you stood shoulder to shoulder with me and I never feared that you would falter."

I nodded, "I would prefer a gun!"

He laughed, "And, my friend, had we had your guns then this would have been over sooner, but you have to hand it to the Captain-General, for someone who was not born a soldier, he has a good mind, and his horsemen won this battle for us!" He held out his arm, "I am Diego and if you ever need my help then just ask!"

We headed back to the coast the next morning. We were not defeated but we had lost many men and our leaders needed more men to retake Tenochtitlán. We learned that over twenty thousand Aztecs had been killed. Most of their chiefs and leaders lay on the battlefield but as there were few priests amongst the dead then I knew that the Aztecs would still continue to fight until the last priest was eliminated!

Chapter 16

It took us more than a month to reach Vera Cruz. The horsemen and our Captain-General were there in a very short time, but we marched on foot with the wounded. My leg and that of Fernando meant we could not move quickly and, indeed, there was no need. The Tlaxcalans protected our flanks on the march and we were feted at every village. The word of our enormous victory preceded us. I felt like a fraud because had the Aztecs wished us dead on the battlefield then we would have been despite the heroic efforts of Hernán Cortés and our horsemen. The Aztecs' religion had prompted their defeat. They had wanted us as live, human sacrifices on their bloody altars. As we trudged back the three of us discussed our future, but we did so privately. Before he and his lieutenants had left for Vera Cruz, Captain-General Hernán Cortés had made it quite clear that the three of us would be the captains of his new artillery train. He had plans for more guns and horses. He was an astute man.

"He can ask all he likes, Tomas, but when we reach Vera Cruz then I will take ship for Isla Juana and my family."

I said nothing. Katerina's death had changed me. I had always understood family, I had followed my father to this new world, but I had not understood the hold a woman could have over a man. I had entered the marriage reluctantly but through the short time I was with her and, indeed, adversity, I had come to love Katerina and the unborn child. I suppose the babe would always be perfect for, in my mind, I gave the child all the best of me, my father and Katerina.

Jose nodded, "And I will be a gunner, but I think, father, that I will try Spain. I will serve King Carlos and fight civilised enemies who do not sacrifice their victims!"

I remained silent for I wanted to go back to England, but I knew that relations between Spain and England were not good and I could not see how I would manage it. The English had not sailed across the Great Sea.

"And you, Tomas, will you return with Jose to Spain and thence to England?"

"As much as I would like to, I fear that I am too well known to do so without discovery. Can you see the Captain-General allowing me to leave his service?"

"What of us? Will he not try to stop us too?"

"You are wounded, Fernando, and I am the one he regards as his lucky charm. I fear that while he would make it hard for you and Jose, he would not actively try to stop you."

"If that is true then how will any of us leave Vera Cruz?" Fernando was a practical man.

I remembered de Bilbao, "There is a way. We would have to stow away on a ship. However, if we were found and brought back, then we would be punished."

"I think that the punishment would be financial rather than physical."

I looked at Jose whom I had seen grow up from a youth to a man, "What do you mean?"

"He wants you as a gunner. If you were caught deserting, and let us be honest, that is what it would be, then he would incarcerate you as you told us happened when you first served de Bilbao, but he would not hurt you. You would become his gunnery slave!"

That somehow made me even more determined to escape the clutches of Hernán Cortés.

By the time we reached Vera Cruz, I was no closer to an answer to our dilemma. We reached a town that looked nothing like the place we had first taken before our fateful march west. It was now Spanish with the Spanish flag flying and Spanish officials bringing order to it. Governor Diego Velázquez de Cuéllar might have sent a fleet and men to defeat our Captain-General but he had also been astute enough to send officials who would bring coins into his Isla Juana. Therein lay hope. If we could reach Isla Juana, then we might be safe.

The remnants of the army were camped close to the walls of the new stronghold. We were far from the Aztecs but as we had discovered the previous year, the Aztecs were more than capable of launching attacks on our new settlements. We made our camp and then Jose and I headed to the port to see what ships lay at anchor. There were just three and even as we approached, I saw our Captain-General speaking to the captains at the quayside. I had avoided meeting him for I hoped that he might forget me. Watching from the shelter of the wooden roof of a newly erected tavern I saw him clasp the arm of one captain who returned to his ship. As the gangplank was raised, I knew that the ships were returning to Isla Juana, for more men and supplies. Then it came to me that they might be sailing further east to find the men they needed. When Governor Diego Velázquez de Cuéllar had sent the men to defeat us he must have taken most of the soldiers, horses, and guns from his island. The ships would either have to sail to Spain or to the lands to the south. If they did sail to Spain, then I would have longer to try to make an escape. We bought some ale and wine from the tavern and headed back to our camp.

The visit to the tavern provided us with much information. Pánfilo de Narváez's men had brought with them smallpox and that disease had proved deadly. Many of the Indians who had come into contact with those soldiers had been infected and were dying in their thousands. It was an indiscriminate disease and struck ally and enemy alike. The tavern keeper had met our Captain-General a number of times and told us that Hernán Cortés saw it as a sign that God favoured our expedition and was punishing the natives. We returned to our camp and Fernando.

We had been back less than a week when a rodelero sought me out. It was the one to whom I had loaned my sword, Diego, and he beamed when he found me, "Englishman! You have brought me good luck. Since I used your sword, I have been appointed to the staff of Captain Gonzalo de Alvarado. It is he who has sent me to find you. Our Captain-General wishes to speak to you."

My heart sank, even though I gave the rodelero a weak smile, for I knew that Hernán Cortés had not forgotten me and my chances of escaping him were now slimmer. I nodded to Jose, "I shall return and, hopefully, I will have more supplies for us." Food was scarce and we were loath to reveal that we had gold. There were men in Vera Cruz who had not fought with us and they might take the opportunity, if they discovered we were rich, of relieving us of our gold!

The building used by the Captain-General was the largest in the town. The official sent by the Governor who had built it and lived in it had decided it would be prudent if he allowed Hernán Cortés to use it. Our victory at Zempoala had been a lesson to all that Hernán Cortés was a lucky man and it was better to back him than a Governor who sat, impotently in Santiago! I was recognised by many of the guards and soldiers in the building. Any hope of anonymity was long gone. That I was greeted warmly was gratifying but not comforting. How could I escape?

The Captain-General was seated in a large room with a fine desk. He was surrounded by priests and secretaries who scratched away. He seemed to be dictating to them. He stopped when he saw me, "Ah, Tomas, you are still alive! Why did you not seek me out? I hear you have been camping with the others. That is not right. We shall find you rooms closer to the port."

I opened my mouth and spoke. Even as I said the words, I regretted them, "I am afraid I cannot for I have Fernando and Jose with me." My two friends could have remained hidden until then. Now they would find it as hard as I would to escape.

"Good, then I have three gunners who can be the heart of my new gunners. Lieutenant Diego, find them a house close to here."

"Yes, Excellency!" Diego was a good soldier and now he was learning the right things to say. He would climb the greasy pole and soon join the de Alvarado brothers at the heart of the Captain-General's circle!

"Sit!" The Captain-General waved over a servant who poured me wine. He clapped his hands, "You may all leave and have food. You have half an hour and then you must return." He turned over the glass and the sand began to trickle through it. The eight men scurried off.

Hernán Cortés smiled and sipped the wine. He shook his head, "Not the best of wine but, when we have taken more gold from the Aztecs then we can afford to import better wine from Spain. Who knows, we may even import vines and grow our own. This land has such potential and yet only a few of us have seen it!" He leaned forward. "Captain Tomas, you shall be richly rewarded when we take back Tenochtitlán! I have made plans as we headed here after our great victory. The Tlaxcalans who escorted me home told me of lands to the north which are even richer than those ruled by Moctezuma! When we have eradicated Aztec power, we shall take the tribute from those tribes."

"But we have no army yet and no guns!"

He waved an airy arm, "We will get them. I have sent ships to both Spain and Castillo de Oro. Our success will draw both men and weapons. As for guns. There are some four here and I have ordered another ten from Spain. It may take months for them to reach us, but we have the winter to prepare."

That gave me hope. I would go along with his plans and hope that an opportunity arose in the next six months.

"I plan on leaving in the Spring. The first ships I sent should be in Spain now. With favourable winds, they may be back within a month or two."

"May I be frank, Captain-General?"

A frown furrowed his brow, "Of course."

"Governor Velázquez ordered us not to sail and he sent an army to defeat us!"

The smile returned, "Which we defeated!"

I nodded, "Yet ships from Spain have to land on Isla Juana, first."

He stood and walked around the tables and parchments, "Tomas, you do not understand how the court works. King Carlos has received gold from me. We lost much when we left the Aztec city, but I made sure that I sent plenty back to Spain. The Governor will not interfere with men and guns sent by the King of Spain!" He smiled and pointed to the new scar on my face, "You need time to heal. Until the men and guns arrive enjoy yourself for you have earned it. I am sorry that you lost your fortune, as did we all, but we will more than make up for it when we return."

We talked, until his clerks returned, about his plans and how he intended to conquer the whole of the Aztec Empire. The deaths of the two Aztec leaders meant he was now in a better place to do so. When the leaders and priests had been killed at the battle of Otumba it had left a void. I was now, more than ever, convinced that the Emperor had been murdered on the orders of Hernán Cortés. He had miscalculated but his clever mind had reversed the disaster.

Lieutenant Diego arrived with the clerks which suggested that our new home was not far from the Captain-General's. That was confirmed when Diego walked just eighty paces to the home he had requisitioned. It was a small house with just six rooms, but it was comfortable enough. Diego told me, cheerfully, that it had belonged to one of the supporters of the now-imprisoned Pánfilo de Narváez who had fled when the Captain-General had returned, "There are three Spanish servants who decided that serving our general would serve them better than serving a failed one."

We brought our gear to the house and had four months of peace. We had neither fighting nor work. Once a week I was summoned to the Captain-General's residence where along with the de Alvarado brothers and the other leaders I was kept up to date with the progress of his plans. The first men arrived in January. Eager to be a party to the plundering and looting, they were rough, tough, and hard men. They would show no pity to the Indians they fought. Thankfully the guns and gunners the Captain-General had promised me did not arrive. Fernando's leg healed although he still suffered occasional headaches and blackouts from the blow to the head.

It was in February that disaster struck. I was laid low with illness. It was the dreaded sweating sickness. Neither of my companions had the experience of it but they had heard of it and when the physician sent by Hernán Cortés confirmed it before scurrying out then they knew that they, along with the servants would have to tend to me. That they stayed with me showed how close we were. They could have fled, and I would not have blamed them. There was little that they could do for there was no treatment. It appeared to be a disease that was in the hands of God. They changed my clothes, they washed me, and they gave me water and broth. I did not know it at the time, but I spent February between life and death. They had no idea if I would live or die but as neither they nor the servants showed any symptoms the whole house was devoted to my recovery.

It was March before I was able to leave my sickbed and another four days before I was able to walk. It would be a long recovery. Lieutenant Diego visited us once the Captain-General received word. "Englishman, the Captain-General is happy that you are recovered, and it shows that God smiles on you. We have just had word that the ships with the guns and the powder will land next week. There is a gun park built on the west side of the town. We leave for the hinterland in April! Is that not good news? We will soon be as rich as a king!"

It was a disaster. My sickness had meant that we had been unable to foster our plans to escape and the euphoria of my recovery was spoiled with the depressing thought that we would have to face the Aztecs and there would be little likelihood of escape.

Hernán Cortés himself was with us as the ships arrived. There were five of them. He went aboard to ensure that what he had ordered had been delivered and then returned to me, "The Commodore tells me that it will take four days to fully unload the ships for the guns were placed low in the hold to ensure a balanced voyage. You need to work with the ships' crews. I will send soldiers and slaves to move the guns. You three go aboard now and speak with the Commodore and I will see you in five days!"

He was the most cheerful I could remember, and he left for his residence.

We trudged aboard and my head was down. It was not until a cheerful voice said, "Tomas, you are still alive!" that I looked up and saw Captain Pedro, now in a much finer uniform.

"Captain Pedro, I thought you were going back to Spain to enjoy your riches!"

He laughed, "And I did! I bought another four ships and I now make more money transporting soldiers and colonists west and gold and silver east. The four ships all have guns and we can defend ourselves."

"Come to my cabin. I have some fine wine and I would like to talk to you!"

Hope rose within me.

The four of us sat in a richly appointed cabin at the stern end of the ship below the aft castle. "If you did not already have employment, Tomas, I would offer you a position on my ships. Hernán Cortés spoke highly of you and your skill. I will not embarrass myself by offering you such a position. Only a fool would trade the riches of Mexico for the life on a ship!" He laughed.

"Then we three are fools, Captain Pedro. We would leave with you and I, for one, would accept your offer."

Jose said, "And I another."

"For myself," added Fernando, "I would be happy for a passage to Isla Juana!"

The Captain was clearly taken aback. He emptied his glass of wine and nodded, "Then I have a problem. I now know that Hernán Cortés will not even contemplate losing the three of you and I cannot afford to offend him." He looked at me, intently, as though trying to see into my soul, "I like you and I will try to help you but I, we, must be cautious. We have four days before the holds will be emptied. That gives me the time to come up with a solution." He lowered his voice and leaned forward, "This stays in the cabin. Act as though you intend to stay here and serve the Captain-General. If I can find no other solution, then I will take you aboard and lose the business." He shrugged, "There are other places we can make money."

"And we would be grateful."

He nodded, "I do not like Hernán Cortés. He gives himself a title he does not deserve and seems as treacherous as a viper. I will do what I can!"

With hope on the horizon, the three of us threw ourselves into doing the best job that we could with the guns. We organised the Indians into teams and made certain that each gun, as well as the powder, was carefully carried to the artillery park which had been made. We then had wheels and trails made. It made perfect sense to me but the two gunners who had arrived with the guns were a little surprised. They had seen rough carriages on guns used at sea but not the wheels and trails we had developed. Once we showed them how to make them, then the three of us were able to concentrate on shifting the guns and powder from ship to shore.

The Captain-General visited us on the second day and was pleased with our efforts, "I am pleased that the three of you will lead these gunners. It gives me confidence. I promise the three of you land when I am made Governor of this new land."

My eyes widened, "Governor?"

"Of course. I have correspondence with his majesty, and it is only a matter of time. But for our unexpected flight from Tenochtitlán, I would be Governor already." He shrugged, "I not only have enemies here in the west but also in Spain. Do not worry, Tomas, I shall prevail!"

On the evening of the third day, Captain Pedro sent for us. The slaves and guards had already gone back to the artillery park and we were just assessing how to move the last guns which were in the bottom of the largest carrack. We entered his cabin which was guarded by his first mate. Captain Pedro was seated at his table and we thought him alone until a figure ghosted from the shadows.

"This is Captain Iago of the *'Santissima Trinidad'*. He offers you berths on his ship."

The slight figure said not a word. He was thin featured with a scar running down his cheek. Half of his hair was white. I hoped and believed that Captain Pedro had explained the situation well, but I had to be sure.

"You know that if you help us that you may well be making an enemy of Hernán Cortés?"

He smiled and I saw that he had lost half of his teeth, "He is my enemy already although he does not know it." He leaned forward, "The man is a snake and not to be trusted. He cheated my brother out of the family fortune when he lived in Spain and then fled west where he used my brother's money to gain power and to ingratiate himself into the good offices of those sent here by King Carlos to manage this land. My brother died as a result of the treachery of Hernán Cortés. I have been seeking a way to get back at him and whilst this will not completely fulfil my need for vengeance, it is a good start which costs me nothing."

I looked at the other two who shrugged and nodded. The motives of Captain Iago were not important. It was his offer which was.

"Besides, he may not know that I actively helped you. I sail on the afternoon tide, tomorrow. It will be just before sunset and few other ships will sail at that time. Captain Pedro assures me that the last of the gun and powder will be emptied by the early afternoon. I will be giving my crew their last opportunity to enjoy wine and women and I shall be alone on my ship. They have until the middle of the afternoon to enjoy themselves and enjoy themselves they will. You will take a boat and board from the seaward side. No one will see you as you board. You will secrete yourself below decks until I send for you and then you can appear as stowaways. I shall, of course, feign anger and, instead of sailing directly to Spain will land in Santiago where I will take you personally to the Governor. That you will be well received by Don Diego will not be known by my crew."

It was a good plan, "And you will do this out of a need for revenge?"

"My brother died years ago. My anger was hot and now it is cold, and I have realised that as much as I want the man dead, I cannot do that. Instead, I have made it my business to do all that I can to hurt Hernán Cortés and I will hurt him with a thousand cuts. I brought the army sent to destroy him. They failed but now I have another chance to hurt him. I have heard of you, Englishman. You are the boy with the mind of an ancient warrior. The de Alvarado brothers hold you in high esteem and Hernán Cortés thinks you are his lucky charm. Taking away his lucky charm gives me satisfaction!" He stood, "And while you are aboard you can give pointers about gunnery to my gunner." He smiled, "Of course you will be ordered to do so by me as payment for your illegal passage!"

We clasped hands and he parted. None would think anything was amiss for the two captains were friends. Under cover of darkness, we slipped back to our home and brought all that we could manage back to the ship. We hid it on Captain Pedro's ship and then headed back to our home to sleep.

We were almost found out for Captain Gonzalo met us as we neared our home, "You three work too hard! The others have enjoyed their evening meal and yet you are still toiling. The Captain-General is lucky to have three such hard-working gunners. Come with me and let me buy you wine."

We could not refuse, and we went with him to his much larger home which he shared with his brothers. It was not a relaxed night as I was afraid that one of us would say something which might alert the very clever brothers. We had to talk as though we planned to be on the expedition and were excited about it when, in fact, we were about to desert. It was with some relief that the night ended and with a knotted stomach I fell into my bed hoping that this would be the last time I slept in the land of Mexico.

As the last gun was finally hauled aboard the carts and the slaves and soldiers headed back to the artillery park I shouted, "We will see if there is any powder left aboard any of the ships. We will follow later."

The officer in charge waved and we went, not below decks but the seaward side where our bags and weapons, looking as though they had been discarded, awaited us. Captain Pedro had a small dinghy tied up there with his first mate at the helm. We clasped hands with Captain Pedro. There were few words for we had said all that we had to say the night before. "I will see you, Englishman, when I dock in Isla Juana. I will take you east if you wish."

I nodded and clambered over the side. Jose and I took the oars and we rowed to the *'Santissima Trinidad'*. It looked like a ghost ship. Three ropes hung over the seaward side then we grasped them and began to climb. The first mate said, "Go with God and may you remain lucky!" He tied the bags to the three ropes, and we hauled them aboard as the dinghy sailed away.

Captain Iago had deck cargo which hid us from any prying eyes along the quayside and he had the hatch to the hold already open. There was no sign of him, and I guessed that he would be in full view of the quay to remove any hint of collusion in our escape. Leaving the hatch open to give us light we scurried like mice down the ladder into the Stygian darkness of the hold. There were crates and boxes as well as sacks. The Captain had described the lay out but, in the darkness, it was hard to move carrying, as we were, helmets, bags and food. We had to move crouched as the hold was not high enough for us to stand. It was when I found the wall of sacks containing maize and the aromatic vanilla pods, that I knew where we were. There was a wall of them and a void behind. We sank down as Captain Iago, at least I guessed it was him, closed the hatch and we were plunged into darkness.

We spoke but it was out of nervousness. Once we heard the tramp of the feet of the crew as they returned then we would have to stay silent. "I do not like the dark."

"Jose, my son, fear not. Once dawn comes then Captain Iago will discover us, and we shall see daylight."

With panic in his voice, Jose said, "What if we need to make water?"

I was arranging my gear to make a bed and my hand found a pot, "I think that Captain Iago has thought of that." My eyes had grown used to the dark and I could see the shapes of my companions. I handed the clay pot to Jose. "View this as a chamber without a light. We go to sleep and, when we wake, as your father says, we shall be hauled before the captain and have to endure a tongue lashing."

"What if this is a plot to kill us?"

I laughed, "The one thing we know is that it is not a plot. What Captain Iago is doing would not please the Captain-General. I believed his story and we will reach Isla Juana. What happens then, Jose, is in the hands of God and Governor Velázquez. Do not forget we were part of the army that disobeyed him. We may be punished. That is the only part of the plan with which I am unhappy, but Captain Iago seems to be confident. Let us trust him."

"Tomas is right, now make your water and then sleep. I shall dream well for come what may soon I shall see your mother again and that makes me happy. When the Aztec club laid me low and I fell I dreamt that I would die and never see her. I am content!"

I had made water before we left Captain Pedro's ship and after taking off my brigandine and boots, I laid down, the motion of the ship at anchor rocking me to sleep. I had barely dropped off when a hand roused me. I could hear, not the feet of seamen but shouts which sounded angry. I did not speak but my hand went to my dagger. It was just a reaction. I was no longer the naïve Devon boy who had left Falmouth with his father. I looked for danger around every corner. Suddenly the hatch was pulled open, light flooded in, and I heard Captain Iago's voice, "Look down there if you will but all that you will see is the cargo intended for Cadiz!"

The next voice I heard was Captain Gonzalo's, "The Captain-General believes that three of his men are trying to desert. The English and his two friends failed to return to their guns! I will search. Hand me a candle."

I heard a laugh from Captain Iago, "And if I do then the rest of the crew and I will leave you Captain Gonzalo for there is also powder down there."

"I could have the hold emptied, Captain Iago!"

"Aye, and I would miss the tide but at this late hour, I am not sure that there are slaves ready to do the work. They are all in their slave pens. Look, Captain Gonzalo, if we do not leave in the next hour then we miss the tide. Look all you like but be quick."

I heard footsteps descending the wooden ladder. Our little den was close to the bows at the far end of the hold. I heard the boots of the soldier as he came down. Then I heard a crack and a curse. The height of the hold had deceived Captain Gonzalo. He was just on the other side of the bags of maize and vanilla. I could smell his sweat. All he had to do was take another few steps and he would see us. I heard him hiss, "If the three rats are aboard this ship then I pray they never return to Vera Cruz. All debts are paid!"

When I heard his feet on the ladder and then darkness fell as the hatch was closed, I knew that we were safe. He had known we were there. Just as I had smelled him, so he had smelled us. He had paid the debt to me even though I had not asked it. I said a silent prayer to God as I heard the order given to cast off. When the motion of the ship became more noticeable then I knew we were at sea and I laid down to sleep once more. I knew that the other two would be as anxious as I was to speak but this was not the time. Captain Iago's plan had nearly unravelled, but luck had been on our side.

Deserter

Chapter 17

Captain Iago sent men to find us as soon as dawn broke. The dark became light as the hatch was opened and we heard Captain Iago's voice, "Check that the sacks of vanilla pods have not shifted."

Two men came down and we feigned shock as we were discovered. "Captain, we have found the three stowaways the Captain-General sought!"

"What! Bring them to me!" The captain had missed his calling. He could have been an actor!

We were hauled up on deck. We left our swords and gear in the hold as the captain had advised us.

I dropped to my knees, "Mercy, Captain!"

Had I not known that it was an act then I might have been terrified. "Mercy? You are stowaways and, who knows, traitors to the crown! I would be well within my rights to have you thrown overboard!"

The reactions of his men were interesting. Some showed glee at the thought of three men being hurled into a shark-infested sea while others looked pained.

"Death is too good for you! You will work your passage and then I will take you, myself, to the Governor of Isla Juana. You are gunners?"

We looked suitably terrified and nodded.

"Then you can train my gunners and work the new guns I have just acquired. The treasure from the west invites pirates from everywhere."

"Thank you, Captain! God will reward your mercy!"

He snorted, "Let us see if you think it is mercy for when you have done training my gunners you will clean my decks. The voyage east may only take a week, but it will feel more like a month to you!"

The ship had four guns and no gunners. It seemed that different men worked the guns when they went into action. They were falconets and, as such, easy to fire. The captain allocated four men for us to teach and we spent the day showing them how to use wedges to adjust the angle of fire and the correct amount of powder. The correct amount of powder was half a pound but no gunner worth his salt actually used scales. In battle, there was no time, and we used our eyes. We all used the same method. Our hands were good scales and one of my handfuls was, give or take a gram or two, half a pound. We used some of the deck salt for them to get used to the measurement. We then showed them how to load the balls although the captain was using round stones collected from beaches. They would never be as accurate as a cast ball, but they were cheap.

The captain fed us, twice, and we were told that we would be locked in the hold. If this had been real imprisonment, then we would have viewed it as a joke for where could we go?

We were halfway through the morning and had just loaded the four guns for a practice fire when the lookout spotted the sail to the east. Had the sail been from the west then there might not have been a cause for concern, but the east made it more likely to be a pirate and Captain Iago acted accordingly, "Arm yourselves. You stowaways have the chance to earn my good favour. If these are pirates, then we will have to fight! I hope that you are ready!"

The three of us supervised the loading of the stones and we chose the ones which offered the best fit. There had to be windage, a gap between the ball and the barrel, but not too much. I chose Juan who had seemed the most interested of our apprentices to hold the linstock of the fourth gun. It was on the larboard side and with the wind, the way it was the captain would, in all likelihood, turn so that the two starboard falconets would fire.

The guns loaded and aimed, I walked back to the stern. I was playing the stowaway trying to impress the captain, "Guns are loaded and ready, captain. I just await your command if it is a pirate."

Captain Iago said, almost casually, "She is a pirate; a Portugee. Captain Pedro told me of her. She shied away when she saw he had company, but she will see us as a goose to be plucked. Save us, stowaway gunner and we shall see if that gives you an easier life aboard this ship." He gave me a wink as I turned.

Fernando and Jose had not as much experience of using cannons at sea as I did. When I reached the bows I said, "She will try to sink us and will attempt to dismast us before closing with us." We had few bags of grapeshot and I wanted them as a last resort. "We fire the stones, but we use the water to help us."

"Water?"

I smiled at Jose, "You remember skimming stones as a boy?" He nodded. "It is the same principal. If we fire on the up roll then we might hit their mast or sails but if we fire when we are just beginning the down roll then the stone will skim across the water and, with luck, hit her below the waterline." I pointed to the barrel of stones we had to use. "We have forty stones. If we waste a couple firing at long range it will not hurt us. Let us try."

I knew that as the pirate had the wind, he could choose his moment to pounce and I also knew that he would have far more men on his ship. I could not see any cannons but that did not mean that he was unarmed. Like '*The Falcon*' they could be disguised. I had lived the life of a pirate.

I guessed the range, which was closing, was about half a mile. "Fernando, let us try. Take your time and learn from the first ball!"

The pirate had obligingly turned a little to take his ship around our stern. I waited until our ship had begun its descent and then fired. Fernando's gun fired a moment later. Even while the falconet was being sponged out I stared at the two balls. Fernando's had been fired just a little too late and crashed into a wave. Mine did hit but it was a glancing blow along the side. It did have an effect for the pirate turned away a little. I would fire the next ball when we were almost horizontal to the horizon.

"Fernando, I will say, 'now' when I intend to fire."

"Aye, Captain. You make this look easy, yet it is not."

The ball loaded I waited for a shorter time before I shouted, "Now!" and touched the linstock. The two falconets had barely a heartbeat between their cracks. I watched and saw that my ball struck just below the waterline while Fernando's made a spectacular crack halfway up the side of the pirate. The difference was the heartbeat and the fact that his gun was ten feet further away from the target.

"I think I have it now, Captain!"

Our two shots made the pirate change his plans and he turned to come directly at our starboard side. It meant we had a smaller target, but he would have to approach more slowly and when he did turn, we would be able to fire two guns at a side packed with men. This time I fired on the uproll. I intended to use the length of the pirate to cause as much damage and death as I could. My ball was true; it was the last of the perfectly round stones. It landed just behind the figurehead. I did not see but I assumed that it would bounce down the ship. I saw the foresail flapping and knew that I had hit a stay along the way. Fernando's ball, fired on the down roll, hit just below the figurehead. The pirate was now less than a quarter of a mile away.

"Jose, turn your gun and see if you can hit him. Even if you cannot it may make him worried."

"I have been watching you too. Let us see what I can do." He had his men turn and drag the falconet to the same side as us.

"Juan bring your gun too!"

Our disparate approaches meant that the pirate had no idea what each bang and flash entailed. The next falls from Fernando's and my gun hit the bow above the waterline but one of those fired by Jose and Juan hit the gunwale and I knew that men would have been hurt, perhaps even killed by the flying splinters of wood. I do not know if the helmsman was hurt but suddenly the pirate lurched to larboard and presented, at a range of three hundred paces, his starboard side. The three of us were all experienced enough to know that you took any chance presented to you. Our three guns fired almost as one and Juan's was but a little way behind. One ball hit the foremast while the other three hit the hull and the gunwale. The foremast fell and the sail hung in the water acting as a sea anchor. It pulled the pirate around and Captain Iago, seeing his chance headed as far away from the pirate as fast as he could go. The wind was now treating us equally but the damage to his mast, hull and sail meant that he would be slower. We had bloodied his nose and he would be wary now of attacking a ship with guns.

The men working the guns crowded around us and bombarded us with questions about what we did and how we did it. I realised then that my father had given me an apprenticeship when he had taken me aboard *'The Falcon'* and it had been as rich a gift as any chest of gold and jewels. We were no longer regarded as stowaways and were treated equally for the rest of the voyage. Captain Iago kept his distance, and I knew why. Our little charade had to be played out to the end so that he could take us to the Governor and in doing so he would show that he was innocent of any complicity in our escape. We saw no more pirates and the other ships we saw were in convoy taking men and guns to Cortés. Captain Iago informed them about the Portuguese pirate for there was a brotherhood of the sea.

Santiago hove into view at noon a day after we had spoken to the last convoy heading west. As we tied up at the quayside I heard some of the crew imploring the captain to let us remain on board. It was touching. Captain Iago played the hard man and refused to countenance their request. He did relent when he told them that he would speak to the Governor on our behalf.

As we headed up to the Governor's residence he spoke warmly of the fight, "Had I been able then I would have kept you aboard for you handled yourselves well. The guns were not cheap, and I thought to save money by not hiring gunners. I see now that it was a mistake."

"Juan learned much when he worked with us," I told the captain, "and the men are keen to fire their guns again in anger. It will take the gunners time to become as good as we are but, as you saw, you have good guns which can keep a pirate at bay."

"Aye, well, when I return, I will call here and see if any of you tire of a life in Isla Juana."

We were left in an anteroom while Captain Iago spoke to the governor. Nerves took over as we waited for I wondered if this was a mistake and the Governor would punish us for being part of the expedition which disobeyed him. It was too late to do anything about it for Captain Iago was in the room for the briefest of times. He came out and clasped our arms, "Thank you for saving my ship. I will be back in four months! I will look for you then."

"Come!" The Governor's voice boomed. It had been a couple of years since I had seen him, and he had aged. His face suggested that we were in trouble. "So, Englishman, once more you are brought before me. It seems that you are always at the heart of my problems."

I had nothing to say in my defence, but I was gratified that I was bearing the brunt of his attack.

"Captain Iago told me of your action in saving his ship and for that, I too, am grateful although as you were a pirate yourself then it is understandable that you know how to defeat them. There still remains the problem of your disobeying of my orders." He looked at me and seemed to be willing me to find an answer.

"Governor Velázquez, you hired us as gunners, and we served you, but our commander was Hernán Cortés. Had we disobeyed his orders we could have been executed. When the army you sent was defeated then the survivors all happily joined his men. If you were to punish all who followed Hernán Cortés, then you would need to build a gaol the size of Santiago to house them."

That elicited a smile from him. "You make a good case. Are you a lawyer too?"

"No, Governor, but the words were easy to find for they were the truth."

He nodded, "And tell me, is the land of the Aztecs as rich as I hear?"

We all nodded, and Fernando said, "Richer, Governor, for when we fought them, we found that even the meanest warrior wore precious metals about them as though they had just picked them from the ground."

"And will this man who abandoned my sister-in-law, take the Aztec Empire?"

There was a pause and I nodded, "He will for he has good leaders, and the man knows how to win."

The Governor's shoulders slumped for he knew that I spoke the truth and with an Empire at his command then King Carlos would make Cortés Governor of Mexico. "All your misdemeanours are forgiven, and I pardon all of you of any crimes you may have committed." With a wave of his hand, we were dismissed.

As we headed out Jose said, "What crimes?"

I shrugged, "I was a pirate, but I had been pardoned already. Perhaps he meant joining the army of Hernán Cortés. It was just a man who realises he has lost giving himself a small victory." I put my arm around Fernando, "Come let us find Maria and then I can seek a room."

Fernando laughed, "No, my friend, you shall stay with me. You stayed with me when I was wounded, and I owe you more than I can say. Let us find the priest."

Father Rodrigo had promised to look after Maria when she arrived. When we had left his wooden church had been built to the height of a man. Now it towered over the nearby buildings. He was holding a service when we arrived, and we stood at the back while he finished. The cool interior of the church was a good place to contemplate our futures and we each stood silently. I knew not what the others were thinking but I was working out how long it would be before Captain Pedro docked and he could make good on his promise to take me back to Cadiz. Cadiz was not England but the voyage from their home was short enough that I could contemplate success.

The service over Fernando approached the priest. The smiles from both told Jose and me that all was well. Fernando had left money with the priest but that had been a couple of years earlier. Maria had children to care for and the gold Fernando had left would be long gone.

"She lives just on the outskirts of Santiago and she is a seamstress! She was always resourceful and with this gold," he patted his chest, "we can buy a small farm! Come." He turned to Jose, "Your mother will be pleased to see you, but she will not be happy that you will be leaving soon."

Jose smiled, "I have seen a new life and you have given me skills." He nodded to me, "You both have. If I were to stay here, then those skills would be wasted."

His father nodded, "I know that but... come this is idle speculation and I am anxious to see Maria and my children."

The reunion was magical. Maria was a beautiful woman and her love for Fernando was clear. Tears flowed and I stood back feeling like an intruder. His daughters and other son had grown in his absence and Fernando kept shaking his head in amazement. I thought to slip away, quietly, and find an inn for I did not wish to be a spectre at the feast. It was Jose who must have realised what I planned as I edged towards the door, "And this, mother, is the man who saved us in Mexico, kept us safe and brought us home. This is Captain Tomas, the master gunner!"

All eyes swung to face me. Fernando said, "Aye, Maria, do not be fooled by his youth. We would not have this gold I bring home but for him."

She took my hands and kissed them, "Then you are doubly welcome in our home. It may be small and mean but while you are here it is yours."

Fernando took off his brigandine and slipped his satchel from his shoulders. We had worn them thus since our flight from Tenochtitlán. He emptied the contents onto the table. Gold, silver, rubies, and other precious jewels tumbled out. Jose and I had seen them before, but Fernando's wife and children were dumbstruck. Fernando said, "And tomorrow we buy some land and have a house which can accommodate us."

Jose grinned and took his satchel to open it. There was as much in his as his father's and he showed it to his mother, "And whatever else you need, I shall provide!"

The next week saw a whirlwind of activity from Fernando and his family. They went to speak to those who owned land and found a farm within a mile of Santiago. The owner had gone off to seek land in the isthmus and not returned. The price was reasonable, and the house had the potential to be enlarged. Fernando showed that he had learned from Mexico. He bought slaves and set to work immediately.

I was not needed, indeed, I was in the way for they tried to include me in everything. I took the opportunity to spend a tiny part of my riches. I bought good boots, clothes, a cloak, a fine hat with metal sewn around the edge and a new sword. This sword would be for show. I had a sword for war. I also went to the quay for the reunion of Fernando and Maria made me even more desperate to get home. Over the first days after our arrival, I made myself a regular visitor to the inns close by the quay. I was flattered that my name was known. The battles against the Aztecs and the other Indians had been recounted by those who had returned from the west and the young English gunner had been part of those stories. When a small carrack docked and said that Captain Pedro and his fleet were just a day away, I hurried to Fernando's new home.

"Captain Pedro will be here on the morrow. I know that he will not leave straight away but my time here is limited."

Jose nodded, "And I will be leaving too, mother, I seek a life as a gunner."

Maria burst into tears and hugged him, "But I have seen so little of you! Can you not wait a while?"

Fernando put his arms around them both, "Maria, Jose needs to do this. He has the skill and he will return. God did not save us from the savage Aztecs for him to die easily. He will come back to us and when he marries, we shall have grandchildren."

Maria could not simply allow the two of us to leave without a feast and it was too late to gather all that she needed that day and so it was planned for the next one. Jose and I had little to do with the preparation as we waited, at first light, by the quay, watching for Captain Pedro's small fleet to appear. The sails were not seen until noon. The two of us were both dressed in smart new clothes. We had shaved and had our hair cut. We looked like young nobles rather than the gunners who had trudged into Vera Cruz in rags. I doubted that any would recognise us unless they knew us well. Captain Pedro would know us,

"So, Jose, you still plan on joining the Spanish army?"

He shrugged, "I do not mind. If there are opportunities aboard a ship, then I will take that." He gave me an embarrassed look, "Tomas, I am grateful for all that you have taught me but I need to command men. If Captain Pedro will allow it, I would serve on a different ship from you. I need to learn how to command and if you were there then I would be looking over my shoulder each time I gave a command."

I smiled, "I understand, Jose. I did not learn to command until my father and the other gunners who taught me died. I will miss you, but I understand, and I know that you will be a good gunner. If you were to join the Spanish army then I could see you rising high in its ranks!"

He looked relieved, "I wish I had spoken earlier for I worried how to tell you."

"If there is one thing that I have learned it is to speak rather than hiding your words. There are times I should have spoken but did not. My father might be alive now if I had said that we had gathered enough gold." I waved a hand at my new clothes, "I have more than enough for a comfortable life in England. It will not be a rich life and I will have to work but that is good for a man. A life of indolence seems to me to be a sin."

We watched, as the sails appeared, for them to draw closer. The winds, it seemed, were against us and it took an age for them to tack and then enter the harbour. Eager as we were, we knew that Captain Pedro would have much to do and we waited and watched from the land while he spoke to the port officials and the cargo intended for Santiago was unloaded. We saw the cargo waiting to be loaded. When he sailed, it would be with a full hold. The lateness of the hour meant that it was unlikely he would be able to sail until the same time the next day when the tide was right. He had seen us waiting and, as the last of the Santiago bound cargo was unloaded, he waved us aboard.

Once again, we were taken to his cabin although this time there was no first mate to keep out any curious crew. They were all too busy cleaning out the hold ready to load the cargo. Captain Pedro smiled, "When you hid you roused a wasp's nest alright. I had my ships examined from top to bottom by two of the de Alvarado brothers. When Captain Gonzalo went to Iago's ship, I felt sure you were doomed. How did you evade capture?"

I had thought about this a great deal on the voyage to Isla Juana, "I think Captain Gonzalo knew we were there. We stank and even the smell of vanilla pods could not disguise that. I believe he let us go out of a sense of honour. I had saved him and his brother once, and perhaps he thought he owed us."

He nodded, "The Captain-General is now marching west. The new men who are arriving daily are being ordered to follow him. He does not want to give the Aztecs the opportunity to regroup." He put his hands flat on his table, "That is the past. Now, what about your future? Do you stay here, or will you come with me as gunners on my ships?"

Jose spoke and it showed his newfound confidence, "We would sail with you, Captain Pedro, but I would like a different ship to Tomas for I wish to learn to lead."

The Captain frowned, "There is no ill-feeling?"

I shook my head, "Far from it but Jose is right. My aim is to sail with you to Cadiz and then make my way back to England, but Jose sees this as his future."

He looked relieved, "Good, then you have but one night ashore. We leave on the morrow on the noontide. Tomas, you shall sail with me on my ship, *'The Golden Hawk'* and you, Jose, on Captain Philip's ship, *'The Silver Swan'*." He smiled, "I like birds and they bring us luck; all but the albatross that is. It is a bird of ill-omen!"

That night was a mixture of joy as well as sadness. We ate well and drank to excess. We laughed and we sang but we also knew that two of us were leaving to sail across the world and as we had all made the journey west, we knew of its perils. Maria and Fernando in particular showed their fears as Maria kept touching Jose's hand or squeezing Fernando's arm. I felt honoured to be part of this family. I had none left. There was nothing for me in England save England itself but I was English and I felt that I had to sail back if only because that had been the plan of my father and me.

When we rose with thick heads and furred tongues neither Jose nor I knew if we would ever spend another night in this new world. We were returning to an old world which looked, smelled and felt so different. Would we still find it as attractive as we thought? I dressed in sea clothes. My good boots and fine clothes were in my sea bags. My satchel of treasure was also within the bag. I wore a pair of serviceable sandals upon my feet, an old hat to keep off the sun and a simple seaman's shift that went to below my waist. My sword belt, sword and dagger completed my garb.

We said our farewells at the house for partings at the quayside would be in public view and we needed privacy. I spoke to Fernando first and I clasped his arm. "Have a good life, Tomas. You are the only Englishman I know, and I would like you to be a happy one. You will find another woman." He tapped his heart, "I know it here."

I left and waited outside so that Jose could have privacy with his family. This was the first time he had mentioned Katerina's death and although I had not forgotten her, I had put her safely in the back of my mind. I visited her at night, and she haunted my dreams but during the day I worked hard not to think of her for it hurt. When Jose joined me his eyes showed that he had wept and that I understood. I felt like weeping at that moment. I had not been given the chance to say farewell to my father and it still hurt.

I put my arm around his shoulders and said, "A new start for both of us. let us begin with a bold foot and a smile, eh?"

He nodded and we headed for the sea.

Chapter 18

Any maudlin thoughts I might have harboured were dispelled as soon as I boarded the ship for I had much to do. I was allocated space by the bow castle where I placed my bag and my sword belt. I would not need a weapon until there was danger. It was not a cabin I occupied but a void beneath the bow castle where Captain Pedro would place his two crossbowmen if we were attacked. There was a hammock there, but it was not yet tied to the two stanchions. Although open I saw that I could fix my cloak across the opening to give me privacy and to keep me from the worst of the weather. I took out my cloak and made my nest secure before I went to look at the guns.

The captain had spent much of his money on guns and he had four. There were two falcons, and they were on the opposite side of the vessel, midships close to the mainmast. By the sterncastle, he had two esmerils. The smaller bore guns fired a shot even smaller than the falconet, just half a pound and the extreme range of the deck gun was only seven hundred and fifty paces. I knew why he had them. They were easy and quick to fire and firing bags of balls could protect the sterncastle; they also had the height of the high sterncastle which would give them slightly more range. It gave me a problem for I could not be at both places at the same time. I knew that I would be the only gunner and that I would have men allocated to me to be used in battle. These would not be the specialist seamen; the officers, topmen, helmsmen, and the like. They would be the labourers of the sea, the jacks of all trades who could do a little of everything. The two ship's boys whom I saw racing around the deck carrying orders would be two of the ones I would be able to use. The captain would be too busy to deal with my problems until we were at sea and so I checked the four guns. They were new and, as far as I could tell, had not been fired. The lack of soot and carbon told me that. Once at sea I would remedy that. I then sought the powder and ball. I did not ask for help. The crew were busy and besides this would give me the opportunity to explore the ship.

'*The Golden Hawk*' was bigger than the '*Falcon*' had been. The hold was divided up into sections. It meant that even if a cargo shifted during a voyage it would not unduly affect the handling of the ship. I would have expected nothing less from such a captain. The powder and shot were kept by the bows and that made sense. It was as far away from anything which could ignite it and, so far as I was aware, there were just half a dozen of us whose accommodation was at the bows. The others were crammed into the bow castle above my head. I searched and found some sacks. I spent the time until we sailed making up bags of powder that could be carried easily on deck and would minimise the risk of leaving a powder trail. When I heard the call to prepare to leave the harbour, I piled the bags together and headed to the deck.

Captain Pedro waved me over. He was by the helm with his helmsman, a squat barrel of a man whose feet were firmly planted wide apart. "Stand with me as we sail. Pepe here knows his business and he will not foul another ship!" There was a smile as he said it and Pepe rolled his eyes. The two knew each other well. I remembered the old man from the voyage west. "You are settled in?"

Nodding to my cloak covered nest I said, "Aye and I have examined the guns. They have not been fired."

"We had no need on the voyage west for pirates only attack when we return laden with riches. The Portugee we saw fled when he saw our numbers. It is why I am happy that I employed you and Jose. If we find danger, then the '*Hawk*' and the '*Swan*' will protect my other two chicks."

The other ships were smaller carracks and, so far as I could tell only had two esmerils for defence.

"And are we likely to need our guns?"

"I hope that our numbers will deter any pirates but if they think we have treasure aboard then they might collaborate to take it from us."

There was something in his voice that suggested we had such treasure, "And we have gold aboard?"

He nodded, "The Governor has collected taxes to send back to the king. Your friend's success in Mexico has made the Governor fear for his position. The gold was brought aboard the '*Hawk*' and the '*Swan*' last night under cover of darkness, but such information can be bought." He patted the gunwale, "These are good ships, but they are not swift. There are many small boats which could outrun us. The islands which guard the eastern side of this sea afford many places where pirates could gather."

I nodded for I remembered well the discussions we had on '*Falcon*' when we first spied the islands.

"Captain?" The first mate appeared.

"Aye, give the order to cast off! We leave the land and the next time we step ashore it shall be on Spanish soil!"

"Cast off! Loose topsails."

People had gathered at the quay. Some had been there to load and to earn a few coins. Others were there because the ships were a connection to Spain. There was a ragged cheer as the sails began to fill and Pepe took us to sea on a tide that was already tugging us from the shore. Captain Pedro looked up at the sail and nodded when he saw the gap to the quay widening. Then he turned his attention to the rest of his fleet and only when they were in a line astern did he speak again.

"Once we have sea room, I will send you your gunners. The men are all chosen by me. I am not giving you the dregs of the mess. Be patient with them and you may test fire. I suspect young Jose will wish to do the same."

I looked astern at the next ship. I had almost forgotten Jose! He would have the same problems as I had but would he know how to deal with them?

"I will see the men by the starboard falcon."

The first thing I had to do was to fetch the powder and stone from the hold. Although the captain had bought iron balls he had also laid in a supply of stones. I knew that I could also descend below the hold and take some from the ballast which lay there. I took just two of each of the stones. That done I performed the most dangerous part of firing a gun at sea, I lit the linstock. The men would still be busy with other duties and so I waited and checked that I had wedges close to hand. I dragged a pail through the sea and found the swabbers. In a perfect world, we would use fresh water, but a ship needed water for the crew. We would have to fill a pot with urine and use that but for this exercise, I needed something closer to hand. The salt in the seawater could cause corrosion. Finally, I tied the cloth around my ears and then donned my hat again. I watched the sea begin to change colour as we left the land and headed into slightly deeper waters. Here we were still protected from the worst of the huge sea that separated our home from the new world and the waves were gentler than we might expect further east.

When Isla Juana became a smudge on the horizon the first mate shouted, "Gun crews to the master gunner!"

Eight men and the two boys came towards me. I had to trust in the captain. He knew the importance of what we did and the crews, I hoped, would do all that I asked of them. They gathered around me. "My name is Gun Captain Thomas. I fought against the Aztecs and the Indians of the South Sea. I know my business and, when I have taught you, then you, too, will begin your journey to becoming gunners." I pointed to the two ship's boys, "You two will be assigned to the falcons!" I patted the barrel. "What are your names?"

"Carlos."

"Stephano."

"Your task when we are to fire the guns will be to go below decks and fetch the powder and ball." I held up two examples. "I have fetched these already and I have the other things we shall need. These guns have never been fired. Today, we shall visit each one and fire it. You will have an easy afternoon for I will do all that you need to do. You will watch and learn. Tomorrow, when the captain allows, we will let you fire the guns!" I could see that they were excited. I spoke calmly and patiently to them. I showed them how to clean out the barrel with the swabber and water. The fact that we had not fired the guns yet was irrelevant. This was a vital task. I went to the centre of the deck where I had placed the bags of powder. I held the hessian bags in two hands to show them the weight. "I will always weigh out the bags of powder. That is a precise measurement." Once the powder was in place, I chose the roundest stone I could. It rolled down the angled barrel, but I still used the swabber as a rammer. "We are now ready to fire. I have put the wedges in so that the ball will arc. It may well bounce for that is a technique we use when firing at other ships. We are now ready to fire. Stand away from the falcon for it will move backwards and sparks could fly." I had deliberately not told them to do as I had done and tie a cloth about their ears. It was better that they experience it once and then they would know the reason I did as I did. I was as interested as any for this was a new gun. I said a gunner's prayer that the barrel was well made and would not explode. If it did then that would be my last thought. Standing away from the gun I put the linstock to the touch hole. There was a spark, a flash and then a boom as a cloud of thick, stinking smoke enveloped the side of the ship. Some of the men recoiled at the sound and the assault on their senses by the smoke. I concentrated on the flight of the stone. The barrel seemed true and the ball skipped across the water. I was satisfied.

I led them to the second falconet and I went through the procedure again. When I was ready, I said, "Some gunners tie a cloth about their ears. I am one such!"

Those who had a piece of cloth to hand emulated me and I knew the others would seek to find protection for their ears. This time the men did not recoil so much for most had stood further away. The larboard falconet was as good as the starboard and I led my gunners back towards the esmerils. The afternoon was wearing on and I doubted that they would get a chance to actually fire the guns themselves. However, the esmerils were so small, little bigger, in fact than an old harquebus, and so simple to fire that, even though the sun was lowering to the horizon I took them back to the larboard falconet. As I did, I heard Jose firing his guns. As much as I wished to watch him, I had a job to do aboard this ship.

"Who wishes to fire the gun?"

This was a test and only two men raised their hands: Paulo and Guido. Both were Italians who came from the land around Nissa. While I sent the ship's boys for more powder and stone, I chose Paulo to be the gunner who fired the gun first. "When we are in action then each of you will have a job to do. The gunner will load the powder, a second will load the ball. The gunner will aim and touch the linstock and then one of you will have a wettened swab to clean out the barrel. All will haul the gun back into position."

It was a beautiful sunset but as Paulo put the linstock to the touch hole we had a sunset of our own as the barrel belched flame and the stone ball, glowing with the heat, bounced away across the water. It was spectacular and I was pleased that I had tried it for the ones who were my men cheered and clapped each other, and especially Paulo on the back.

I roared, "Clean out the barrel and use the ropes to secure the gun." They were silenced, "You did well and tomorrow, Guido, we will let you fire the starboard falconet and then the two of you can fire the esmerils. That will be all the practice that you will be given. Now make water in the pot for from now on we use that to swab out the barrel and not seawater which will make the barrel rust!"

When they had finished doing as I asked, I waited until their buzz had moved down the ship. The captain had reefed sails while we had been firing and I was alone at the bows. I stroked the barrel of the larboard falconet, "I hope, father, that I will do as good a job with these men as you did with me."

A lonely seabird called from on high and I made the sign of the cross. Old sailors believed that the dead inhabited the bodies of birds. Until that moment I had doubted but now...

I went to the stern where the captain was giving his orders to the first mate who would have the next watch. A sailor was hanging a lighted lamp from the stern so that *'The Silver Swan'* would not run us down in the night.

"The guns looked and sounded good but were they, Master Gunner? Was my money invested wisely?"

"They are good guns and the men you have chosen are made of the right stuff."

"And they will fire them if we are attacked?"

I shook my head, "It is unlikely that both falcons will fire at the same time. They can load them but when and if we go into action then I will be the one to fire. The esmerils are a different matter. They are closer range weapons. Paulo and Guido will fire those." He nodded. "How is it that you have two Italians on your ship?"

"It is not unusual. Genoese and Nissan sailors are well respected. The two sought me out when I had my new ships built. I think they sought the treasures of the west. Many men are of the same mind. I have promised each man a share of our profits rather than pay." He looked at me, "You have not asked how much you were to be paid."

I shrugged, "I assumed I was working my passage. I need to get home."

He laughed, "And, of course, you have your bag of treasure."

I gave him and the first mate a sharp look. I had thought it a secret. He shook his head, "Fear not your treasure is safe here. There is a code amongst sailors and if any transgress that code they will be fed to the sharks. You could leave your gold in plain view and none would be tempted. Now when you step ashore…No, my friend, you shall share in the profits from this voyage too. It will not be the same share as me or my officers but more than the crew for you are a gunner. The amount will depend upon the price we receive when we dock. Who knows, it may be enough to tempt you to remain aboard, we shall see." Food was being carried from the sterncastle. The captain smiled as he explained, "We eat on deck when we can for the air is more wholesome. Eat well now for if we hit adverse winds when we leave the islands we may go on short rations."

I joined the men and found myself the centre of attention. It was not just the fact that I was a gunner but also because I had fought alongside the de Alvarado brothers and Hernán Cortés. They wanted to know all that had happened. When I told them of the priests and their macabre decorations it made some of them make the sign of the cross. I think the ones who contemplated leaving the sea to seek treasure on the land reconsidered at that point. This was something I could not have anticipated when I had been dragged aboard the first Spanish ship. Then I had been reviled and despised; here it was the opposite.

The next morning was once more a pleasant one with wind moving us along sharply and the waves were not too big. A good day to try out my new gunners. Paulo and Guido proved to be good listeners and when I gave them the chance to fire the esmerils themselves they did all that I asked of them and I was satisfied. As I had expected the small stones did not travel far but it would give us two more teeth and might deter a pirate. I gathered them around me as I sat on the steps leading to the bow castle. "We have practice fired for the last time. We cannot afford to waste powder and shot. Each day we will practice when the captain allows, the act of loading and firing but we will not use powder, stone, or light the linstock." They nodded. To them, it was a diversion and a distraction from their normal routine, and they saw themselves as special which, indeed, they were. "Paulo and Guido, you two shall command the esmerils. They are short-range weapons and, if we have to fight, you will wait until I shout the command before you fire. I will fire the falcons. We will be very unlucky if we are attacked on both sides." I looked at the two ship's boys, "You two will be kept the busiest for there are four guns you will need to service. One task for all of us is to make bags of stones. I have collected the smaller stones from the ballast, and I have some sacks we can sew. The sailmaker has needles we can use. Paulo and Guido, you make smaller bags to fit the esmerils. Believe me, these bags of stones can save our ship. We do not fire them until an enemy is less than fifty paces from us. If a horde of pirates try to board us they will clear the decks."

Understanding why we did what we did was as important as knowing that they had to obey orders. Each day we spent an hour at practice and making bags of shot. We grew close and there was banter between them. That was always a good sign. The two Italians were competitive and were keen to outdo the other.

We had been protected on our leeward side by Hispaniola and the islands which were known, for obvious reasons, as the Leeward Islands. When we spied the cloud-topped island of Nuestra Señora de las Nieves then we knew we were about to leave the relatively benign waters of the Spanish Sea to strike the more unpredictable Atlantic Ocean. I joined the captain at the sterncastle as we passed the island which had no sign of Spanish dwellings upon it. There were just a few Arawak Indians living there.

"Well, Tomas, you and your gunners are ready?"

"Ready, Captain Pedro?"

"The time for practice is over. Your gunners will have to work hard from now on. The sea will become rougher and you alone will have to tend to your guns."

The sailmaker had fashioned covers for the guns, but I knew they would have to be checked each day and the ropes which secured the guns to the deck would need to be inspected.

I nodded and said, "And pirates?"

"They are not fools, and they know that the place to attack us is when we are close to the end of our voyage. Many ships are in a poor state by the time they pass the archipelago of the Azores and that is where they wait. Our small fleet is well-armed, but my fear is that we become separated. The two smaller ships have just crossbows for defence and would be easy for a pirate to take. I will take no chances and we shall keep in company all the way across even if it slows us. Better to arrive with some spoiled cargo than lose a ship! If I can I will take us well to the south or north of the islands. I do not want to make life easy for them."

Perhaps I had forgotten the voyage west on *'The Falcon'* or maybe it was not as bad as the one as we sailed east but we were barely two days beyond Nuestra Señora de las Nieves when we began to be battered by the Atlantic storms. Troughs appeared so deep that when we descended, I wondered if we would ever rise again and the waves we climbed appeared to be as mountains. I was called upon to help haul on ropes and to try to replace canvas torn and ripped. There were no passengers on this ship. The first storm lasted for two days and when it subsided, albeit briefly, the crew set about repairing the ship. It took a day for the other ships to rejoin us and we all looked as though some nautical giant had shredded masts and sails. Two of our ships were relatively new but you would not know it. As we began to head east again, we saw black clouds ominously gathering ahead of us and even more worrying, pieces of wreckage coming west. I tried to dry my clothes whilst there was little spray and no rain. Already I spied mildew forming on my cloak and boots.

We had respite for a day and a night and then the next storm brewed up from the southwest. Captain Pedro was worried for normally the storms, at this time of year, came from the west and had the saving grace that they made for a faster passage. These storms were more violent and slowed us. This second storm was worse than the first. When the foremast tumbled down I was lucky for I was at the base of the bow castle and the brunt of the damage was borne by the cabins above my cubby hole. None were hurt for all were working the ship, but we had to clear the mast and salvage as much of it as we could. When the storm abated and if we survived then we would have to jury rig it for the rest of the voyage. As Captain Pedro told me when he toiled with the rest of the crew to salvage as much of the rope and sail as we could, "This will delay our voyage back, Tomas!"

I shook my head, "Will we reach Cadiz?"

He nodded, "This is a well-made ship, and the damage is not disastrous, at least not yet!"

The savage storm lasted for three days and by the end of it, there was no dry part of the ship save the hold. The boatwright had done a good job and our cargo was safe. The crew were not so lucky. One of the crew had a broken arm while another had been swept overboard. His disappearance had been both silent and unseen. I could not imagine the death, floating around in a boiling black sea, totally alone and without hope.

There was no sign of any of the other ships but, as we saw blue sky the captain set to repairing the mast and replacing it. We would not be able to sail as well with a shortened foresail, but we would, at least, be able to sail. With lines out to catch fish and an anchor to hold us steady, we worked for two days to remast the ship. The second day saw an equally battered *'The Silver Swan'* appear. She had lost her bowsprit and the topmast from the mainmast. She hove to next to us and while the captains exchanged words at the sterncastle, I went to the bow castle to speak with Jose. I cupped my hands to make my voice heard.

"How goes it?"

"I think that Mexico has appeal, Captain Tomas, for there it is just the Aztecs who are trying to kill you! Here the sea and the weather do the job!"

I nodded, "Does it make you wish to return to the land? Do you still intend to join the Spanish army?"

"Aye, the men I have trained are good and I now know that I can be an officer. I am no sailor. And you?"

"It was terrifying, but I trusted to God and my father was a sailor. I am not sure. I still intend to return to England and buy land. We shall see."

I had little more time to speak to Jose as we still had much work to do repairing our ships. We had almost finished when the third ship, the tiny carabela, *'The Blackbird'* appeared on the horizon. She had just her mizzen mast that was whole and her mainmast was a mere stump. Men were sent aboard her to help with the repairs. The last ship in our fleet, *'The Grey Goose'*, never appeared. She must have perished in the storm. By the time we headed east, once more, the seas were becoming livelier but at least the storms had abated. We were almost at journey's end and even though a quarter of the vessels had been sunk Captain Pedro still had a valuable cargo he could sell.

As we neared the Azores, we saw that not all of our enemies were natural. A carrack led five smaller ships from the lee of the southernmost island. The captain had been right and the storms had meant he had been unable to avoid the islands. We were trapped. The pirates were waiting and like a shoal of sharks were gathering to take the wounded ships! My guns would be called into action!

Chapter 19

There was no beating to quarters for everyone knew that if each of us did not do our job then we would all die. I shouted as I ran to my nest for my sword, "Fetch powder and ball. Keep bringing it until I tell you to stop." The two boys hurtled through the hatch like a pair of rabbits down a burrow. "Paulo, Guido, man your guns. Load them and await my order."

"Aye, Captain!"

I turned and saw Captain Pedro point to the starboard side. I nodded my understanding. He would use the wind and allow us to fire at the carrack from that side of the ship. It flew no colours and for all I knew could be manned by Englishmen. I had promised myself when I first served Spain that I would not fire on a king's ship. Pirates were another matter. I could not count on these pirates being as merciful as One-Eyed Peter had been. Captain Pedro used his speaking trumpet to speak to *'The Silver Swan'* to give instructions for the other two ships. Like a small herd of deer attacked by wolves, we all had to act together for the pirates would try to pick out the weakest of us. This would be Jose's first real taste of a serious sea battle. The damaged carrack at the rear would have to sail as close to the stern of *'The Silver Swan'* as she could and trust in God!

I examined the ships. The carrack was the same size as we were, and the others were two-masted ships that had a tiny bow castle. They would have no guns but the carrack might; they would be armed with crossbows and if they were English, bows. She was the real danger although the smaller ships were nimble and could close with us and board us just as easily as the carrack. I planned on firing as soon as I could. The sea was calmer than it had been earlier and there was a chance that a bouncing ball might do some damage. The smaller pirate ships were close to the carrack, like dogs in a pack. As soon as the first ball was brought up, I examined it and put it to one side. The second was better. "Boys, choose the roundest balls!"

"Aye, Captain Tomas!"

I carefully loaded the powder and the ball. I nodded to Philippe who rammed it home. I adjusted the wedges and then looked at the pirates who had closed with us. We had the weather gauge, but we had to pass them, and we were slow ponderous milk cows. They were lithe terriers who could cut across our bows and attack from two sides. If they did that then we were finished. The pirate carrack was a big one and I wondered if she had guns. If she had then she would try to dismast us and pick us off by using sheer weight of numbers.

When the carrack was about fifteen hundred paces from us, I said, "Stand clear!" They all stood back, and I touched the linstock to the powder. Smoke filled the space before me. "Clean her out!" While the gun was swabbed, I peered to see the ball. It bounced along the waves and looked to be heading directly for the carrack. Of course at that range, the flame and the smoke would tell the pirate that we had fired, and any decent captain would turn his ship. He did so but the smaller boats emulated his turn. They were slightly behind him and the ships were echeloned like an arrow. My ball hit one boat. A waterspout rose and the boat rocked. That told me we had struck her below the waterline. A single hole can be temporarily repaired by the use of cork and cloth but that took time and before it could be completed the ship would take on water. The ship I had hit slowed and both our crew and the one behind cheered. It put heart into the men but I knew it would make the pirates change their tactics.

Sure enough, the pirates began to spread out in a longer line to catch us. It made it harder for me to fire a hopeful shot and catch, as I had done, a lucky hit. The time it took to do so allowed us to close a little more. I knew that the captain would choose his moment to turn to starboard and that would give us even more wind. He would have done so already if it was not for our damaged consort. I loaded the next ball and saw that the range was down to less than a thousand paces. There was a crack from behind us as Jose fired. He used common sense and instead of trying to bounce fired on the uproll. It was a riskier shot, but he was rewarded when his ball smashed into the gunwale of the pirate carrack. I saw then that the pirate had at least one gun. I fired another bouncing ball. I watched the ball strike the carrack just above the waterline. The angle meant that the ball did not penetrate the hull but bounced off. The carrack would have weakened timbers, but we would need to hit the same spot to see results.

"Stand by to come about!"

We ran to the larboard gun and I quickly loaded it. The move had taken us closer to the pirate but once the wind caught us it would take us further away until the pirates did the same and then they would have the wind too. As I adjusted the wedges I shouted, "Guido, fire as you bear!"

Guido had the larboard esmeril and he shouted, "Aye, Captain Tomas!"

Captain Pedro had taken the pirates by surprise and they were slow to turn, perhaps mindful of the dangers they had of a collision. The small, damaged ship was now four hundred paces astern of the nearest ship and, with luck would take no further part in the attack. I saw that the carrack was almost broadside onto me. I fired and saw, through the smoke, a double flash as he fired two cannons. Our crack was heavier and that told me that the pirate had falconets. They could still hurt us. As I watched my ball bounce and then strike the pirate carrack below the waterline, I heard the smaller cracks as his balls hit the sails and snapped a rope.

"Fix the rope!" A topman raced up the rigging to repair the rope for failure to do so might lose us way. The hole in the sail would not hurt us, yet.

The esmeril fired and it sounded more like a pop than a crack, but Guido had aimed well. He was higher than I was and there was little point in trying to bounce. He was at the extreme range of his weapons and he dropped a small ball into the middle of the deck. The effect could not be seen but a half-pound of metal striking a wooden deck would, at the very least, send splinters to scatter into faces, eyes, and limbs! Jose's next ball was aimed at one of the smaller pirates who was also broadside on. The effect was spectacular. It hit amidships and just above the waterline. The ship must not have been well maintained for even at a range of seven hundred paces I could see that the hole was larger than it should have been. The ship began to sink.

We now had a chance. There was a slightly damaged carrack and three smaller ships to fight us but soon they would be chasing us down and we would be left with just the esmerils with which to fight. I loaded again and fired, not at the carrack, which was bow on and therefore a small target but at one of the smaller ships which was still broadside on as it tacked. I bounced the ball and was overjoyed when my lucky shot struck the foremast and cut it in two. It fell and acted as a drag anchor to swing the boat around. Guido's esmeril and the one on Jose's ship fired at the ship which presented an inviting broadside. Both balls hit and I saw men falling overboard. We now had a more even fight, three ships against four.

The problem we now had was that our stricken chick, which had the least armament was closer to the pirates. I loaded both falcons and then ran back to the captain. He nodded as I approached, "I know what you are going to say, Tomas. We cannot let the pirates take *'Blackbird'*; I am taking in sail to slow us down." I saw that the crew were already racing up the rigging to reef the sails. "That way *'The Silver Swan'* and we will be able to protect the little one. We will sail a parallel course. Can you hurt the pirates again?"

I grinned and nodded to Guido, "Aye, for Guido has shown us that the esmerils have a bite. If we are close to *'The Silver Swan'* then four guns can fire at the leading pirate."

Guido asked, "Do you wish to take over now, Captain Tomas?"

I shook my head, "Why? For I have two gunners here who can do the job." The two Italians each grew a couple of feet at the compliment.

Captain Pedro shouted, "Tell Captain Philip to take in sail and let *'The Blackbird'* get ahead of us!" A seaman nodded and the captain turned to me, "If I get the chance, I will turn so that your bigger guns can bear

I hurried forrard for whilst there was no target for us at the moment, I knew that we might get a chance again.

I spoke to my gunners as soon as I reached them. "We are hurting them, but we must draw them on to our guns. We shall be alert and the first sight we have of an enemy we shall fire." I had the larboard falcon traversed so that it was pointing as close to astern as we could manage. There was no target but once the smaller ships tried to overtake us and board us then we would. I did not relish a fight on the deck. We would be seriously outnumbered and having killed some of the pirates they would be intent upon vengeance.

I heard the cracks as the esmerils opened fire. They would be too small and too high to sink any of the pirates, but they could weaken the ships and, perhaps, the pirates resolve. More importantly, they would ensure that the pirates were circumspect and wary when they approached. I was relieved when the battered little *'Blackbird'* edged ahead of us. The storm had almost sunk her and had the pirates caught her then she would have been an easy victim. Even if they caught us, she might escape and that gave me solace. It was as she hurried by that I realised the implications of her move. She was under restricted sail and was still faster than we were. It meant that the damaged pirate would be able to join the others and they could go faster than we! The odds would be in favour of the pirates once more.

It did not take long for the pirate to change their tactics. I spied the smaller two-masted pirate as she appeared from behind our stern. She was swift and using the wind to come abeam of us. I think they must have worked out our range for she was tantalisingly out of reach and was only beam on for a short time. The captain cleverly tacked and turned so that, as he raced to try to get ahead of us, I only had a good sight of his hull for a short time. When a second appeared I knew their plan. The two ships would get ahead of us. They knew that we could not fire at a target that lay directly ahead. I traversed the gun back to its original position. I would not waste a ball on a small target but once they were abeam of us, I would risk one. I would have to calculate when she would turn and so, as the two ships moved to get in the lead I counted in my head.

"I intend to fire a ball when the leading two-masted ship is abeam of us. As soon as I do I want the barrel swabbed. Boys, bring up the bags of shot. We shall need them." The two ship's boys raced to the hatch. As soon as I fired the pirates would turn and close the gap to us. Just as I had calculated their predicted turn so they would know how long it took for us to reload. I said to the other gunners, "Make sure you are armed. When they board us the guns will no longer be effective." The men I led had a variety of weapons, axes, swords, knives, and the like but two of them went to the mainmast and each took a boarding pike. It was a good weapon to keep a pirate, attempting to clamber aboard us, at bay.

The boys had returned when I decided to fire. The leading pirate was just a thousand yards from us and had sailed directly at us. I fired as the two-masted ship began to turn. I watched the ball bounce towards the ship. I had no way of knowing where it would hit and I prayed that it would strike. The second pirate was also turning and there was a chance that I might hit both. There was a great deal of luck in gunnery at sea. The shape of the ball, the charge used, the roll of the deck and rogue waves could all make a good shot miss or a poor shot strike home. I watched the ball bounce just fifty feet from the pirate. It did not strike the hull nor the sail but it smashed into the rail at the side. I saw one man hit by the ball and when I saw the mainmast shiver a little knew that the ball had hit it as its course was deflected. I prayed that it might be damaged.

Ahead of us *'The Blackbird'* was heading east as fast as it could manage and I heard Captain Pedro shout, "Full sail!" We had given our damaged consort a chance and now he was giving us one.

The two pirates abeam of us took evasive action and headed away but they were still on a parallel course and being that much smaller would not run the risk of our guns. They could afford to use their speed to get ahead of us. I knew that Jose and Captain Philip would have two ships doing the same on their side. The carrack would be waiting for one of us to break and then it could use its own guns. I wondered then about having a ship with at least one gun facing forward. Perhaps one could be mounted on the bow castle. Even as I was loading my falcon, I worked out that it would have to be a falconet. A falcon or anything bigger would be too heavy for the flimsy bow castle. I traversed my falcon for I wanted another shot at the damaged pirate. I would have one chance when she turned, ahead of us, to cut us off from our escape route. The extra sails were making us move faster and that would also make my job a little harder. It might come to a fight with a sword after all. I took comfort in the fact that no matter how many pirates there were, they could not be as terrifying as the Aztecs I had faced at Otumba!

The chance came when the two ships were just six hundred paces from us. I could have risked a shot at their sterns, but it was a tiny target compared with the whole hull and as they made their last turn to disappear behind our bows I fired. This time the bounce worked for me and the ball sailed up over the hole I had made in her gunwale and struck the already damaged mainmast. There was a crack we could hear from our ship and then the cross tree and upper section tumbled into the sea, dragging the sail down with it. The pirate that was following had to take evasive action, but the captain was skilful, and he disappeared behind the stationary and stricken ship. My men quickly swabbed out and I reloaded as quickly and carefully as I could. Our speed had brought us closer to the damaged ship whose sail acted as an anchor and held her as still as she was ever going to be. My next shot was at a range of five hundred paces which was, almost, point-blank range. I saw, through the smoke, the call strike the waterline. The waves and the water began to pour into the hole. Taking a bag of shot I reloaded the gun as the pirate sank deeper into the sea. We passed just three hundred and fifty paces from her and had I seen any sign that she was salvable I would have raked her with shot, but she was already beginning to turn turtle as the sail dragged her over. I counted at least twenty men clinging to her wreckage and that was a warning of the numbers on the other ships. If the two-masted ships had so many men then how many would be aboard the carrack?

The lookout shouted, "Ware ahead! The other pirate is sailing towards us." I looked up and saw that another of the two-masted ships had got ahead of us and was sailing directly at us. They knew that there were no guns in the bows. I saw that the ship had a figurehead. It looked to be a mermaid.

I heard the crack of crossbows as the men in the bow castle tried to hit the crew of the pirate. It was like throwing snowballs at a fire! I turned and saw Captain Pedro point to larboard. I nodded and said, "The other gun!" I grabbed a sack of shot and ran to the starboard gun as the captain began his turn. I saw then that *'The Silver Swan'* was mirroring our turn and heading to starboard and beyond her, I saw the sails of the last two two-masted pirates closing with Jose's ship. When I heard the crack from behind us, I knew that the pirate carrack had also turned to bring his gun to bear and another hole appeared in our sail, this time the mizzen.

The mermaid pirate, who was sailing towards us, was presenting a target as he tacked towards us, moving slowly as he headed into the wind, but my gun would still not bear as *'The Golden Hawk'* began a laborious turn to larboard. It was a race. I shouted, "Arm yourselves for they will board!" I knew that no matter when I fired, they would be close enough to grapple. The two-masted ships might be small but as I had already seen, they were tough.

I heard Jose's gun fire as yet another ball smacked into our mizzen, this time severing a rope and a sailor who was working the sail. We had lost our first man in this battle. Would it be the last?

The clever captain of the two-masted ship with the mermaid figurehead approaching us kept his ship safe by tacking and turning as he approached. They were going to hit and when I saw the sails lowered on the pirate and the sterncastle appear I knew that they would board. All that I saw was a mass of men clinging to ropes with knives in their mouths and swords in their hands. I touched the linstock when there was still a gap between us and as the grappling hooks soared in the air to grab us. The belch of flame and the smoke obscured the pirates, but the screams told me I had hit some. I had told my men to arm themselves and so I quickly used the swab to clean out the gun. We would not be able to run it out again. As I retracted the swab, I saw that the sterncastle was almost destroyed and, more, the flame from the falcon had started a fire. I loaded the gun again as a French voice ordered the pirates to attack us. The grappling hooks bit and we were dragged closer to the pirate, I now knew was French. I touched the linstock and this time the wall of smoke appeared thicker. I heard the thud of feet on the deck and I drew my sword and dagger as a pirate raced through the smoke towards me. Had this been before we had fought the Aztecs then I might have been terrified into immobility, but I had fought ferocious priests. I used strokes that had been effective against the Aztecs and I used my sword to block the swinging cutlass as I ripped my dagger across the unprotected belly of the Frenchman. I saw that the pirate ship was now on fire and the risk was that it would spread to our ship. All around me men were fighting and the cracks of the esmerils, Jose's gun and the pirate carrack told me that the battle hung in the balance. I slashed my razor-sharp sword across one rope which twanged in the air. Smoke was all around us and it was like fighting in fog.

"Captain Tomas!" The ship's boy, Stephano's, warning saved me as a boarding pike was swung at my head. I dropped to my knees and brought my dagger up between the French pirate's legs. I kept pushing until my hand was stopped by his pelvis. I stood and swung my sword at the other rope which held us bound to the stricken Frenchman. This time the burning ship was pushed away from us by the wind, but we had still been boarded.

"Captain Tomas! Fire your other gun!"

Captain Pedro's voice came from the murky smoke filled sterncastle. Our ship was wreathed in smoke and I knew not if that was because we were afire.

"Gunners to me! Man the larboard gun."

I knew that if the carrack grappled and boarded us then we were lost. Jose and his ship, along with our damaged consort might escape but the remaining pirates would overwhelm us. It was time to take a chance. After using a little extra powder I loaded the larboard gun with ball and shot. I saw the bowsprit of the French carrack appear and heard the crack of its gun. It was no longer firing at our mast but our stern for Captain Pedro had not yet managed to bring us around enough to prevent it. The ball smashed through the sterncastle. Although the esmerils and the helm appeared intact, the ball flew the length of the ship, nicking a lump from the mainmast as it passed. The French gave a cheer, but I concentrated on choosing my moment well. The Frenchman was turning his bows to bring his ship alongside ours. I could not see the smaller pirates and assumed they were attacking *'Swan.'* I touched the linstock when the carrack was at an oblique angle to us. The side was crowded with pirates ready to board us. I feared I had put too much pressure on the falcon for the noise and flame was bigger than any I could recall. As with the two-masted pirate, the flame touched the Frenchman's gunwale and set it on fire, but it was the shot and the ball which did the damage. They scythed through the boarders, flew the length of the ship and the ball smashed into the sterncastle. Such was the force that the French carrack began to move away from us, and Captain Pedro took advantage, turning us away from the attack. Guido and Paulo were quick-witted enough to fire their esmerils with shot and they completed our work, clearing the quarter deck as the stricken carrack passed within thirty paces of them.

The two smaller pirates had been badly handled by Jose and his gun; they joined the stricken carrack. It was out of control and I guessed that the ropes to the rudder had been severed. The fact that Captain Pedro was able to turn our ship told me that we had been luckier. My gunners and the two boys crowded around me clapping me on the back and cheering. I turned and saw Captain Pedro bow to me. We had not only survived, but we had also won. Six pirates had thought to take the treasure from us. The two sunken ships and the damage to the rest had given them a lesson they would not forget. All that they gained was the experience that you do not attack ships that are armed. As we began to clear the debris and the French dead, I wondered if, perhaps, this would lead to more pirates buying cannons. If they did then life on the sea could become even more parlous.

Chapter 20

Cadiz 1521

The repairs on our ships took almost two days to complete and they were a nervous couple of days as we were uncertain if the pirates would return to finish the job with reinforcements. They did not and we finally reached Cadiz. As soon as we docked Captain Pedro reported the attack to the port official. He was a mine of information and as he made a note of the number and size of ships, he told us that the Empire and England were now at war with France. It explained the larger than normal numbers of French pirates. They were acting as privateers and that meant they had the backing of the French king. There would be an increasing number of such ships until there was peace. The sea would not be a safe place to be! I helped the crew to unload the precious cargo. It would take some days to sell and so I would stay aboard the ship. I had a decision to make. I met up with Jose as soon as the ships were emptied. We had moved the ships to the berths used for repair and Captain Pedro bought a new mast for his small ship and carpenters and shipwrights came aboard to make permanent the temporary repairs we had made.

Jose looked and sounded different, "You know, Tomas, I have changed my mind about joining the Spanish army. I think I will stay aboard the ship. Captain Philip treated me as an equal and the men all looked up to me despite my age. I know that if I join the army I will have to begin at the bottom and earn the respect which I now enjoy. I command four guns and men who can be moulded into good gunners."

I nodded, "I understand."

He grinned, "It is what you did with me! I can see that now." I nodded and smiled. "And you? You will still return to England?"

"This war has put a spoke in that particular wheel. With the war between England and France, it will be hard to make the journey safely and, besides, I still await my pay from Captain Pedro."

And so we waited in Cadiz. It was a lively port for with all the ships now crossing the Atlantic it was the main port for the new trade and as the trade was mainly in gold and exotic foodstuffs then it was filled with men trying to make money. Jose and I were happy to stay aboard our ships where life was safe and we enjoyed the company of two crews who, because of the battle, were now closer to each other. We had hot food each day cooked on the quayside. Life was good although as the new year arrived, we had to endure colder weather than I expected in Spain.

It was two days into the New Year when Captain Pedro and his other captains held the meeting to distribute the pay. It had taken longer than we had expected to sell all that we had brought but the profits were much higher than any had expected. Captain Pedro could now afford to buy more guns. *'The Blackbird'* would now be armed. My pay, as master gunner equated to half that which I had brought from Mexico meant I could look to buy a good manor in England rather than the small farm I had anticipated. When the bulk of the crew left, their purses bulging with coins which many would waste on wine, women, and the roll of a dice, Jose and I stayed with the three captains. Jose had made his position quite clear and all their eyes turned to me.

"Tomas, I know that you had planned on returning to England, but I wondered if you could delay that by a month or two?" Captain Pedro's voice was almost pleading.

"I am anxious to get home but is there a good reason for I would like to help you if I could?"

He nodded, "I have seen the wisdom in purchasing more guns. You spoke to me of having a gun facing forward and rather than buying a new ship to replace the one which was lost I would arm all my ships. I would have you select and mount the guns and then train my gunners. What say you? I will pay you for your time."

I confess that like Jose I had grown close to the crew of *'Hawk'* and Captain Pedro in particular. I was tempted and the thought of a wintery journey through hostile waters did not appeal. "Of course, I will help you and when it is done, I shall sail back to England." The joyful response humbled me. I had been a slave when I entered Spanish service and now, I was an honoured craftsman. Life is strange.

It was easier to source guns in Cadiz than in Mexico, but they were slightly different from the ones we had bought in England. They had different names; the falconet was a falconete, a culverin was a culebrina, but they were essentially the same. Jose and I visited the foundries to see the range and when we had selected the ones we wanted Captain Pedro came to negotiate a price. As we needed to place at least two of the guns on the bow castles of our larger ships I chose the falconet. *'The Blackbird'* was also given a pair of falconete pieces as well as two serpentines. These were slightly larger than the esmeril but could be managed by a couple of men. We bought two for our larger ships too.

While we waited for them to be delivered, we had the shipwrights make the bow castle decks stronger and fit the metal rings which would be used to haul the guns back and forth. I contemplated asking for hinged openings to protect the guns from the worst of the weather and seas, but I realised that we needed to be able to move our guns up and down the decks. The battle with the pirates had been a lesson for me. We made the carriages and trunions. When the guns came then it was Jose and me who supervised the mounting of them on the ships. It was only when the ships were ready for sea and the crew returned that we were able to begin training the new men. All of this took time, and I was not in a position to return to England by March. The new men on *'The Blackbird'* were keen enough but unlike the ones on the two larger ships they had no experience of guns and it was taking longer than I expected.

It was about this time that Jose found a young woman he took a fancy to. Juanita was one of the whores who worked in the inn close to where we were working. She was one of the younger ones who served the tables and for a price, she served men. She and Jose soon became close. He paid for his first visit but, thereafter, he did not. I did not comment but I chose not to go with him each night. I was not disapproving but the other girls wondered why I did not wish to enjoy their company. It was easier to stay aboard the ship. When I saw him during the day I knew that the two were growing closer. I wondered at that. Would Jose use his treasure to but somewhere where he and Juanita could be together?

Captain Pedro told me that the ships would be sailing west at the start of April. We would be transporting, ironically, guns and powder for Mexico. The Captain-General had destroyed Tenochtitlán and was expanding the empire. There were rumours that he was now the Governor of Mexico and I knew that Diego Velázquez de Cuéllar would not be a happy man!

Over the last months, as a result of sourcing materials and the like, Jose and I had become familiar with the streets of Cadiz. One evening in March when we had finished our work for the day Jose went to spend time with Juanita while I decided to have a last walk around the port I had come to know well. The ships would be sailing soon. Already Jose had bought a small house close to the docks for Juanita. I was not sure that his mother would approve but a man had needs and the couple seemed to be fond of each other. Indeed I wondered if they might marry before he sailed. The memory of Katerina kept such desires in me dormant.

It was a pleasant evening and, donning a cloak, I headed into the main part of the port. I had my sword strapped on as well as my dagger and a smaller one concealed in the top of my boot. I now knew how to defend myself. I did not have to travel far to lose the sounds and smells of the sea and I found an inn that had tables outside. I found the air more wholesome than inside and I was able to sit with my back against the wall. The protection was for my purse as there were many cutpurses in Cadiz. I was drinking a fortified wine from the Xerez region. I never drank a great deal, but it was a warming drink and I liked its flavour. I also bought a plate of small mouthfuls of food; mainly ham and cheese. Tomatoes, which we had brought from Mexico were becoming popular, but they were so expensive as to be considered, by me at least, as a waste of money. Captain Pedro had been approached to bring back live plants. The price was the same as for a bar of gold. I knew that the seeds of the exotic plant fetched ridiculously high prices but as the kings and queens of Europe demanded these new foods then the price would be paid.

I had just finished and was heading back to my ship when I spied a well-dressed man emerge, furtively, from a fine walled house. He was not young; I would have said he was of an age with my father or Fernando. It was his furtiveness that attracted my attention. He glanced up and down the road and when he saw that the street appeared empty pulled up the cowl of his cloak. I had just stood and was donning my cloak and so he did not seem to notice me. He headed off towards the harbour, some half a mile from where we were. It was as I was fastening my cloak that I saw three men, this time not well dressed and patently not gentlemen, appear from a house and follow the furtive man. I recognised the type. They had swords but they also carried clubs and bags of sand with which to lay low their victims. They were thieves and robbers. Had I seen them approach from the opposite direction then I would have crossed the street to avoid them. They were not interested in me but seemed intent on following what was clearly a gentleman. I know I should have just shrugged and headed back to the ship but as they were heading in the same direction I was already taking then I followed. I did so silently.

The streets were never well lit. There were burning brands hanging at the intersections of the streets and roads, but their light faded quickly.

Cadiz had fine houses but, as it was a busy port then some buildings which had been noble houses had been bought by merchants and those seeking to profit from the New World. There were no people there at this time of night and that meant there were places where a man could be attacked and there would be no help to hand. The smartly dressed man appeared to know where he was going but when he took a sudden turn to the left, close to a house that was the home of a slave trader then I did wonder. This was not an intersection and there was no pool of light. The three pursuers ran when the man appeared to dart down the street. Even as I followed, drawing my own sword, I heard the hiss of steel as a weapon was drawn ahead of me down the darkened passageway. The voice I heard spoke Spanish but was accented. He was not a Spaniard.

"Why are you following me? Has the Frenchman sent you or are you simply after my purse? If so then it is yours for there is little enough within."

Turning the corner I could not see the man for the bodies of the three hulking brutes filled the narrow street.

One of the men laughed, "The purse, sword, fine boots and clothes we will take when you are dead, Englishman. All that the Frenchman wants is your death. We can make it quick for there are three of us and you are no longer a young man."

I had thought to help the man if I could but knowing that it was an Englishman made me throw caution to the wind. I tapped the man in the centre on the shoulder with my sword and said, "I think you have the odds wrong. It is three to two!"

The three men whipped their heads around as one and that was a mistake for the well-dressed man lunged with his sword and whipped the blade across the sword hand of the brute on my left. The Englishman must have had a well-sharpened sword for the hand was almost severed and the sword dropped to the ground. One raised his sword to bring it down to hit me while the other whipped around to face the Englishman. As I blocked the blow with my sword, I drew my dagger and tried to stab my opponent in the arm. His left hand came across to block it and my dagger drove through his palm. He was a street fighter and I saw his head draw back as our sword hilts locked. He intended to head butt me. I twisted and turned my dagger as I withdrew it and the man screamed in pain as his head came at me. I dropped my head so that his forehead connected with the top of my skull. I felt the blow but my hat, with its metalwork, took the bulk of the force and the metal scratched his head. Even so, I stepped back.

The man who had almost lost his hand was trying to stem the flow of blood. The Englishman was more than holding his own with the other and my man was wounded. I tried to reason, "My friend, you have failed, and you are hurt. I do not wish to kill you. Leave now and have your friend's wound tended to lest he dies."

For some reason that seemed to infuriate the man who roared and ran at me like a wild bull released after a long voyage. I merely turned my body and pirouetted as his sword flailed at fresh air. His back was to me and I slashed down with my sword at his shoulder. I felt the edge bite on the bone. The man turned and attempted to backhand me with his sword, but his fingers would not grip and his sword dropped. I put the tip of my blade to his throat, "I give you one more chance, my friend, go to your friend and help him or, so help me God, you shall die."

At that moment the Englishman riposted and disarmed the third one. His voice was laconic as he drawled, "The young man is right and if the Frenchman sent you then you know that I am Lord Christopher Collingwood and not without influence. Take your friend and leave Cadiz. There are many ships heading for the west. Board one for, on the morrow, I will speak with the Alcalde and you will be arrested and tried for attempted murder. I do not think that the Frenchman would like that, would he?"

Supporting the one with the severed hand and after retrieving their swords the three left.

We both waited until they had gone and then sheathed our swords. Lord Collingwood put his arm around my shoulder and led me back to the larger road we had left. "I am in your debt, my young friend. Come to my home for I have a fine brandy that we can drink while I find more about you and discover why a total stranger should help me!"

He had spoken in Spanish and as we reached the better-lit street and I spoke in English he stopped, "I helped you because I am English, my lord."

He stepped back and looked at me, "I never would have guessed. I took you for a Spaniard. Your skin is tanned, and you dress like a Spaniard. Your Spanish is like that of a local." He shook his head, "Come, we have not far to go and this promises to be an entertaining story."

211

He was right we had but a few hundred feet until we came to an imposing building with a solid looking door. When Lord Collingwood knocked, I heard bolts drawn back and the man who faced us was clearly a soldier or had been one in a previous life, "Captain Hogan, this man just saved my life. He is a friend." He spoke in English. "Foster, brandy!"

A disembodied voice answered, "Yes, my lord."

The scowl which had been on the man's face disappeared to be replaced by a broad grin. His voice had the twang of Ireland as he said, "Then you are welcome, my friend. Let me take your cloak," he nodded at my sword, "and your weapon for you shall not need it in here." He seemed to be the sort of man you did not argue with and I gave him my cloak and sword belt.

The house was well apportioned, and the furnishings were as fine as those in the home of Governor Diego Velázquez de Cuéllar, the richest man I knew. A fine fire was burning, and Lord Collingwood led me to a pair of chairs before a fire. A servant, another soldier, appeared with a tray, two goblets and a bottle of brandy. He poured one for each of us.

As the man left Lord Collingwood raised his goblet and said, "Your health!" We drank. "And, of course, your name and then your story."

I shook my head, "I am unimportant. Why were those men after you and who is the Frenchman?"

"First, young man, your name and your story." He was used to commanding and having those commands obeyed.

I shrugged, "There is little to tell. I am a gunner on the Spanish ship, *'The Golden Hawk'*. We have just returned from the New World where I served in the army of Hernán Cortés." His eyebrows raised but he said nothing and continued to sip his brandy. "My name is Thomas Penkridge, and I am from Devon."

His brow wrinkled, "From Devon?" I nodded. "Was your father a gunner also, John the Falconet?"

It was my turn to be surprised, "Aye but how…"

He beamed, "This is fate. I knew your father and he was a good man. When I was a young man, I served old King Henry on his ships and I came to know your father. A better gunner I never knew. Now I serve Young King Henry. I left the ship when Ned Edmundson had him whipped. There was an evil man!" he shook his head as if to clear the memory. "Give me your tale for I believe that you were sent to me for a purpose."

It took longer than I expected to tell him all. The fact that he had served with my father made me tell him the true story of our dalliance with piracy. He did not appear shocked, but he was genuinely upset when he heard of his death. I told him of the intrigues on the Isla Juana and the battles with the Aztecs. I finally ended with the battle against the French pirates.

He emptied his goblet and offered me another. I shook my head; I had consumed three goblets already and I felt I needed to keep a clear head. "You have been honest with me and I appreciate your candour. An admittance of piracy could result in the stretching of your neck." He saw my eyes widen and he held up his hand, "Your secret is safe with me and now I will answer your questions. I serve King Henry and that is why I am surrounded by soldiers like Hogan and Foster. I inhabit a dangerous world. Tonight was a foolish act and a result of itching loins. I was visiting...let us say a friend and went alone."

"What is it that you do for our King?"

He smiled, "I gather information. Old King Henry was a wise old king, but his son is as sharp as the blade you so adeptly wielded this night. The young king knows that information can be as valuable as gold. He is allied to the king of Spain, at the moment and we fight France. The Frenchman who seeks to end my life is Comte de Valois and he does for the French King what I do for King Henry. The difference is that the men he employs are crude footpads and cutpurses. I like to employ those who are soldiers or, in your case, a sailor."

"Me? I am heading back to England to buy a farm and marry. My days of war are over."

He merely smiled, "You have the look of your father you know. I can see it now and I wonder do you have the heart? He was an Englishman who fought for King Henry."

"Until he fell out with an English lord."

"I know about that and it is sad. You have shown, from your own tale, that you are not only a gunner, like your father, but something else, you are a warrior. By your own admission, you fought in a Spanish line and defeated many thousands of Indians. Can you honestly tell me that you will be happy counting sheep and watching beans grow?"

His words shocked me for they showed me that I had not thought this through. I knew nothing about farming. The smallholding my grandparents had worked involved milking a cow and growing just enough to feed us. A farm was a different prospect. Had I gone through the terror of Mexico just to lose my fortune when my crop failed, or my animals died of some disease I did not understand? Perhaps I should just go back to England and live off the profits I had made thus far.

Lord Collingwood reminded me of Francisco Pizzaro. He was a clever man who read people well. "Even now you are wondering about the farm, are you not?"

I nodded, "But you know not what it was like fighting the Aztecs!"

"Yet you have left that world and from your story, you are now respected by your shipmates. You could have a life like your father's if you choose it. You defeated twice your number of ships when the pirates attacked and from what you say your ships are now better armed. You made money from the voyage?" I nodded, "Then go back to sea and also serve England."

I had almost accepted that his advice was sage, but I could not see how I could serve him and England. "What would I do for you and for my country? I am at a loss to understand."

"Gather information! Spain has managed to lead the rest of Europe in its discoveries. One day England will want lands to the west. You are a sailor. You can copy maps and bring them to me. You can let me know of the successes of the Spanish armies and what they discover. We are allies now but that may not always be true. All that I ask is that each time you return you visit me here, discreetly of course, and allow me to pick your brains."

"And will you always be here?"

He laughed, "You will make a good spy for you are clever. You mean what if the Frenchman succeeds and slips a blade in my ribs?" I nodded. He shrugged, "There will be a successor and Foster and Hogan will let him know of your existence. I will also let the king know of your service."

I stared at the fire. The offer was tempting but my father and the rest of the crew of *'The Falcon'* had made the mistake of staying in the western seas too long. Would I be making the same mistake? I smiled, "You are tempting me Lord Collingwood for I should like to serve my country and my king, but I have had much to drink this night and I would like to look at it again in the cold light of day."

"That is understood. You said that your ship is *'The Golden Hawk'*?"

"It is."

"Then after lunch tomorrow I shall walk there with Hogan and Foster. If you wish to serve me then come and speak to us as fellow Englishmen." He smiled, "I will make sure that we talk loudly close to you so that your approach will not elicit suspicion and it might be better if you did not return here in daylight. When those three return to the Frenchman he will have me closely watched and he will seek you out! I take it you do not wear this garb on the ship?"

"No, my lord."

"Good." He stood and clasped my arm. "Until the morrow then and I pray that you answer in the affirmative. I will have Hogan walk back to your ship with you."

"There is no need, my lord."

"You are a potential investment and I protect all that is valuable to me."

The Irishman was silent as we walked the short way to the sea, but his eyes were constantly moving as he scanned the sides of the street for danger. When we reached the ship he merely nodded and said, "Thank you for what you did. Lord Collingwood is the best of men!" He turned and left.

It was Guido who was the sentry at the gangplank, and he leered as I approached. Sniffing he said, "Brandy and, I am guessing, that you were with some doxy."

Realising that the truth would arouse more suspicion than a lie I nodded, "You have caught me out but let it remain our secret eh?"

He grinned, "Of course, Captain Tomas!"

I rose early the next day for I had endured a tormented night as I wrestled with the decision I had to make.

Captain Pedro greeted me as I left my cubby hole, "Tomas, as you know we sail in a very few days and while you have said that you wish to return to England, I still hope that you may relent. May I try to persuade you?"

"Of course, Captain Pedro."

He beamed, "Come." The bow castle had been damaged during the fight and had been rebuilt. Carpenters had toiled away from dusk until dawn. We climbed the steps to a small door. He smiled, "You may have to crouch to enter."

I opened the door and ducked my head just a little. It was a cabin and there were two small windows on the bow side to let in light. There was a chest and a chair. A hammock was slung already. I looked in amazement at the changes which had been wrought. Four seamen had used the cabin before and there had been no windows.

The captain had not entered, and he waved for me to join him outside. "This is for whoever commands my guns. I hope that it will be you but if not, then someone will be grateful for a snug nest."

I was speechless and left the cabin to stand with him on the deck. "It is a fine gesture."

He nodded, "You would be worth the effort and the cost and there is more. I am happy to double your share of the treasure. If you have to fire the guns, then it will be trebled."

"But if we lose?"

He shrugged, "Then I will not have to pay the bonus." We walked back down the length of the ship. "I have spoken with my officers and all agree that it was you, with some help from Jose, that saved us. The storm took a quarter of my fleet but without you, we would have lost every ship, every man and all the treasure. That is why I beg you to give me a year of your time." I already had an answer but felt, somehow, guilty about accepting the offer. It felt as though I was accepting under false pretences. The needs of my country and Lord Collingwood's words had almost convinced me and it would have taken just a hand and a smile to confirm it. "You can have until tomorrow if you wish."

I shook my head, "I am decided, Captain. You are a good man and I like the crew. You shall have your year."

His delight was clearly shown on his face and he clapped me about the shoulders. "Move your gear into the new cabin while I tell the officers. We shall celebrate this night."

I took great delight in organizing my cabin. It would be the first time since I had left England that I had enjoyed any semblance of privacy. Thinking back it was the first time for when I had lived with my grandparents, we had all shared one room! Just before noon I left the cabin and was gratified by the smiles which greeted me. It was clear that the crew were happy that I was staying. As I looked to the quay, I saw Lord Collingwood, Hogan and Foster approaching. I had to play a part for Lord Collingwood did not wish anyone else to know of our association.

He came to the gangplank and spoke to the seaman there. Eduardo shrugged and shouted, "Captain Pedro, there is an Englishman here and I cannot understand a word he says."

The Captain spoke English, but he waved me over, "Tomas, perhaps you can translate for your countrymen." I nodded. Captain Pedro shouted, "Come aboard, my lord." He did not know that Lord Collingwood was a knight but he dressed like one and Captain Pedro knew how to flatter."

"I am Lord Collingwood. I now live in Spain where I deal with King Henry's interests in Spain. I understand that you are sailing to Mexico." He addressed Captain Pedro, but I translated.

"Yes, we sail tomorrow."

"I would like some plants bringing back to grow in England." He had a list written in English. "These are the items. Can you furnish them?"

Captain Pedro was a shrewd businessman, he gave them to me and I translated for him. He nodded, "The problem is that we cannot guarantee that plants will survive. If I procure them for you and they die, then it is I who will lose money and not you."

Lord Collingwood nodded as I translated. He took out a purse, "Here is silver to ensure that you do not lose out, but I would hope," he looked at me, "that I would not be cheated."

I answered as myself, "I can guarantee that we will do all that we can to make certain that the plants have the best chance of survival."

His eyes bored into mine as he sought the information he needed, "Then you will be sailing with the ship?"

"I will."

"Then I am satisfied," He handed me another piece of paper. "This is my home. When you return then send a messenger to me. When can we expect you back?"

I translated and Captain Pedro said, "Not less than six months."

Lord Collingwood held out his hand and shook Captain Pedro's, "May the seas be kind to you and bring back my hopes for a rich future!"

When he had gone Captain Pedro asked, "He is a lord then?"

"So he said. He certainly sounded like one."

"And do you trust him?"

I said, reasonably, "I do not know him, but he seemed genuine. Besides we have nothing to lose for we have his silver. I do not think it would be wise to cheat the representative of the King of England, do you?"

He laughed, "You are right and see the luck you bring us. We can buy plants cheaply in Isla Juna and Mexico. All we need is luck to bring as many back safely as we can. Perhaps this may prove as lucrative as bringing gold."

"Perhaps. They would have to be carried on deck, but it seems to me there are many places we could use which are, as yet unoccupied."

"Tonight we feast. I have invited Jose and my other captains. This is the start of a great venture which will make us the richest men in the world!"

My smile was genuine, but I was not just working for myself. I was now a spy for the King of England, and I wondered just how that would change my life.

We left Spain on the noontide. The three ships, freshly painted and with the added teeth of new guns, looked formidable as we headed west. The last time I had done this had been with my father and we had been intent on life as pirates. This time we were going as merchants and conquistadors. The name given in fun might now be said to be a true description of Thomas Penkridge, Devonian, Englishman and Master Gunner. I now served both the King of England and the King of Spain! What a change in a few short years! What would the future hold for me?

The End

Glossary

Burgular – burglar
Cabacet- Spanish helmet -an early version of a morion
Gong scourers – the workers who collected human faeces at night
Harquebus – an early and primitive handheld gun
Isla Juana – Cuba
Maquahuitl - Aztec sword club edged with obsidian and having a point
Morion - a Spanish helmet
Pukara – An Incan fortress
Rodeleros – Sword and buckler men (singular rodelero)
Sweating sickness – A disease that ravaged England from 1485 - 1551
and then disappeared. The symptoms/disease either lasted a day or
resulted in death.
San Juan Bautista – Puerto Rico

Historical Note

All the events battles etc. really happened. Everything from the hunting dogs of de Bilbao to the murder of the Emperor is real. The nautical battles are fiction and the characters both real and fictional have been given their characteristics by me. I have tried to mould Pizarro, de Bilbao, Hernán Cortés and the other real figures into believable men acting in unbelievable times. That the Spanish with a tiny army were able to subdue the incredibly sophisticated Aztec Empire is nothing short of remarkable.

Gunnery was new in the fifteenth century but was developing rapidly. Soon it would dominate the battlefield. For men on ships, it was a new experience. The *'Mary Rose'* had many guns but that was some years after the time this novel is set.

The next book in the series will see our hero reunited with Francisco Pizarro as he encounters the mighty Incan Empire.

Griff August 2021

Other books by Griff Hosker

If you enjoyed reading this book, then why not read another one by the author?

Ancient History

The Sword of Cartimandua Series
(Germania and Britannia 50 A.D. – 128 A.D.)
Ulpius Felix- Roman Warrior (prequel)
The Sword of Cartimandua
The Horse Warriors
Invasion Caledonia
Roman Retreat
Revolt of the Red Witch
Druid's Gold
Trajan's Hunters
The Last Frontier
Hero of Rome
Roman Hawk
Roman Treachery
Roman Wall
Roman Courage

The Wolf Warrior series
(Britain in the late 6th Century)
Saxon Dawn
Saxon Revenge
Saxon England
Saxon Blood
Saxon Slayer
Saxon Slaughter
Saxon Bane
Saxon Fall: Rise of the Warlord
Saxon Throne
Saxon Sword

Medieval History

The Dragon Heart Series
Viking Slave
Viking Warrior
Viking Jarl
Viking Kingdom
Viking Wolf
Viking War
Viking Sword
Viking Wrath
Viking Raid
Viking Legend
Viking Vengeance
Viking Dragon
Viking Treasure
Viking Enemy
Viking Witch
Viking Blood
Viking Weregeld
Viking Storm
Viking Warband
Viking Shadow
Viking Legacy
Viking Clan
Viking Bravery

The Norman Genesis Series
Hrolf the Viking
Horseman
The Battle for a Home
Revenge of the Franks
The Land of the Northmen
Ragnvald Hrolfsson
Brothers in Blood
Lord of Rouen
Drekar in the Seine
Duke of Normandy
The Duke and the King

Danelaw
(England and Denmark in the 11th Century)
Dragon Sword
Oathsword
Bloodsword

New World Series
Blood on the Blade
Across the Seas
The Savage Wilderness
The Bear and the Wolf
Erik The Navigator
Erik's Clan

The Vengeance Trail

The Reconquista Chronicles
Castilian Knight
El Campeador
The Lord of Valencia

The Aelfraed Series
(Britain and Byzantium 1050 A.D. - 1085 A.D.)
Housecarl
Outlaw
Varangian

The Anarchy Series England
1120-1180
English Knight
Knight of the Empress
Northern Knight
Baron of the North
Earl
King Henry's Champion
The King is Dead
Warlord of the North
Enemy at the Gate

The Fallen Crown
Warlord's War
Kingmaker
Henry II
Crusader
The Welsh Marches
Irish War
Poisonous Plots
The Princes' Revolt
Earl Marshal
The Perfect Knight

Border Knight
1182-1300
Sword for Hire
Return of the Knight
Baron's War
Magna Carta
Welsh Wars
Henry III
The Bloody Border
Baron's Crusade
Sentinel of the North
War in the West
Debt of Honour
The Blood of the Warlord
The Fettered King

Sir John Hawkwood Series
France and Italy 1339- 1387
Crécy: The Age of the Archer
Man At Arms
The White Company
Leader of Men

Lord Edward's Archer
Lord Edward's Archer
King in Waiting
An Archer's Crusade

Targets of Treachery
The Great Cause
Wallace's War

**Struggle for a Crown
1360- 1485**
Blood on the Crown
To Murder a King
The Throne
King Henry IV
The Road to Agincourt
St Crispin's Day
The Battle for France
The Last Knight
Queen's Knight

Tales from the Sword I
(Short stories from the Medieval period)

**Tudor Warrior series
England and Scotland in the late 14th and early 15th century**
Tudor Warrior
Tudor Spy

**Conquistador
England and America in the 16th Century**
Conquistador
Inca

Modern History

The Napoleonic Horseman Series
Chasseur à Cheval
Napoleon's Guard
British Light Dragoon
Soldier Spy
1808: The Road to Coruña
Talavera
The Lines of Torres Vedras

Bloody Badajoz
The Road to France
Waterloo

The Lucky Jack American Civil War series
Rebel Raiders
Confederate Rangers
The Road to Gettysburg

Soldier of the Queen series
Soldier of the Queen

The British Ace Series
1914
1915 Fokker Scourge
1916 Angels over the Somme
1917 Eagles Fall
1918 We will remember them
From Arctic Snow to Desert Sand
Wings over Persia

Combined Operations series
1940-1945
Commando
Raider
Behind Enemy Lines
Dieppe
Toehold in Europe
Sword Beach
Breakout
The Battle for Antwerp
King Tiger
Beyond the Rhine
Korea
Korean Winter

Tales from the Sword II
(Short stories from the Modern period)

Other Books
Great Granny's Ghost (Aimed at 9-14-year-old young people)

For more information on all of the books then please visit the author's website at www.griffhosker.com where there is a link to contact him or visit his Facebook page: GriffHosker at Sword Books

Printed in Great Britain
by Amazon

19232702R00132